A MILLION BLESSINGS

A Million Blessings

Angela Benson
Marilynn Griffith
Tia McCollors

KENSINGTON PUBLISHING CORP.
www.kensingtonbooks.com

DAFINA BOOKS are published by

Kensington Publishing Corp.
119 West 40th Street
New York, NY 10018

All Kensington titles, imprints, and distributed lines are available at special quantity discounts for bulk purchases for sales promotion, premiums, fund-raising, educational, or institutional use.

Special book excerpts or customized printings can also be created to fit specific needs. For details, write or phone the office of the Kensington Special Sales Manager: Kensington Publishing Corp., 119 West 40th Street, New York, NY 10018, Attn. Special Sales Department. Phone: 1-800-221-2647.

ISBN-13: 978-0-7582-4211-2
ISBN-10: 0-7582-4211-5

First Printing: March 2010
10 9 8 7 6 5 4 3 2 1

Printed in the United States of America

CONTENTS

Showers of Blessings

ANGELA BENSON

Chapter 1

"It's me again, Lord," Andrew Gooden said, lowering his forehead to rest against the steering wheel of his leased burgundy 5 Series BMW, which was parked in front of a run-down Bankhead convenience store. He'd chosen this neighborhood and this store because of their distance from his home and stomping ground in the decidedly more upscale suburb of Alpharetta. There was no chance he'd run into anyone he knew here. "I know I said I wouldn't end up in this situation again, but here I am. I don't know how it happened, really. I had been so good for so long and then I just fell off the wagon."

Andrew lifted his head and stared out the window at what appeared to be two homeless men ingesting their beverages from brown paper bags. He felt as destitute as they looked. He leaned forward and picked up the two completed lottery forms resting on the passenger-side dash. "I need your help, Lord. I don't have to tell you how much. The repo guys are looking for my cars. The house is teetering on foreclosure. My bank account is overdrawn. Things have been bad before, but never this bad. Sandra's threatening to leave me if I don't do something fast." He held the lottery forms up and double-checked the numbers. "All I'm asking, Lord, is that you bless these forms and these numbers. I'm counting on you for a miracle."

Andrew closed his eyes and bowed his head. "Please, Lord." With those final words, he picked up the hat and sunglasses he'd brought with him and put them on. Though the possibility was slim that he'd run into someone he knew, he couldn't take the chance. He was an assistant pastor at Praise City, a well-known megachurch in metro Atlanta. As much as his senior pastor raged on the sins of gambling and playing the lottery, he'd be put on blast if someone caught him purchasing lottery tickets.

Andrew got out of his car and headed for the store entrance, careful to keep his head down. So as not to be obvious, he went to the soda case and picked up a liter bottle of orange soda, his kids' favorite. To give the current customer at the counter time to complete his transaction, Andrew stopped and browsed the snacks. He picked up a family-sized bag of chips. When the checkout counter was clear, he made a beeline for it. "Two lottery tickets," he said, handing the forms to the cashier as he put his two items on the counter.

"Hope these are winners for you," the cashier said.

From your mouth to God's ears, Andrew thought. "Thanks," he said, not wanting to get into a conversation that would extend his time in the store or give the clerk any reason to remember him. He wanted his lottery tickets and he wanted to get home. As the clerk ran the lottery forms and rang up his purchases, Andrew opened his wallet and pulled out the last of his credit cards that wasn't charged to the limit. At least, he hoped it wasn't. He and Sandra had been living on credit for months. This card had to be pretty close to the limit by now. When the clerk took the card, Andrew silently prayed that his purchase would be authorized.

He released a breath when the clerk asked for his signature. He quickly signed the receipt, took his purchases without waiting for them to be bagged, and rushed out of the store. He slid into his car, took off his hat and glasses, and breathed deeply again. "Thank you, Lord," he whispered. He put the key in the ignition and was about to turn it, when someone knocked on the driver-side window.

"Pastor? Is that you, Pastor Gooden?"

Andrew couldn't believe it. He'd gotten so close to making a clean getaway. He turned toward the window and saw one of his male parishioners grinning at him. Though he couldn't come up with a name, he knew the face. He pressed the button to lower the window.

"I thought that was you," the man said, still grinning. "What are you doing in my neck of the woods? It's Wednesday night. I figured you'd be in Bible class. Don't you teach on Wednesday nights?"

Andrew forced a smile. "I'm on my way to church now, brother," he said, wondering if the man had seen him coming out of the store with his hat and glasses. "Are you going to make it?"

The man shook his head. "Not tonight. The wife has already gone. She doesn't like to be late."

Andrew looked at his watch. "I'm going to be late myself if I don't get moving."

The man stepped back from the car. "Don't let me hold you up," he said. "I'll see you on Sunday."

"I'll look for you," Andrew said, starting the car. He nodded to the man and pressed the button to raise the window. It was then he realized he still had the lottery tickets in his hand. He glanced back up at the man, whose grin had settled into a smile. Had the man seen the lottery tickets? Andrew wondered.

Shaking his head in answer to his question, Andrew guided the car toward the main street. He didn't breathe again until he was on the interstate, far away from that Bankhead convenience store and his unnamed parishioner.

Chapter 2

Sandra Gooden waved one last time to her children, eight-year-old Matthew and ten-year-old Andrew, Jr., as they headed off in the backseat of her father's car to get ice cream and then she closed the front door. She lowered her eyelids and leaned back against the door, taking a moment to rest.

"Tired, dear?" her mother asked.

Sandra sighed and pushed away from the door. "I'm fine, Mother," she said. "I appreciate you and Daddy taking the kids for a few weeks."

Ida waved off her thanks. "It's no bother. You know we love having those kids. I'm just glad we could help."

Sandra was glad, too. Her kids were old enough to know things weren't right around the house, and her excuses were wearing thin. Besides, it was embarrassing to coach your kids not to answer the phone unless they recognized the name on the caller ID. It would be more than embarrassing if they knew their parents were being hounded by creditors.

"Sandra," her mother began. "You know I don't like to dip in your marriage, but Andrew needs to get some help. He's gambling again, isn't he?"

Sandra regretted ever sharing her husband's vice with her mother. But at the time, she'd had to tell somebody and her mother had seemed the safest choice. Andrew's problem was certainly not something she could share at a prayer meeting with the members of Praise City's leadership team, not if she wanted to maintain their standing among them. No, this was a secret they had to keep.

"I don't want to talk about it, Mother," she said, walking past her mother and toward the kitchen.

Her mother followed her. "I know you don't want to," she said, "but you need to. You can't keep all this bottled up inside. You're hiding it from the people who care about you and you're hiding it from your kids. You need to let it out, Sandra."

She turned on her mother, throwing up her arms. Her mother's doggedness defied her short stature. "What am I supposed to say, Mother? That my husband is a gambler, and a poor one at that? Should I announce in church that he's so far gone that we're on the verge of losing everything—again? Should I tell them that Andrew's fallen so low that he's even gambled away his children's college funds? How can I tell anyone all that?" she cried. "How can I admit that I tied myself to a man who is so fatally flawed?" She turned away from her mother. "Some days I wonder why I married him. This is not the life I signed up for, Mother. Andrew and I should have our own congregation by now, and we would if not for his problem. I thought he'd overcome it last time when he brought us to the end of our rope, but here we are again."

Her mother walked over to her and rubbed her shoulders. "You married him because you loved him."

"I don't even know him," Sandra said. "How can I love him?"

Her mother pulled away. "Are you thinking about leaving him?" she asked.

"I have to think about it, Mother. I can't keep on like this. My kids deserve better than this. I deserve better than this."

"Andrew is a good man, Sandy. He just needs to get some help. You both need to get some help."

Sandra pulled away. "I'm not the person with the problem, but I certainly have to deal with the fallout. I'm tired, Mother. Tired. I can't go through this again with Andrew. I don't have it in me."

"You know your daddy and I had some rough years, but we made it through."

Sandra remembered those rough years when her father was a functional alcoholic, and they weren't good memories, either. She wanted better for herself and her children. "I admire you, Mom, and what you were able to endure and to work through, but I'm not you." *I don't want to be you*, she added silently, not wanting to hurt her mother's feelings.

"Well, what can I do to help?"

Sandra pressed a kiss against her mother's forehead. "You're already doing it. You're taking care of the kids."

"I have a little extra money that your father doesn't know about," she said, reaching into the pocket of her jeans and pulling out a check.

"I can't take your money," Sandra said, though she was sorely tempted. She was sure they were at the limit on their last credit card, and she had less than a hundred dollars in cash. She didn't know what they were going to do.

Her mother took her hand, put the check in it, and folded the hand closed. "It's only five hundred dollars. It's not much, but it'll help."

Sandra felt tears well up in her eyes. This wasn't the way things were supposed to be. Here she was a thirty-five-year-old married woman with children taking cash from her mother. As the daughter, it should be her turn to help her parents. "I can't, Mom—"

"Shh, yes, you can. It's done. You take that, and if you need more, you let me know. I'll see what your father and I can do."

Sandra began shaking her head. "You can't tell Dad, Mom. You promised."

"I know what I promised, and I'm going to keep my promise, even though I don't think it's wise. Your father could talk to Andrew, help him out, especially since he doesn't have a father of his own."

Andrew was an orphan, brought up in foster care. She and the children were his only family. His need for family was one of the traits that had attracted her to him. He valued what he'd never had. She saw in him solid husband and father material. What she hadn't seen was his fatal gambling addiction.

"Andrew would be devastated if Dad knew how badly he was handling his family duties. I can't do that to him. His pride is battered as it is." Besides, it had taken her father years to warm up to Andrew. If he knew about the gambling, he would revert to his earlier opinion of her husband. She was sure of it.

Her mother lifted a brow. "Those aren't the words of a woman getting ready to leave her husband."

Sandra frowned. "Oh, but they are. I know what it means to reach the end of your rope. That's where I am."

Chapter 3

Andrew knew something was wrong when the boys didn't rush him at the door as soon as he entered the house. "I'm home," he yelled out, hoping against hope that his family was just otherwise occupied. Thoughts of Sandra's threat to take the boys and leave chilled his heart. She hadn't really done it, had she?

He marched through the kitchen, peeked into the family room, and seeing no one there, headed upstairs to the bedrooms. "Sandra," he called out from the stairs. When she didn't answer, he quickened his steps. When he passed the boys' rooms and saw their beds were empty, his heart raced. She'd done it this time. She'd really left him.

"Please, Lord," he prayed. "Please, please, please, don't let them be gone. I won't ever gamble again. I promise. Just don't let me lose my family."

Andrew stopped short when he entered the master bedroom and found his wife curled up on the bed reading a book. "Didn't you hear me calling you?" he asked.

Without glancing up, she said, "I heard you."

"Then why didn't you answer?"

She looked up at him then, and the disappointment he read

in her eyes made him wish she hadn't. "What's the point?" she asked. "I'm tired of your excuses."

Okay, he deserved those words. He accepted them with a swallow. "Where are the boys?"

"They're staying with my parents until we straighten things out."

He didn't like that she had shipped the boys off without consulting him, without giving him a chance to say goodbye. "Don't you think we should have talked about this?"

She closed the book, put it on the nightstand, and then sat up in the bed. "I sent them away because we need to have a serious talk about this marriage and our family. The bottom line is that I can't keep going through this with you. You promised me the last time that it wouldn't happen again. Yet here we are."

He came to the bed and sat facing her. "I know I've let you down," he said. "But I'm going to fix this. I have a plan—"

She began shaking her head. "Not another plan. Andrew, you need help. Professional help. I believed you before when you said you could stop. I don't any longer. You're destroying this family. Can't you see that?"

Andrew shook his head, refusing to believe God would let him lose the only thing that mattered to him—his family. He took his wife's hands in his. "Trust me one last time," he pleaded. "And if you can't trust me, trust God. Expect a miracle with me, Sandra."

He saw the wariness in her eyes. "What have you done, Andrew?" she asked. "What kind of miracle are you expecting?"

"I want you to look for a miracle that only God can provide."

She laughed a dry laugh. "I guess you want me to believe that God is going to drop money from heaven for us the way he dropped manna for the Israelites."

"That's exactly what I want you to believe," he said.

She pulled her hands away. "Come on, Andrew. You should know by now that God doesn't work that way. That's how we got in this situation in the first place. You're always looking for the big score, instead of building slowly. You need to change the way you operate."

Andrew reached for her hands again. "Okay, if this doesn't turn out the way I believe it will, we'll try it your way."

She squinted at him. "What have you done, Andrew? What scheme are you working on now? Please don't tell me you've borrowed money so that you can gamble."

He chuckled, shaking his head. "This deal only cost me two dollars."

"Two dollars? What are you talking about? I don't understand."

"I had a vision," he said, taking a bit of leeway with the truth. "In that vision God told me to play the lottery this week and he gave me the numbers to play."

Sandra snatched her hands away and jumped up from the bed. "That's the last straw, Andrew. Now you've started lying on God. You know as well as I do that God did not give you any lottery numbers. Have you lost your mind?"

Her words hurt, but he brushed them off as best he could. God was not going to let him down. He could feel it.

"If playing the lottery is your way of getting us out of the hole you've put us in, we're in more trouble than I wanted to believe. I think it's best that I go stay with my parents and the kids and give you some time to figure out what you want from us and what you're willing to give. We can't build a future for our family on a lottery scheme. We don't even believe in the lottery."

Andrew glanced at his watch. "Turn on the television," he said.

When she just rolled her eyes, he reached on the far-side nightstand, picked up the remote, and turned it on himself.

"They should be announcing the lottery results in a few minutes. Believe with me."

"I believe you've lost your mind," she said. "That's what I believe."

He pulled the two lottery tickets out of his pocket and handed them to her. "You hold the tickets," he said. "I'm too nervous."

Grudgingly, she took the tickets and sat down next to him on the bed. "I don't believe I'm doing this," she said. "Pastor McCorry would fall out of the pulpit if he knew his assistant pastor was at home waiting for the lottery numbers to be announced, rather than at church teaching his Bible study class."

Pulling her close, Andrew chuckled. "There was no way I could teach tonight. I'm too anxious about the lottery results."

"How much is the lottery for this week anyway?" Sandra asked.

"Not much," he said. "About twenty million."

She laughed out loud. "Sounds like a lot to me."

He laughed, too. "It's a lot to us but not for the lottery. It's not like it's one of those hundred million dollar weeks when everybody plays. This is an average-sized jackpot."

She peered up at him. "You know, it bothers me that you know so much about the lottery. Something tells me this isn't the first time you've played."

"Watch the television," he said. "They're about to call the numbers."

She did as she was told. "Here," she said to him. "You hold one and I'll hold one."

He took his. His heart began to sink as the announcer read the numbers. He hadn't won. He glanced over at Sandra, and from the look on her face he gathered she hadn't, either. He couldn't believe it. He'd been so sure God was going to come through for him.

"We'll just play the numbers again next week," he said. "We can't give up now. I really believe in these numbers." When his wife didn't respond, he looked down at her and saw she was crying. Her tears broke his heart. "I'm sorry, Sandra," he said. "I'll fix this. I promise I will."

Sandra began shaking her head, and then she began to laugh. Andrew wondered if her disappointment had made her delirious. He grew uneasy as her laughter grew and she threw herself at him. "We won, Andrew," she said. "We won the lottery!"

Chapter 4

"We won," Sandra screamed, wrapping her arms around her husband's neck. "We won." She hopped up from the bed, pulling him with her. "We're rich," she said, dancing him around the room. "We're rich."

Andrew stopped dancing, forcing her to stop, and looked down into her eyes. "I told you I wouldn't let you down," he said. "I told you."

She pressed a hand against his cheek. She loved her six-foot chocolate drop, warts and all. "I know you did, baby, and you came through for me and this family. I never should have doubted you."

He turned her hand over and kissed her palm. "You never should have doubted God," he said. "When a door closes, He opens a window. We just have to look for it."

"It really is a gift from God, isn't it?" she asked.

"You bet it is," Andrew confirmed. "Man couldn't do this. I couldn't do this. God had to do it."

Sandra lifted her arms heavenward. "I'm so happy I could shout it to the world." She reached for the phone on the nightstand. "I have to call Momma and Daddy. They won't believe it. Then we have to call Pastor McCorry and Vickie."

She glanced back at her husband. "You know we're going to have to tithe this money, don't you?"

Andrew grabbed her hand before she could dial and forced the phone back on the cradle. She looked up at him. "What are you doing?"

He sat on the side of the bed and pulled her down with him. "Think about it, Sandra. What are you going to tell your parents? What are you going to tell Pastor and Vickie?"

"I'm going to tell them God blessed us to win the lottery."

He didn't say anything, just looked at her.

"What?" she asked.

"You're going to tell Pastor 'Lottery means Hell' McCorry that God blessed us to win the lottery? I don't think so."

Sandra slumped back against her husband. "I see your point," she said, a dark cloud trying to push away her happiness. "They wouldn't understand."

"No, they wouldn't," Andrew said. "That's why we have to keep this to ourselves."

"That's going to be impossible, Andrew. We're going to have to claim the lottery winnings." She covered her face with her hands. "And they're going to put our pictures in the paper. Everybody's going to know and we'll be kicked out of the church. What are we going to do?"

"We're not getting kicked out of the church," he said. "The first thing we need to do is talk to an attorney about our options. I'm sure there's a way we can collect our winnings and keep our identities hidden."

"I hope so," Sandra said, some of her glee fading. "God really wants us to have this money, doesn't he, Andrew?"

Andrew pulled her close. "Of course he does. We needed it and he opened a window to give it to us. All we have to do is use it the right way."

"We're going to tithe it," Sandra said. "The church could

use the money and there are some other ministries I'd like to bless."

Andrew kissed her forehead. "You have a good heart, babe. That's why God knew He could trust us with the winnings. We'll use it to build His kingdom. I think it's time for us to start thinking about starting our own church."

She looked up at him, her joy returning. "Are you serious, Andrew?"

He nodded. "Dead serious. It's always been our prayer to have our own church. Well, there's nothing stopping us now. We can use this money to serve our congregation. That's what God wants."

Sandra hugged her husband's side. "Oh, Andrew, I can't believe this is happening. A few hours ago, we were on the verge of bankruptcy or worse, and now we're millionaires getting ready to start a church. I can't believe it."

"Believe it," he said. "God works in mysterious ways."

Sandra pushed away the uneasiness she felt at her husband's words. While she was on board with using the money for good, something about God providing it did not set well with her. "What are we going to tell folks when we start doing all these things? They're going to wonder about the money."

Andrew hugged her close. "I've been thinking about that," he said. "We'll tell them that a long lost relative of mine left it to me."

She peered up at him. "Everybody knows you're an orphan, Andrew, and that you don't have any family."

He shrugged. "That's all the better. We'll be as surprised as anybody. Folks will be happy for us and will praise God for providing a way out of no way. They'll believe us. Why shouldn't they?"

Sandra knew there was something hypocritical in lying about a blessing, but she didn't see any other way for them. "I guess we've got everything covered then," she said. "All we need now is a lawyer who'll help us claim the winnings without anyone knowing who we are."

Andrew pressed her down on the bed. "We'll talk to the lawyers tomorrow. Tonight I want to celebrate. Since the kids are at the grandparents', Mommy and Daddy have play time."

Sandra giggled. "You're so crazy."

His face sober, he said, "Crazy about you." He wiped a finger down her cheek. "I love you, Sandra, and I love our family. I'm sorry for the pain I put you through. I promise you and I promise God that I won't ever do that to us again. I know He's giving me yet another chance, and I'm not going to blow it. This is a new start for us. We've been blessed and we're going to be a blessing to others. We're going to walk in faith and believe the promise of God for our ministry. Today is the beginning of a new journey for us. We're not looking back."

Sandra felt the tears roll down her cheeks. This was the man she married. Not only had God blessed them with money, He'd given her back her husband. She pulled Andrew down to her. Kissing him, she said, "Let the celebration begin."

Chapter 5

Sandra's head was still spinning when she and Andrew pulled into her parents' driveway after leaving the attorney's office on Peachtree Street in downtown Atlanta. When Andrew turned off the engine, she said, "Is this real, Andrew?"

He chuckled. "Very real," he said. "We're rich, Sandra. We'll never have money problems again. Our kids are provided for and so are your parents. And we have the money to start our own church. God is good."

"The lottery is good," she said.

Andrew picked up her hand and kissed it. "Same thing."

She met his eyes. "I don't like lying to my parents."

"Neither do I, but what choice do we have?"

She sighed deeply. "I know," she said, "but I still don't like it."

"Well, I bet your parents will like hearing what we've done for them and their grandchildren. I can't wait to see the look on your dad's face when we tell him about the horse farm."

Sandra smiled. "They're going to be so excited. Let's go in and tell them."

Wanting to surprise her parents and the children, they rang the bell instead of using their key. Her mother opened the door. She looked between the two of them. "What are you two doing here?" she asked. "We weren't expecting you."

Sandra laughed. She kissed her mother's cheek and said, "Nothing's wrong, Momma. In fact, everything is right. Where are Daddy and the kids?"

Her mother accepted a kiss from Andrew and then closed the door after they were both inside. "Your father took the kids out to Harper Farms so they could go riding. They left early this morning."

"And won't be back until late," Sandra finished. Her kids had inherited her dad's love of horses and riding. She'd had that love, too, until her drunken father had put her on a horse too spirited for her and she'd taken a fall, breaking her arm. She pushed the thought aside, not wanting to dampen the joy of the day. Those days were long gone, anyway.

"Have you two eaten?" her mother asked as they settled themselves in the family room. Her mother took the plush club chair while she and Andrew took the couch.

"We had a fancy lunch down on Peachtree Street."

"What were you doing down there?" her mother asked.

"We had lunch with an attorney," Sandra said.

"An attorney?" her mother asked, her eyes wide. "You two aren't getting a divorce, are you?"

Andrew touched his mother-in-law's knee. "No way," he told her. "I love your daughter and she loves me. We've been through a rough patch lately, but God has opened a door and cleared up all our financial problems."

Her mother met her eyes. "What's happened?" she asked.

"Well, Mom," Sandra began. "We met with an attorney this morning who informed us that Andrew has inherited a substantial sum of money, very substantial."

Her mother turned to Andrew. "Who left you some money? I thought you didn't have any family."

"I didn't think I did, either, but apparently there was a distant cousin. Believe me, I'm as surprised as you are. Surprised and blessed. And we're going to use our blessing to bless others." He went on to tell her about their plans for a church.

"That's wonderful, Andrew," she said. "You have a good heart. I know you and Sandra will make good use of your money."

"It's *our* money, Mom," Andrew corrected. "Mine, Sandra's, the kids, and yours and Dad's. It's ours. We want you to share in it, too. The first thing we want to do is buy you and Dad that horse farm he's always talking about. We want you two to start looking for it immediately."

Ida dabbed at her eyes with her fingers. "You can't be serious."

Sandra sat on the arm of her mother's chair and pulled her close. "Dead serious," she said. "We want you and Dad to have everything you've always wanted. As soon as the paperwork is finalized, we'll put a share of the money in an account for you so you can spend it as you see fit. For now, though, we want you and Dad to find that horse farm you want. And I want you to have the house you want. If you find property, we can even build from scratch. Whatever you want."

Her mother began to cry. "Oh, Sandra, you don't have to."

Sandra glanced at her husband, tears in her own eyes. Then she said to her mother, "We want to, Mom. You've always been there for us. Let us be there for you and Dad. It's time for you to have what you want."

"I don't know what to say."

"There's nothing to say," Andrew said. "Just thank God for the blessing. That's what we're doing."

"Grady is going to be beside himself when he hears this. He's dreamed of owning a horse farm forever, but it was never anything but a dream. I don't think he ever imagined it would actually happen."

"I know, Mom, but it is happening. Today is a new day for all of us."

"I wish Dad were here now so we could tell him," Andrew said. "I can't wait to see the expression on his face."

"Well, why don't we drive up and spend the rest of the

day with him and kids at Harper's. We can reserve a room at one of those bed-and-breakfast places and hang out a couple of days."

"That's a great idea, babe," Andrew said. He turned to Ida. "What do you think, Mom? Are you ready to tell Dad that Christmas came early this year?"

Chapter 6

Still on an emotional high from the weekend spent with her family celebrating their newly found riches and looking at horse farms, Sandra had high expectations for her and Andrew's meeting with Pastor McCorry and Vickie. The older couple were their role models in the faith, so their opinion meant a lot. She listened with a smile on her face as Andrew told them their good news and their plans. When he finished, she turned to the pastoral couple and awaited their congratulations.

"Have you checked out this relative, Andrew?" Pastor McCorry asked, rubbing his chin. "There are so many scams going around these days. You can never be too careful."

Sandra's smile faded a bit. That wasn't the response she'd expected.

"You should consider hiring a private detective to verify everything, including the attorney who contacted you," the pastor added.

Andrew cleared his throat. "We've done enough checking," he told them. "The attorney is from a very reputable firm here in Atlanta."

Sandra lowered her eyes at her husband's half truth. She wished they could tell Pastor and Vickie the truth and be accepted, but she knew the older couple were too judgmental and set in their ways to accept their lottery win as a blessing from God. In fact, as she thought about it, she realized Pastor and Vickie were judgmental about everything related to being a Christian. They were always preaching about what you should do and where you shouldn't go. And some of the stuff they talked about wasn't even in the Bible. No, they had their own rules and tried to make everybody abide by them. Sandra raised her eyes, met Vickie's, and smiled. She was glad she and Andrew were starting their own church. They'd be better shepherds than the judgmental McCorry's.

"This is a blessing from God, an unexpected blessing, and we're going to accept it, not question it. Isn't that what you've taught us over the years?" she challenged the pastor.

Pastor McCorry peered at her from over his glasses. "I've also taught you to use wisdom. All I'm asking is that you move with caution."

"We're moving in faith," Andrew said. "You know it's always been on our hearts to start a church. We're going to use this money to build God's kingdom by doing exactly that."

"Whoa," Pastor McCorry said, lifting his right palm toward Andrew. "Money is not a calling to start a church. How do you know this is what God wants you to do at this point in time? I'm your shepherd and He hasn't let me know any such thing. I don't think you're ready," he said bluntly. "Either of you."

Pastor McCorry was being judgmental again, Sandra thought. Who was he to tell them they weren't ready? "Maybe you're just jealous," she muttered before she could stop herself.

"What did you say?" Vickie demanded.

Sandra met Vickie's eyes again. "I said maybe you and Pastor are jealous of the good fortune that has come our way. Maybe you want to be the big Pastor and First Lady with all the little peons bowing at your feet."

"Sandra!" Vickie shot up out of her seat. "I can't believe you're saying that. You know us better than that."

Andrew patted her knee to calm her but she pushed his hand off. "What I know is that nobody in our congregation has as big a house as yours and nobody drives cars as expensive. Why is that?"

"You're out of line, Sister Gooden," Pastor warned.

Sandra turned her attention to him. "I'm not out of line," she said. "I'm just telling the truth. Maybe you two don't want us to have a church. Maybe you're afraid it'll be bigger and better than Praise City."

"That's enough, Sandra," Andrew said. "Pastor and First Lady have a right to their opinions." Then he said to Pastor McCorry, "I believe God is telling us it's time to move on and do a new thing. We wish we could have your blessing as we go, but we'll go without it. We have to follow the path God has for us."

Pastor began shaking his head. "I can't support you in this move or encourage you," he said, "because I don't think it's the right time. It's not right in the spiritual realm and it's not right in the practical realm. Look, you don't have a church building and you don't have any members."

"And your hearts are not right," Vickie tossed in. "I had no idea you two held us in such low esteem. You need to work out the issues you have with us before you try to start your own church. You want to build it on a sound foundation. Right now, your foundation is pure sand."

Sandra opened her mouth to tell *First Lady* Vickie about sand, but Andrew stopped her with a tight squeeze on her thigh.

"We have the money to buy a building," he said, ignoring Vickie's words. "And we're trusting God to bring the members."

Pastor McCorry shook his head. "I don't know what else we can say."

Andrew stood and Sandra stood with him. "I don't think there's anything left to say. We appreciate all you've done for us." Andrew extended his hand. "I hope we can part friends and brothers. I could benefit from your counsel as we move forward with the new church."

Pastor McCorry shook Andrew's hand. "If you can't take my counsel now, Andrew, I don't see any point in seeking it later. We'll always be here if you need us, but we can't help you with this church of yours."

"I'm sorry you feel that way, Pastor," Sandra said. Though she wasn't really feeling it, she leaned in and gave him a hug. "Thanks for everything. You've been a good pastor to us." She glanced at Vickie, but couldn't bring herself to hug her.

"Even though I know you won't come," Andrew said, "we'll invite you to our opening service. You're a doubter like Thomas in the Bible. You're going to have to see to believe. Well, we're going to make believers of both of you."

Feeling proud of her husband, Sandra took his hand and followed him out of the McCorry home.

Chapter 7

Andrew stood in the back of the ballroom he and Sandra had reserved for the dinner that was now in progress. This meal was about much more than food, though. Andrew had considered the things Pastor McCorry had said and knew he was right. He couldn't take Kevin Costner's "If you build it, they will come" approach if he wanted the new church to be a success. He had the money for a building and he believed that God would send members, but he needed a leadership team to help him and Sandra build the ministry. The two of them had discussed their options and decided to ask five couples in leadership at Praise City to join with them in their new ministry, which they were calling Showers of Blessings.

They knew Pastor wouldn't like their stealing members from Praise City, but what else could they do? They needed folks they knew and trusted and who knew and trusted them. They also needed folks who believed in their vision. So their first step had been to invite twelve couples and their children to a backyard barbecue. The five couples having dinner with them tonight were the couples from the barbecue that had shown the most enthusiasm and support after hearing their plans. Tonight he and Sandra were taking it to the next level.

These were the five couples they wanted with them in Showers of Blessings. Now he had to sell them on the idea.

Sandra looked up from her conversation with Monica Ray and saw him. She waved him back to the table. When he joined them, she leaned over and said, "Everybody has dessert. When are you going to speak?"

"I guess now's the time," he said. He stood and tapped his fork against his glass to get everybody's attention. "The evening is not over, but I wanted you to know how much Sandra and I have enjoyed your fellowship tonight."

A bunch of "thank you"s came from the gathered couples.

"While you're finishing your desserts, I'd like to talk to you some more about Showers of Blessings. We're excited about the path God is leading us on, but, like Moses when he was leading the Israelites, we're going to need help." He paused, taking the time to make eye contact with each couple. "We've invited you here tonight to ask you to take part in this vision and join the Showers of Blessings leadership team."

Sandra came and stood next to him. "Because we always want to be honest with you," she said, "we want to confess that last week's cookout was your interview. As Andrew said, we want folks with us who believe in the vision God has given us. Your response to our news last week showed us that you were believers. We want you with us, if you want to be with us."

"We'll understand if you turn us down," Andrew added, "and there'll be no hard feelings. This has to be right for all of us. If you don't feel it's right for you, then I have to believe that it's not what God wants for you. It's that simple."

Then Andrew went around the table telling everybody what their positions would be. The Moores would serve as associate pastors of Christian Education; the Thomases, associate pastors of Music and Praise; the Salleys, Youth Pastors; and the Rays, associate pastors of Outreach. The Wilsons would serve as Assistant Pastors and be their closest advisors.

"That's it," Andrew said, after he informed the couples of their proposed duties. "Do you have any questions?"

Jacob Wilson posed the first question. "Starting a new church takes a lot of time and effort, Andrew, and we all have full-time jobs. How much of a commitment are you expecting from us?"

Andrew turned to Sandra and chuckled. "How could you let me forget the most important point?" She just shook her head. He turned back to the group. "These will be full-time positions. We're asking you to take a leap of faith with us and we're prepared to compensate you. Because the Lord has blessed us financially beyond what we could have asked, we want to share that with you. Therefore, we're offering each of you five-year guaranteed contracts at three times your current salary and twice the benefits."

Murmurs went around the room.

"That's generous," Gloria Moore said.

"Very generous," her husband echoed.

"Any other questions?" Andrew asked.

"I've never been involved in the formation of a new congregation," George Salley said. "I want to join you but I'm not sure I have the skills."

"You have the heart," Sandra said. "You can be trained in the rest."

"In fact," Andrew said, "we've planned a four-week retreat in Hawaii for next month. It'll be a time of teaching and learning, prayer and fasting, and fun and fellowship. We have to be a closely knit team if we're going to achieve this vision."

"Hawaii!" Jackie Thomas called out. "Sign us up now!"

Everybody laughed at Jackie's enthusiasm.

"What about a building?" Michael Ray asked. "Where will we be meeting?"

"We'll have to find a building," Andrew said. "We've found five properties that could work but we wanted to get you all on board before we made a final decision." He glanced around the table. "I'm not asking for a commitment tonight. I know you need some time to consider what's best for your families. Your contracts will be delivered to your homes tomorrow so you can review them as you make your decision. We don't want to put pressure on you, but we need your answer within the next two weeks. The sooner the better."

Chapter 8

Sandra stood on the lanai of the Waikiki bungalow her husband had rented for their retreat, looking beyond the soothing blue ocean. Despair settled around her when she should have been at her happiest. Her children were sleeping soundly in their rooms. Their leadership team was installed in identical bungalows down the beach. Her parents were in the bungalow next door. Everything was going as she and Andrew had planned. Except she hadn't planned on the casino nestled on the grounds of their resort.

Andrew was doing so well that she hadn't given much thought to his problem. She'd been too busy working with him to build the ministry. They'd gotten their team together and found a building. From what she could see, Andrew didn't have the time or the inclination to gamble. He was totally committed to the ministry. *Stop torturing yourself,* she said silently. *He's not going to start gambling again.*

She was beginning to believe she was right until that afternoon when the group had decided they wanted to spend the evening in the casino. She'd tried to talk them out of it to no avail. So now she stood here on the lanai while her husband dressed for his night out, without her.

She turned when she heard him cross the threshold onto the lanai. "Don't go, Andrew. You can make an excuse."

He came to her and pressed a kiss on her forehead. "Stop worrying. Everything will be fine. I'll be fine."

"You have a problem, Andrew. Twice we almost lost everything because of it. I can't live through a third time."

He sighed. "There's not going to be a third time. I've got it under control. We're just going out to have a little fun."

She tried another tact. "Do you think it's appropriate for the pastor and leadership team of Showers of Blessings to be hanging out in a casino?"

He leaned back against the railing. "You don't lose your faith because you walk into a casino, Sandra. Showers of Blessings is not going to have any Christian litmus test, other than the Bible. I thought you wanted us to be different from Praise City, with all its do's and don'ts."

Andrew had an answer for everything, just as he always did. "That's not the issue," she said. "The issue is that you have a gambling problem and you shouldn't be in a casino."

He checked his watch, a new Rolex, and then moved away from the railing. "Come with me," he said. "Even your parents are coming. You'll have fun and you can keep an eye on me."

Sandra shook her head. "I can't."

He kissed her forehead. "I won't stay out too late," he said. And then he left her standing alone on the lanai.

Sandra turned back to the ocean, wiping at the tears that now rolled down her cheeks. They had everything and she was afraid they were going to lose it. How could Andrew even take the chance? Didn't he realize the severity of his gambling problem? It wasn't something that he could get over by the sheer force of his will. He'd tried. And failed. Twice.

Sandra turned when she heard the door open, her heart growing light. Thank God, she thought, Andrew had changed his mind and decided to stay home.

"Sandra," her mother's voice called. "Where are you?"

Sandra's heart sank. "I'm out on the lanai, Mom." She wiped her tears away and prayed her mother wouldn't be able to tell she'd been crying.

"I just saw Andrew," Ida said when she joined her. "He said you were staying in because you weren't feeling well. What's wrong?"

"Just tired, Mom. Nothing to worry about."

Her mother came closer, studied her face. "You've been crying. What's wrong, Sandra?"

Sandra took a deep breath, debating how much to tell her mother. "I'm worried about Andrew."

"Ahh," her mother said, "because he's going to the casino."

"Bingo!"

"He hasn't gotten help, has he?"

Sandra shook her head. "With the money and the new church, I thought everything would work itself out. He promised me that the lottery would be the last time."

"Lottery?" her mother asked. "What are you talking about?"

Sandra debated lying to her mother, but quickly decided she needed to unburden herself. "Andrew didn't get an inheritance, Mom. When all was lost, he bought two lottery tickets and we won. Twenty million dollars."

Her mother dropped down in a wicker chaise. "You won the lottery?"

Sandra nodded.

"Why did you lie about where the money came from?"

"Because we were ashamed. With Andrew being a minister in a church that preached regularly on the evils of gambling, including playing the lottery, how could we explain our winnings to the pastor and the congregation?"

"So you came up with this elaborate lie?"

Sandra hated the look of disappointment in her mother's eyes. "We're doing good things with the money, Mom. Showers of Blessings is going to be a blessing to a lot of people."

Ida shook her head. "You're deceiving yourself, Sandra. How can it be a blessing when it's based on a lie? How can it be a blessing when Andrew's vice is its foundation?"

Her mother was voicing all the concerns Sandra had willfully pushed out of her mind. "God knows our hearts," she said. "That's what matters."

"What matters is that you're lying on a daily basis," her mother corrected. "Doesn't that bother you?"

Sandra sat on the chaise next to her mother. "But we're lying so that people will be helped. How many people do you think would go to a church founded with lottery money?"

Her mother shook her head. "A lot of people, I'd guess. Sure, some folks might be skeptical about a pastor who plays the lottery, but telling the truth would have given you and Andrew an opening to talk about how gambling had damaged your family."

Sandra knew her mother was right, but it was too late for her and Andrew to make that choice. They had to stick with the road they had chosen. That is, unless Andrew blew it by going back to his old ways. "Are you going to tell Dad?" she asked.

"I know I should, but I won't. I think you should, though."

"I can't," Sandra said. "I just can't."

Her mother got up and kissed her on her cheek. "I'll just wait until the day you can. You're a stronger woman than you think, Sandra. I hope you believe that one day."

Sandra watched her mother leave the lanai. While she knew the older woman had a point, Sandra had more pressing issues. She had to keep her family together and her husband in line. With a sigh, she left the lanai and headed to their bedroom to dress. She'd call for a sitter and then she'd join her husband in the casino. If he wouldn't help himself, it was her duty to help him.

Chapter 9

A month after leaving Hawaii, Andrew sat in his office at the new church, the phone to his ear, twirling a gold pen through his fingers. "Fifty thousand," he told his bookie. "And don't call me again. I'll make contact with you from here on out."

Andrew hung up the phone, feeling a bit guilty. He'd told Sandra and God that he'd give up gambling after the lottery, but he hadn't been able to do it. He'd tried, but he'd been sucked right back into it while helping his father-in-law search for a horse farm. Not only had they found a farm, he'd found a love for horses, not riding them like his children, but betting on them.

Then that trip to Hawaii had given him a chance to get back in the casino. It was a familiar place, and he'd found himself sneaking off to play a few games when Sandra was otherwise occupied. He had a problem, he knew, but fortunately he had money to lose. At least he wasn't as bad as basketball Hall of Famer Charles Barkley, who lost half a million dollars in a casino. He wasn't that crazy.

His intercom buzzed and he pressed the answer button. "Pastor," his secretary said, "you have a visitor who doesn't have an appointment. His name is Luther Williams. He says that he knows you from Praise City."

Though the name didn't ring a bell with him, Andrew knew this was an opportunity to win over a Praise City member. He checked his watch. "I have a few minutes before my next meeting. Send him on in." Andrew stood, as he always did, when someone entered his office. He almost dropped back down in his chair when he saw who Luther Williams was. This was the guy he'd seen outside the convenience store the day he'd bought the lottery tickets. What did he want?

Luther moved easily to the desk and extended his hand. "Thanks for taking the time to talk to me, Pastor," he said. "I knew you'd be busy getting the new church started and all, but I decided to try my luck. It must be my lucky day, huh?"

Andrew motioned Luther to the chair in front of his desk. The man's use of the words *luck* and *lucky* seemed to have some added emphasis but maybe he was reading more into the man's words than was warranted. "Well, it's good to see you again, Luther. What can I do for you today?" he asked.

Luther leaned forward in his chair. "The wife and I are thinking about moving our membership over here with you. We're going through a rough time since I got laid off, and the folks at Praise City don't seem willing or able to help. I'm hoping your church will take care of its members better."

Andrew's ears were alert for any kind of threat, but he didn't hear one. "Of course, we'll take care of our members. That's one of the purposes of the church."

"That's the way I see it, too," Luther said. "It's nice to know that some pastors believe in the church blessing the members rather than the other way around all the time."

"Well, I don't know about other churches, but here at Showers of Blessings things will be different. We've been blessed and we're going to bless others."

Luther nodded. "I guess 'Showers of Blessings—a place to bless and be blessed' is more than a motto."

"It certainly is," Andrew said, wondering where the conversation was going.

"Well, it sure does seem like you've been blessed a lot since I saw you that day at the convenience store. It's like you hit the lottery, but not the real lottery 'cos I know you preachers are against the lottery, you know what I mean?"

Andrew nodded. He definitely knew what the man meant. Obviously, Luther had seen those lottery tickets in his hand that day. What did he want? "I know what you mean," Andrew said. "And I look forward to having you and your wife here at Showers of Blessings. We take care of our own."

Luther stood up. "I'm glad to hear it. The wife and I will be here on Sunday. We're not asking for a handout, Pastor, but we could use a little help with the mortgage. It's tough with just one salary."

"I hear you, Luther. We won't let you down. Just be sure to be here on Sunday."

Luther extended his hand for a shake. "You can count on it," he said. And then he winked.

Andrew wanted to slap him but he shook his offered hand instead. "See you and the wife on Sunday."

Andrew watched as Luther strode out of his office, renewed pep in his step. He shook his head. He'd been blackmailed in his church office. How bold was that? He dropped down in his chair. He had just agreed to pay this guy's mortgage. How was he going to make that work without confirming that he'd won the lottery? All Luther had now was a strong suspicion based on seeing those lottery tickets. Once the church paid his mortgage, he'd have evidence.

Andrew didn't have much time to ponder the question as there was a knock at his door and Sandra walked in. "Who was that guy?" she asked. "He looked familiar."

"His name is Luther Williams. You've probably seen him before. He's a Praise City member who's thinking about moving his membership over here with us."

Sandra gave him a full-watted smile. "Well, that's good news.

I know you gave him the counsel he needed to make the right decision."

Sandra's faith in him was a heavy burden since he knew he didn't deserve it. "I did my best," he said. "The guy is out of work and needs money for his mortgage."

"What did you tell him?"

"I told him that Showers of Blessings takes care of its own."

She lifted a brow. "You know he's going to expect us to take care of his mortgage payments, don't you?"

Andrew nodded, an idea forming in his mind. "What if we did?"

Sandra leaned against the edge of his desk, facing him. "We can certainly afford it, but we'd have to develop some policy around the kind of help we give and in what situations so we would be fair to all our congregation."

Andrew nodded. "We should discuss it with the leadership team."

Sandra stood. "Speaking of which, they're assembling in the conference room now. We'd better get in there."

Andrew followed his wife out of his office and down the hallway to the conference room. Once all twelve members of the team were seated around the conference table, he opened the meeting. "What are our numbers looking like for our first Sunday service?" he asked Michael Ray, the associate pastor in charge of Outreach.

"We're looking at a minimum of two hundred, two hundred fifty folks. Most of them are coming from Praise City, though. Those folks are committed and they've worked hard to get the word out about what we're doing here at Showers of Blessings. It's a challenge, though, because there are so many churches in the metro area. The motto and new building help, but we need more to distinguish ourselves if we want folks to check us out. Religion editors at seven of the eight newspapers we contacted are either coming to the first service themselves or sending a reporter. We should see some benefit out of their coverage, but not this week."

Andrew smiled. He'd just figured out how to solve two problems with one stone, so to speak. "You're right, Brother Ray, but we don't have to come up with a way to be different. We are different. It's right there in our motto, 'Showers of Blessings—a place to bless and be blessed.' We're going to be the church that blesses its members practically and spiritually. We're going to meet people's everyday needs."

"How are we going to do that, Pastor?" Rob Moore, the associate pastor of Christian Education, asked.

Andrew grinned. "This Sunday we're going to ask all the unemployed folks to come to the altar. When they get there, we're going to ask them to put their name and financial need on a slip of paper and put it in a basket. Then we're going to meet those needs."

"What?"

"How can we afford to do that?"

"What if it's a lot of people?"

"Doesn't matter," Andrew said, answering the questions from his team in a single matter-of-fact statement. "We're going to do it, and by doing it we're going to build our reputation as a church that cares."

"And we're going to end up with a lot of poor members who take more than they give," said Associate Pastor Ray.

Andrew shook his head. "It may start that way, but folks with money will be drawn here because they see that we're taking the Bible seriously. You all will have to trust me on this. If we take this approach, our membership will grow faster than we ever thought." *And I'll have a cover for getting Luther off my back.*

He glanced in Sandra's direction and saw her love and pride in him in her eyes. He didn't deserve her, but he was going to do everything he could to keep her. And that included keeping Luther quiet.

Chapter 10

"Good night, sweetheart," Sandra said into the phone. She sat on the floral upholstered chaise in her church office. As usual, she and Andrew were working late. "Mommy loves you, too. You and your brother be good for Grandma and Grandpa."

"We will, Mommy," ten-year-old Andrew, Jr. said.

Sandra held the phone close to her breast after the dial tone told her that her son was no longer on the line. She missed her children, but she understood that they enjoyed staying with her parents on the horse farm. She enjoyed it out there as well, despite the disapproving looks her mother gave her when she thought no one was looking. Sandra had given up trying to make her mother understand that the good she and Andrew were doing with the money more than made up for the lie they told about getting it. The older woman would just have to see for herself.

Sandra yawned. Today had been another busy day, and she was ready to go home. Actually, she was ready to go to their new home, but the contractor had told them just today that it would be at least two more months before they could move in. She was getting the dream house she always wanted, but it was taking some time. She yawned again. She could wait.

She got up from the chaise and headed to Andrew's office. As usual, she would have to drag him out. When she opened his office door, she found him sitting at his desk, head lowered over a pad, a pen in his hand. Her heart grew full as she watched him, thinking of how much their lives had changed in the last few months. Their dreams had finally come true. Her husband was now pastor of his own church, she was First Lady, and together they would make a difference in a lot of lives. They'd show the naysayers, namely, her mom, and Pastor McCorry and Vickie, just how wrong they were.

"Sweetheart," she called as she walked toward her husband's desk. "It's time to go home."

He looked up and gave her a weary smile. "I'm sorry. I lost track of time." He put the pad and pencil on the desk and then rubbed the back of his neck.

When she reached him, she pressed a light kiss against his lips. "It's okay. I've gotten used to it."

He pushed his chair back from the desk and pulled her down on his lap. "I promise I'll do better," he said, rubbing a finger down her cheek. "I was working on Sunday's sermon."

"How's it going?"

He inclined his head toward the pad on the desk. "Why don't you read it and tell me what you think?"

She leaned over and picked up the pad. She read the words of what she knew would be one of her husband's most powerful sermons. A tear rolled down her cheek.

"That bad?" Andrew teased, wiping away the tear.

She turned to face him. "No," she said. "That good. This is wonderful and powerful, Andrew. You're going to bless everybody on Sunday."

"That's the plan," he said, pulling her close. "We are Showers of Blessings, after all."

Sandra eased off his lap and sat on the edge of his desk. "That we are," she said.

He lifted a brow. "I feel a *but* coming. I knew the sermon was missing something."

She met his eyes. "It's not the sermon," she said. "It's this idea of having folks come down to the altar and write their needs on a piece of paper so we can meet them. I had Jacob run some numbers. What you're proposing can get pretty expensive pretty quickly."

"We have the money," he reminded her. "We can afford it."

"I know we can afford it now, but it's not something we can sustain over the long haul. Can't we start smaller so that we do more over time?"

"I'm open to suggestions," he said.

She couldn't help but lean over and kiss him. They were really partners in this ministry, and he considered seriously every idea she had. If she didn't already love him, his respect for her and her ideas would have made her love him.

"What's that for?" he asked.

"Because I love you," she said simply.

"I love you, too," he said. "Now tell me your idea."

"I think there needs to be a closer tie between the sermon and the blessing. Last year, after preaching a sermon on good stewardship, Bishop Long at New Birth asked folks who had gotten themselves into trouble with credit card debt to come to the altar so he could pray for them. He ended up praying for them and paying off their credit card debt."

Andrew leaned forward and kissed her. "Marrying you is the best thing I've done in my life," he told her. "That's exactly what we'll do, but instead of credit card debt, we'll do mortgage debt. This is what was missing from the sermon."

"Paying mortgage debt might be too ambitious, Andrew," she said. "Couldn't we start even smaller?"

He shook his head. "Mortgages are on my heart. You have to trust me on this. It's what God wants."

Sandra still wasn't 100 percent on board with the idea, but she trusted her husband. His gambling days were behind him and so were the lies and half truths that went with them. "Then that's what we'll do," she said, giving him her full trust.

Chapter 11

Andrew stood in the pulpit, his ministerial staff on the platform with him, his brand-new choir robed and seated behind him, his wife and First Lady in the second pew left of the aisle. He looked out on the congregation, his congregation. Since the sanctuary was a little over a quarter full, he guessed the total in attendance was a little less than six hundred. Having this many attendees on the first Sunday increased his confidence that the church would be filled to capacity within six months. He could see it in his mind now and he knew it would happen. He'd bet all the money he had that it would.

Catching himself thinking about gambling, Andrew quickly turned his attention back to his congregation. "The Lord has shown me," he said, "that some of you are struggling with your housing payment. Some of you have asked for help and not gotten it, others of you have exhausted all the help you have, while others of you are too ashamed to let others know you're having trouble. Well, the Lord is speaking to all of you today and he wants you to come down to the altar so that I can pray for you. Your help is coming. You just need faith to hold on until it gets here. You can exercise your faith this morning by coming down to the altar."

As he gave the altar call, his eyes landed on Luther wearing a smug grin as he made his way to the altar. About fifty others joined him. "Don't let pride keep you from your blessing," Andrew added for the benefit of those who might be reluctant to come down. About twice as many more people joined them at the altar.

"The altar call this morning is for each of you. God wants to bless you, and we here at Showers of Blessings want to bless you. We're going to pray for you, but here at Showers of Blessings we believe that prayer, like faith, is dead without works. The blessing God has for each of you standing at the altar is six months' worth of housing payments."

A huge sigh went out among the congregation. Andrew spoke to them. "Some of you sitting out there now wish you had come to the altar, but it's too late. You've missed a blessing because you wouldn't follow the Lord's instruction. The good news is that the altar is still open for you, but not for the housing payments. The altar is open for you to take a step of faith. All you have to do is stand to your feet where you are. The altar of God is all around."

After the congregation stood, Andrew prayed a prayer of faith and blessing on them all. When he finished, the choir began a song as the deacons came around and took names and contact information for everyone at the altar. That done, Andrew said, "Now we're going to open the doors of the church for membership. Showers of Blessings is a new church and we want you to be a part of us. If you feel the Lord leading you to join with us, please come down to the altar as the choir gives us another song. If you're not ready to make that decision today, that's okay. Just keep coming back until you do feel it's right."

More than half of the church came down. After Andrew officially welcomed them, he said, "We're going to give the benediction now and invite you all to share in refreshments with us in the fellowship hall. First Lady Sandra will be there to meet you, and I'll join you shortly. Those of you desiring membership, please stay here until we get your names and contact numbers."

Andrew gave the benediction and then waited for the ushers and Sandra to lead the congregation to the fellowship hall. He noticed that only a few people chose to leave instead of staying to share in refreshments. Another good sign.

Andrew took special care to greet every new member personally. To help him remember names, he had a photographer take a picture of each person, label it with his or her name, and put it in a folder for him to study. He knew it would be a tough job remembering all their names, but he was committed to it. People needed to know that their pastor knew who they were.

After he had greeted the new members, he left them and joined Sandra and the others in the fellowship hall. His wife was encircled by a small group so instead of interrupting her, he made his way around the room meeting the others. He stiffened a bit when he saw that the next couple up was Luther and a woman he guessed was his wife. The wife's eyes were damp.

"Thank you so much, Pastor," she said. "I'm Carrie, Luther's wife. You really blessed us today. We're really going through a hard time. Since Luther lost his job, we've had to use credit cards for things his salary normally covered. Your help came just in time because our credit cards are at the limit. Isn't that right, Luther?"

Andrew blinked twice. Was this woman now asking for help with her credit cards? He glanced at Luther.

"She's right, Pastor. It's a miracle, like God handed down manna from heaven just when we needed it. If we needed those credit cards now, we'd be in trouble because all of them are at the max."

Andrew wasn't stupid. Luther and Carrie were asking for

money for their credit card bills. This couple was going to be a problem. He'd have to figure out a way to deal with them.

"You two just keep the faith. God will open a door for you," he told them. "All you have to do is trust Him."

Chapter 12

Andrew called a short meeting with his leadership team in the conference room after the social hour in the fellowship hall ended. "Numbers?" he asked.

"One hundred and two people came down for the first altar call," Jacob Wilson said. "Those will be getting mortgage or rental assistance for the six months you promised. I estimate that will cost a little over half a million dollars."

"That much?" Rob Moore asked.

"It's money well spent," Andrew said, brushing aside the comment. "What about membership?"

"Three hundred and thirteen people joined, including eighty-two of those who got housing assistance. That brings our total membership to four hundred and twenty-five. That's not bad at all."

Andrew nodded. "No, that's very good. As I stood in the pulpit today, I saw the church filled to capacity. I believe our membership will grow to three thousand in the next six months."

Jacob Wilson whistled. "That would be some growth."

"I believe it," Andrew said, "and I need you all to believe with me. God is doing something here and He's using us to do it." He looked around the conference table, meeting the eyes of each member of his team. "Are you all onboard with me?" He waited while each of them nodded. "Good," he said. "There are big things ahead for all of us. I've got three newspaper interviews lined up next week, and the local CBS affiliate wants to do an on-air interview for their morning show. You can't buy that kind of publicity."

"That's wonderful, Andrew," Sandra said. "I can't believe you didn't tell me."

"I wanted to surprise you. And there's more to the surprise. They want to interview both of us."

"Both of us?" she exclaimed.

"Of course," he said. "What's a pastor without his First Lady?"

"You've got that right," Jackie Thomas said.

Andrew looked back at the group. "For now, Sandra and I will be the face of the church, but I don't want any of you to think that means your contribution is less valuable. It doesn't. We all have different roles to play and it takes all of us doing our part to make this work. Agreed?" Again, he waited for everybody's nod. "Then that's it for today. Thanks for all your hard work. I'll see you all on Tuesday."

Andrew and Sandra stayed in the conference room while the others filed out. "We've had some day, Pastor Gooden."

"Yes, we have, First Lady Gooden. And this is only the beginning. The sky is the limit for us and for this ministry. God has opened the windows of heaven so He can rain down blessings on us. He started with the lottery and He has no plans to close it."

"Excuse us."

They both turned at the sound of Sandra's father's voice. He and her mother stood in the entrance to the conference room. "Come on in, Dad, Mom," Andrew said. "Have a seat and join us. We're just winding down."

"Where are the kids?" Sandra asked after her parents had seated themselves at the conference table.

"They're with the Salley kids. Pastor Salley had some last-minute something to do in his office. Mrs. Salley is watching them."

Sandra nodded. "Thanks, Mom."

Her father cleared his throat. "I want you both to know how proud I am of you and what you're doing here in this church. It was something to see you help those people with their mortgages and rent. So many churches want to pray and do nothing else. I'm glad Showers of Blessings is different."

Sandra shot a quick glance at her mother, but the older woman's face told her nothing.

"Your blessing means a lot, Dad," Andrew said. "It always has."

"It's no secret that I didn't approve of you in the beginning, Andrew," he said. "I thought I saw too much of myself in you, too much recklessness. I'm happy to say I was wrong. You've been a good husband to my girl and a good father to my grandchildren. And now you're going to be a great pastor to the congregation God gives you."

Andrew reached for Sandra's hand and squeezed it. "I couldn't do it without your daughter by my side. I'm a better man with her. I've always known that."

Grady winked. "We're both lucky when it comes to wives," he said, smiling at his wife. "I got myself a winner, too."

Sandra's mother waved off the compliment.

"It's true," Grady said to Ida. "I just wish I had been as good a husband to you as the boy here has been to our girl. I'm sorry for the years I wasted."

Ida blinked back tears. "A marriage is for better or worse," she said. "We've had our share of worse but we've had more than our share of better. I'm happy with the deal."

"So am I," Grady said.

"We should celebrate," Sandra said.

"Celebrate what?" Ida asked.

"Our happy marriages. We don't ever want to take them for granted."

"Sounds like a good idea to me," Andrew said, standing. "Why don't we go out for dinner? Those refreshments didn't do the job for me."

"Me either," Grady said, standing as well.

"I could eat a little something," Ida said. "And those kids are probably hungry from all that running around."

"They aren't the only ones," Sandra said. "Let's get them so we can head out."

"I'll round up the kids," Sandra's father said.

"I need to stop by my office for a quick minute," Andrew said. "I'll meet you all at the entrance."

With that, Andrew left for his office and Sandra's dad headed off in search of his grandkids. Sandra was left with her mother.

"Dad said he was proud of us, Mom," she said, "but you haven't said anything."

"I've said what I need to say, Sandra. Nothing has changed."

"But can't you see what we're doing here?"

Her mother shook her head. "What I see is a church built on a rocky foundation. I just hope you don't face a strong wind."

Chapter 13

"Are you sure I look okay?" Sandra asked her husband when they stepped off the elevator on the fourth floor of the WTAL building that housed the studio for the local CBS affiliate. She wore a cap sleeve cornflower blue Maria Pinto dress identical to the one Michelle Obama had worn to the third presidential debate. In fact, the closet of their new house would be filled with Michelle originals. Clothes were top among the things she'd splurged on since they'd gotten their windfall.

Andrew brushed a kiss against her cheek. "When it comes to First Ladies, Michelle Obama's got nothing on you."

Sandra frowned. "Be serious, Andrew," she said.

"I am serious," he said. "You look wonderful. That color is going to show up well on television."

Sandra wanted to believe her husband's words but she began to second-guess herself and him. Had her arms been in better condition, she could have worn that sleeveless navy blue and white polka-dotted Lanvin Resort dress identical to the one Michelle had worn to that D.C. elementary school the other day. She'd start working out with a personal trainer as soon as they moved into the new house. She already had him lined up. She'd have her Michelle Obama arms in no time.

She and Andrew followed the long hallway to the receptionist's desk. "We're the Goodens," he told the young woman sitting behind the desk.

"Good morning," she said, standing. "We were expecting you. I'll take you to the green room where the other guests are waiting."

Sandra caught her husband's eye, mouthed "green room," and shook her head. He grinned at her.

They followed the receptionist through a set of glass double doors, down another hallway that opened to a lounge where a continental breakfast had been prepared. Sandra's eyed roamed from the delicious-looking pastries to the other couple in the room. She swallowed hard. It was Pastor McCorry and Vickie. Before she could say anything, the young receptionist was making introductions.

"We already know each other," Pastor McCorry said, cutting the young girl off. "In fact, we're old friends."

The young girl smiled. "Well, it shouldn't be long before they call you in for makeup. Enjoy the breakfast and let me know if I can get you anything else."

"Everything's fine," Pastor McCorry said, answering for them all.

Sandra resented the way Pastor McCorry had stepped up to speak for the group. He was no longer their leader and it was presumptuous of him to act as though he was. She glanced at Andrew to see if he shared her feelings, but he was smiling.

"It's good to see you two," Andrew said. He extended his hand to Pastor McCorry, who shook it, and then he placed a soft kiss on Vickie's cheek. "It's been a long time."

"Not that long," Pastor McCorry said.

Contrary man, Sandra thought, *always had to have the last word.* "It seems like it because of all the changes in our lives since we last talked," she said. She hadn't embraced either McCorry and wouldn't. Their lack of support for Showers of Blessings still stung.

Vickie caught her eye. "We've heard a lot about your ministry," the older woman said. "It seems you're off to a good start. You have some strong folks on your leadership team."

Sandra flinched at the dig. Their leadership team had come from Praise City, the McCorry's church.

"They wanted to come with us, Pastor," Andrew explained. "We needed help and they were the best folks we knew."

Pastor McCorry nodded. "I'm not surprised. In fact, I expected some folks to follow you, and I was right. You're a charismatic guy, Andrew. I never doubted your ability, just your timing."

"They believe in the ministry God has given us and believe God wants them to be a part of it."

"Believing doesn't make it the right time," Vickie said.

Pastor McCorry shook his head. "Now's not the time for that, Vickie," he told his wife. Then he looked at Andrew and Sandra. "We didn't think your leaving Praise City was the right thing to do at the time, but now that you've done it, we only want the best for you and your members. I've been hearing nothing but good things."

Sandra wondered who'd been reporting back to the McCorrys. She'd have to talk to their leadership team about where their loyalties lay.

"Everything that I'm putting in place at Showers of Blessings, I learned from you," Andrew said. "My pulpit is open to you anytime you want to join us."

"Thanks," Pastor McCorry said. "I may take you up on that."

Sandra knew that statement for the cop-out it was. Pastor McCorry was never going to step foot in Showers of Blessings.

"It's a standing offer," Andrew said. Then he turned to Sandra and asked, "Do you want some coffee or a pastry or something?" he asked. When she shook her head, he asked the same question of Vickie.

"Thanks, but I'm fine,"Vickie said.

"I'd like a cup of coffee," Pastor McCorry said. "Why don't you ladies take a seat while we get our coffee."

Sandra reluctantly followed Vickie to a table. When they were seated, Vickie said, "Your new house looks like it's going to be gorgeous."

And it's going to be twice as large as yours, Sandra said to herself. "Thank you," she said. "We wanted to get a place that would grow with us and the ministry. You know how that is."

Vickie nodded. "I do. How are you dealing with challenges of being First Lady?"

Sandra gave a false smile. "So far, it's been nothing but rewarding. Andrew and I are closer than ever and that makes it easy." Even if the job had been killing her, she would never admit it to Vickie for fear the woman would use the information against her somewhere down the line.

"Enjoy it while it lasts,"Vickie said. "The challenges will come. I can promise you that. If you need an ear, I've got one to give you."

Sandra thought she heard sincerity in Vickie's voice, but she couldn't be sure. "Even though you don't believe in what Andrew and I are doing?"

Vickie glanced toward the men chatting near the pastry table. "Pastor is right. It's a done deal now, and we all want good things to come from it."

Sandra still wasn't sure she could trust Vickie, but the old saying "Keep your friends close and your enemies closer" came to mind. "We're having a home blessing ceremony a couple of weeks after we move in. Why don't you and Pastor join us? We'd love to have you." As an added bonus, Sandra would get to rub Vickie's nose in the grandness of the place.

"I don't see why not,"Vickie said. "I'll call you later in the week and we can coordinate our schedules."

Sandra nodded. She couldn't wait for Vickie to see how the Lord had elevated her and Andrew. They and Showers of Blessings were new news while Praise City was old school, old news. She welcomed the contrast in the two churches viewers were certain to see when the television show aired.

Chapter 14

Six months later

Andrew paced in front of his desk in his church office. His day had started badly and gotten worse. What was he going to do? His financial situation was nowhere near as dire as it had been before he'd won the lottery, but it was pretty bad. How could he have lost so much money so fast? He wiped his hand down his face.

"Okay," he told himself, "don't panic. You can fix this."

First things first. He had to find five hundred thousand dollars to pay his debt to his bookie. He had the money, but he didn't have easy access to it because it was in a trust for his boys. It would take some legal finagling to get that money without Sandra's knowledge since there was no way she'd sign for him to get it.

So all he had to leverage were the horse farm, their new house, and the church. He had convinced his father-in-law to allow him to get a mortgage on the horse farm, he'd put less down on the house than Sandra thought he had, and he'd been dipping a little in the church discretionary fund. Of course, he planned to repay them all before Sandra, or anybody else, found out. He was just having a turn of bad luck. Things would change for him. He was convinced of it. He only needed time.

He turned at the sound of the intercom on his desk. He walked over and pressed the button. "Pastor, you have an unscheduled visitor. A Mr. Bert Taylor. He wouldn't state his business."

He didn't have to. Andrew knew who he was. "Send him in," he said. "I'll see him."

Instead of greeting his visitor at the door, as he normally did, he went and sat at his desk. He needed the protection provided by the furniture. He pulled a pad out of his desk drawer and pretended to write. He heard the door open but ignored it as if he hadn't.

"Hello, Pastor."

He didn't even look up when he heard Bert's voice. "I told you never to contact me here," he said, still pretending to write.

Out of the corner of his eye, he watched Bert saunter to the desk and drop down in one of the visitor chairs. When Bert leaned back in his chair and put his feet on the corner of the desk, Andrew was forced to give him his attention.

"That's more like it," Bert said, meeting Andrew's eyes. "I don't like being ignored and I don't take orders from deadbeats who don't pay their debts."

"You know I'm good for it," Andrew said.

"What I know is that you owe me five hundred grand."

"Don't I always pay?"

Bert took a toothpick from his shirt pocket and stuck it in his mouth. "You've never owed this much before. And you've never avoided me the way you have for the last month or so. I don't get a call, a visit, nothing. Makes me wonder about my personal hygiene."

Andrew grimaced as Bert laughed at his own joke.

Bert removed his feet from the desk and leaned toward Andrew. "I hope you're not trying to cheat me, Andrew. You've got a good setup here with this church. I'd hate to have to ask your deacons to make good on what you owe. Somehow I don't think they'd look too kindly on a gambling pastor. You could find yourself out of a job."

Bert's words didn't scare him. He'd heard them before. "What good would that do you? Not having a job would make me less able to pay you, not more."

Chuckling, Bert leaned back in his chair. "Church folks hate a scandal. They'd fire you and pay me just to keep me quiet." He leaned forward again. "Look, I'm not here to ruin your gig. I just want my money."

"And I've told you, you'll get it."

"When?" Bert demanded.

"Give me a couple more weeks. I have something in the works, but it'll take a couple of weeks."

Bert stood, flicked the toothpick on Andrew's desk. "I'm not a bank," he said. "But I am going to have to charge you interest. I'd say two weeks is worth an additional hundred thousand."

Andrew jumped out of his chair. "You've got to be joking."

"Do I look like I'm joking?" Bert said. "You pay me in two weeks or I take this to your church. If the church isn't interested, I bet that little wife of yours will be. It's that simple. We clear?"

Andrew nodded. What else could he do? He couldn't let Bert go to Sandra. He'd get the money, even if he had to dip into church funds again.

"Good," Bert said. And then he turned and left the office.

When the door closed, Andrew dropped down in his chair. He would need a miracle to get the money he needed in the next two weeks. All wasn't completely lost. He'd gotten a miracle before. He began to pray.

Chapter 15

Andrew stood in the fellowship hall after service chatting with T. I., the latest celebrity member of Showers of Blessings, about a fund-raiser he'd volunteered to host for the homeless. "We need to sit down and finalize everything next week," he said to T. I. "God's going to bless you for volunteering this way."

"I'm already blessed, man," T. I. said, giving him a two-fisted shake. "I'll hollar at you next week and we'll do this thang."

Andrew smiled as T. I. and his entourage made their way to the door, giving brief greetings to the parishioners they passed. Unlike some churches that had a special up-front section roped off for their celebrity members, Showers of Blessings had no such designated seating. All members were treated equally. Of course, folks like T. I. came with their entourage so they effectively roped themselves off. The rest of the congregation respected the privacy of the celebrities and didn't hound them for autographs. The notice in the weekly bulletin reminding them not to do so helped a lot, he imagined.

He was more than pleased with the way the membership was shaping up. Not only was Showers of Blessings drawing from folks already in church, they were also drawing the unchurched. And while their rolls had a high percentage of lower-income people, there was a healthy percentage of upper-income folks along with quite a few celebrities like T. I. Andrew took that diversity as a sign of the power of the ministry. The church had gone from the roughly six hundred attendees that first Sunday to more than three thousand, exceeding the capacity of the sanctuary. They had gone to two services a Sunday, but Andrew didn't think that was enough. He was eager to talk to his leadership team about expansion to meet their continued growth.

He wanted that growth for spiritual and personal reasons. Personally, an increase in membership would justify his next request for a salary increase, an increase he needed to meet his growing obligations. His luck had turned, but not enough and not fast enough. He was keeping his head above water, but barely. He saw Sandra across the room and smiled at her, relieved that she was unaware of his financial situation. He moved in her direction but stopped when Luther and Carrie Williams greeted him.

"Great sermon, Pastor," Carrie said. "You hit it just right every Sunday. It's as though you know exactly what we need, and you give it to us."

Andrew forced a smile. "That's the Holy Spirit."

"I have to tell you that we've been blessed here at Showers of Blessings more than we've been blessed at any church. And you putting Luther on staff here at the church has helped our family beyond means. I don't know how long we could have gone without him having a job."

Andrew clapped Luther on the shoulder. "We had a need and he was the right man for the job," he said. After running into the man at the dog track, Andrew had figured the best way to keep him from asking for a handout every week was to give him a job. While he was sure Luther was paid more than any other janitor-slash-groundskeeper in the Atlanta area, the cost was more than worth it. Luther did a good job keeping the church and the grounds maintained, and the begging had stopped. Apparently, Luther knew a good thing when he stepped in it. "Luther's doing a great job. He's an important member of the Showers of Blessings family."

Luther actually stood taller at Andrew's words. Amazing, Andrew thought. Luther had gotten the job through blackmail, yet he still valued Andrew's praise. He'd never understand people. Not really. He was about to say more when Sandra walked up and joined them. "How are you two today?" she asked Luther and Carrie.

"Couldn't be better, First Lady," Carrie said. "We were just telling the pastor how much we like it here."

"No more than we like having you here in the Showers family," she said, embracing them with her smile. "I hate to do this," she added, "but I need to steal the pastor for a few minutes."

"We were going anyway," Luther said. "You folks have a nice night."

"Nice couple," Sandra said as they walked away. Then she turned to her husband. "The leadership team is waiting for you. You called the meeting so I think you need to be there. Everybody's tired, and I promised you wouldn't keep them long so we'd better get started."

Andrew followed his wife out of the fellowship hall and to the conference room across from his office. As Sandra had said, everybody was waiting for him. He guessed they'd gotten used to his tardiness by now. He was typically the last one to arrive at a leadership meeting. "I apologize for being late," he told his team while he waited for Sandra to take her seat to his immediate left. After she was seated, he took his place at the head of the conference table.

"It's time we start looking for a bigger building," Andrew

said without preamble. "The second service helps but doesn't totally address our space problems. We are crowding Sunday School classrooms, and the fellowship hall doesn't accommodate all of us."

"We are at capacity with our children's church as well," Sandra added. "We need more space if we're going to serve people the way they should be served."

"Our membership is up, true," Jacob Wilson said, "but so are our expenses. We're barely staying ahead of the curve. I'd hate to see us incur more debt until we build up our reserves."

"Especially if we're going to continue providing social services for our members," George Salley added. "We've paid mortgages, credit card debt, and auto loans. All total, we've spent a little more than two million dollars on these services."

"That's not a lot of money considering the record growth we've experienced in return. And we're going to keep growing so we need to be prepared for that growth. Sandra and I have been looking at buildings. New Birth is getting ready to move to a larger facility, and we should consider taking over their existing complex," Andrew said.

"But that New Birth complex seats twenty thousand people," Rob Moore said. "We're nowhere near that number."

"Not today," Andrew said, "but we'll be close within the next year. If we had a complex that large, we could host events like the T. I. benefit on our property and not have to pay site fees. I'm pretty confident the complex would pay for itself over time." He paused and then took a moment to meet the eyes of each leadership team member. "I'm asking you to take a leap of faith with me, much like the leap of faith you took to join Showers of Blessings in the first place. God didn't let us down then and He won't let us down now. All we have to do is move in faith." He waited another long moment, and then he asked, "Are you ready to move in faith?" As his eyes moved around the table, he got a nonverbal assent from every member. His eyes finally met Sandra's, and they both smiled. Just as they'd hoped, Showers of Blessings was going to expand in a major way.

Chapter 16

"Sandra," her mother said, standing in her closet doorway, "this house is entirely too big. Whatever were you and Andrew thinking to get something so extravagant? I almost got lost trying to find you in here."

Sandra chuckled. She stood in front of the Michelle Obama rack in her closet, trying to decide what to wear to this afternoon's garden party. Andrew had invited their higher income members over to discuss the expansion plans. These people gave a lot of money to the ministry and liked to keep up with where it went. She and Andrew didn't mind obliging them. "It's not that bad, Mom. If you came out here more often, you'd learn the place fairly quickly."

"I doubt it," Ida said, dropping down on one of the two chaises in the closet. "Whoever heard of a closet with a chaise? This closet is as big as our master bedroom. All these clothes and shoes." She shook her head. "I can't believe you bought all of this stuff. You'll never wear it all."

"Which should I wear this afternoon?" she asked her mother, holding up the sleeveless black Michael Kors sheath identical to the one Michelle had worn in her official White House portrait and the blue polka-dotted Lavin Resort.

"The blue is better for the afternoon," her mother said,

shaking her head. "I like Michelle Obama, too, but you've taken it a bit too far."

"I like her style, Momma. What more can I say?" She went over to her wall of shoes and pulled down a matching pair of blue Jimmy Choo slides. "I'm First Lady of a growing ministry. I can't show up looking like a bag lady, especially with the guests we're having this afternoon. These folks place value on presentation."

"I think you've gotten too caught up in presentation. There's a long way from bag lady to designers who serve the First Lady of the United States. Your old clothes were perfectly fine."

Her outfit chosen, Sandra settled down on the opposite chaise facing her mother. "Don't worry about us, Mother. We have the money. We aren't living beyond our means. We can afford the finer things in life so we've bought them. There's nothing wrong with that."

"I know you won a lot of money in the lottery, but I also know you're spending a lot. You bought the horse farm for us, this estate for yourselves, those luxury cars in the garage, this new wardrobe. You've put the boys in a fancy and pricey private school. And I don't even want to think about the money you've put into the church. There has to be a bottom to it, Sandra. You can't keep spending this way forever. You've got to think about the future."

Sandra sighed. Her mother was a worrywart. "You're thinking the way I used to think when I'd look at Pastor and Vickie McCorry. They seemed to have so much more than the rest of us. But that's not the way it is at Showers of Blessings. We have members who have as much as we do and members who have more. More important, we share with those who have less."

"Still," her mother said. "You have to be careful with your money."

Sandra gave her mother an indulgent smile as she got up

to pick out the jewelry she would wear tonight. "We're careful, Mom. And we've planned for the future. We have trusts for the boys and for you and Dad. And the horse farm is yours free and clear. Don't worry so much. Just enjoy. That's what Andrew and I want."

"The farm is not ours free and clear," her mother said.

Sandra turned away from her jewelry safe to look at her mother. "What did you say?"

Her mother held her gaze. "I said we don't own the farm free and clear."

Sandra thought her hearing had gone bad. "Of course you do. I was there when we bought it, remember?"

Her mother looked down at her hands, now folded on her lap. "Andrew took out a mortgage on it last month."

Sandra fell back against the safe, unsteady on her feet. "What?"

"Andrew came to your father last month and had him sign some papers. Your father was uneasy about it, but what could he say? Andrew promised it was a short-term problem and he'd pay off the mortgage within the next year."

Sandra slid down to the floor with a thud. "Why didn't you tell me?"

"Andrew asked your father not to tell you or me. He said he didn't want you to worry about a situation that would be rectified within the year. I had no idea until today."

Sandra didn't like what she was hearing, but deep down inside she knew it was true. "What made Dad decide to tell you?"

"He didn't intend to. But since it's happened, he's grown a bit cold toward Andrew. When he kept making excuses for why he couldn't come today, I was able to get the truth out of him." She met her daughter's eyes. "He feels there's more to this than Andrew is letting on."

Sandra shared her father's skepticism. Her heart told her what the more was, but she couldn't voice it. Andrew had promised it wouldn't happen again. Things were perfect with them. He wouldn't jeopardize it. He wouldn't.

"Do you think Andrew could be gambling again?" her mother asked.

Sandra squeezed her eyes closed, wanting to shut out her mother, Andrew, the world.

"I'm sorry, Sandra," Ida said, coming to sit on the floor next to her.

Sandra turned in her mother's arms and sobbed as the weight of her world crashed down on her shoulders.

Chapter 17

Sandra stayed too long in her sons' rooms tonight, but she needed the grounding that being with them gave her. Whatever might be wrong with her world, her children were not part of it. They were the one perfect gift her husband, the disappointment that he was, had given her. He would always have a place in her heart because of them.

With leaden feet, she headed down the wide hallway to the master bedroom. She didn't know how she'd made it through the party. Had no idea what she had said or who she said it to. Everything was a blur. She hadn't even been able to look at her husband. How could Andrew have done this to them again?

Relief settled around her when she entered the master bedroom and found he wasn't there. She needed a bit more time to channel her anger. If she spoke to him now, she knew she'd say things she'd later regret.

When she entered her designer closet, she felt none of the giddiness she usually felt. What was there to feel giddy about? For all she knew, the repo man would be coming for her clothing and jewelry before the week's end. This house that had meant so much to her could be gone as well. "Damn you, Andrew," she said aloud, pounding her knee with her fist.

She stiffened when she heard the bedroom door open. She didn't move when she heard Andrew call her name. She still wasn't ready to talk to him. She wondered if she'd ever be ready.

She stood as his footsteps neared the closet. She'd come to undress, but she realized she didn't have the energy to undress and have a conversation with Andrew, too. Undressing would have to wait. She forced herself up from the chaise and met him at the closet door. She preferred the much bigger bedroom area for their discussion. There she could put more distance between them. The way she felt now, that distance was as much for him as for her. She wasn't a violent person, but the feelings she felt tonight were violent in their intensity. She had to control her environment as much as she could.

"Did you say good night to the boys?" she asked him as she brushed past him.

He turned and followed her. "Yeah," he said. "You feeling all right? I've been getting a funny vibe from you all afternoon and evening."

She fought the urge to scream at him. "I've been better."

He lifted a brow. "Uh-oh," he said. "What have I done now?"

Lord, she wanted to smack him. Sock him right in the jaw. She took a deep breath. "You tell me," she said.

He chuckled, dropping down on the side of their king-sized bed. "Okay, give it to me with both barrels. What awful thing have I done?"

She turned and stared down at him. "This is no joking matter, Andrew."

He got up, came to her, pulled her into his arms. "Tell me what's wrong and I'll fix it. Promise."

A part of her wanted to stay cuddled in his arms, bury her head in the sand, and pretend there was no problem. She couldn't. She pulled away and walked to the far side of the room, looked out the windows on their grand estate. She batted her eyes at the tears that blurred her vision.

"Okay," he said, "if you don't want to talk then I'll talk. I thought the afternoon went well. You really know how to throw a party, babe. Everybody was impressed with the party and with you. You were the best-looking and best-dressed woman present."

On any other day that kind of praise from Andrew would have had her sailing on a cloud, but not today. Today the things he praised seemed shallow, meaningless. "I don't really care what those people thought, Andrew," she said, turning to him. "I don't even care what you thought."

He took a step back. "O-kay," he said. "I know you're angry, but I have no idea why. Just tell me so we can fix this."

She folded her arms across her chest, took a deep breath. "Did you take out a mortgage on the farm?"

He shrank into himself at her question, and she had her answer.

"How could you, Andrew?" she cried. "How could you?"

He dropped down on the side of the bed again, this time in defeat. "Your father should not have told you."

"He didn't," she said. "He told my mother and she told me. But that's beside the point. Why didn't you tell me?"

He sighed deeply, wiped his hand down his face. "Because I didn't want you to worry, and I knew you would. This is a short-term problem that I can fix."

She met his eyes, held them, not wanting to ask the question she knew she had to ask. When he broke eye contact, she had her answer. "You're gambling again, aren't you?"

He looked at her but didn't quite meet her eyes. "I can fix this, Sandra. I just need some time."

Only the thought of her children kept her from screaming. "How could you do this to us, Andrew? You promised me," she cried. "You promised me."

He came to her again, but this time she wouldn't let him pull her into his arms. "Don't touch me," she spat out. "Don't even think about touching me again. You're a liar, Andrew, a liar and a cheat. You've been lying to me, lying to God, and lying to the congregation. How could you?"

Although she struggled, he overpowered her and pulled her into his arms. He tilted her chin up so he could look into her eyes. "I love you, Sandra. I love you, I love our boys, and I love our life. You have to know that."

She shook her head. "You don't love us, Andrew, not as much as you love gambling."

He held her tighter. "That's not true."

"I wish it wasn't," she said, between tears, "but it is. You're like a man who repeatedly cheats on his wife with the same woman and expects her to forgive him. I can't be that wife, Andrew," she said. "I won't be."

He dropped his arms. "What are you saying? I told you I can fix this."

"I've heard it all before."

"And I've fixed it every time, haven't I?"

"But at what cost, Andrew? The cost is higher each time. I don't have it in me to pay again."

"What are you saying?" he asked again.

"I'm sleeping in the guest room," she said. Then she turned and left him standing in their bedroom calling her name.

Chapter 18

Sandra and Andrew faked their way through breakfast the next morning for the sake of the boys. She even kissed him good-bye when he headed off to the church, resisting the urge to wipe his taste from her lips after the kiss was over. For her kids, she could act. She just didn't know for how long.

Her plan was to go back to bed after the kids were off to camp and forget her troubles in a daylong sleep marathon. Mrs. Willis, their cook, stopped her. "First Lady," she said. "Do you want to make any changes to today's brunch menu?"

Sandra slapped her palm against her forehead. She'd totally forgotten about her brunch plans with Vickie McCorry. After the McCorrys had been unable to make the housewarming, the two women had agreed to brunch. Sandra had eagerly offered to host it, mainly to rub Vickie's nose in her good fortune. She'd planned to show Vickie how God had blessed them despite the McCorrys' lack of support. She'd wanted to show the older woman how much bigger and better everything she and Andrew had was compared to what she and Pastor McCorry had. Now those plans seemed petty and meaningless. She wanted to cancel, but it was too late.

"The menu is fine," she told Mrs. Willis.

"Will you still be eating on the patio by the pool?"

Sandra nodded. She didn't have the wherewithal to make any changes at this point. Her best bet was to stick with what was already arranged. That settled, she trudged back up the stairs and headed for her bedroom and closet. She'd chosen her outfit days before, just the dress to show off her newly toned arms and her newly acquired designer tastes.

She took her outfit—lingerie, jewelry, and shoes included—back with her to the guest room. She no longer belonged in the master bedroom with Andrew. Not after he'd betrayed her again. She placed the clothes across a chair in the guest room and then fell back into bed. She may not have been able to sleep the entire day away, but she'd gladly take the next three hours. She quickly fell into a deep sleep. She didn't awaken until Mrs. Willis knocked on her door.

"It's eleven, First Lady," she said, through the door. "You're going to be late for brunch if you don't start getting ready."

"Thanks, Mrs. Willis," Sandra mumbled into her pillow. "I'm up. I'll be ready."

Sandra stepped into the guest shower and exited refreshed. The warm water had soothed her. Had she known how much better the water would make her feel, she'd have showered sooner. She quickly donned her outfit and made her way down the stairs. The doorbell rang just as she hit the bottom step.

She checked herself in the full-length mirror opposite the door and, pleased with what she saw, pulled open the door, a practiced smile on her face. "You're right on time, Vickie," she said, taking in the woman's appearance. It was obvious she too had dressed to impress. "You look lovely. That's a beautiful outfit."

"Thank you," Vickie said, entering the house. "You look stunning. And this entranceway is marvelous, so majestic. I guessed from the outside that this house was a masterpiece, but my guessing didn't do it justice. I can't wait to see the rest of it."

Sandra relaxed a bit. Vickie's enthusiasm and sincerity took some of the edge off. "Let's do the tour first and then we'll eat," she said.

"That's a good idea," Vickie said with a laugh. "I don't think I could enjoy my meal otherwise. Let's get started."

Sandra started in the foyer and moved left to cover the first floor. When they had made the circle, she took Vickie up the winding staircase to the second-floor living quarters. From there, they took the back staircase down to the patio where they would eat.

"Whew," Vickie said after she was seated at the patio table. "This place is gorgeous, absolutely gorgeous. The floor plan is to die for, and you've done a masterful job with the decorating. Did you do it yourself or did you hire somebody?"

Mrs. Willis brought out tea and served them both a glass, leaving the glass pitcher on the table.

"I hired a decorator," Sandra said. "I can give you her name."

Vickie shook her head. "I'm sure she's out of our price range. You and Andrew are living on a much grander scale than me and Pastor."

Sandra took a bit of satisfaction in those words. After all, she'd wanted Vickie to recognize and appreciate what she and Andrew had accomplished. She became angry again when she thought how Andrew's gambling had put it all in jeopardy. Maybe Vickie would have the last laugh after all when she and Andrew were evicted from this majestic estate. She shook off the negative thoughts. Maybe Andrew could fix it. She hated to admit it, but she liked their lifestyle and didn't want to lose it. "You and Pastor taught me and Andrew to dream," Sandra said honestly, surprising herself. "You showed us what was possible with God."

Vickie took a sip of her tea. "Now you're making me feel bad."

At that point, Mrs. Willis brought out a cart with their meal. In her desire yet again to impress Vickie, Sandra had instructed Mrs. Willis to prepare a variety of exotic dishes for sampling. She'd gone to a luncheon with a similar menu a couple of weeks ago and had been bowled over with both the presentation and the tasty dishes.

Vickie's eyes lit up. "What is all of this?"

Sandra smiled. "Just a little something, something. There are a variety of dishes from more than fifteen different countries. I had Mrs. Willis label them for us. Feel free to try everything. If you don't like something, don't eat it."

Vickie grinned at her. "My fear is that I'll like everything. Are you trying to get me fat?"

Sandra laughed. A fat Vickie would be a sight to see. She handed Vickie a designer plate and took one for herself. "I guess we'll be fat together."

Both women laughed as they loaded their plates.

"Everything is delicious," Vickie said. "Your cook will have to give me all the recipes. I'm going to have to host a luncheon like this for the ladies at Praise City. They'd love it. I guess you can teach an old dog new tricks."

"I wouldn't call you an old dog," Sandra said, wiping her lips with her linen napkin.

Vickie put down her fork. "I owe you an apology, Sandra," she said. "I've come to realize that some of the things you said the night you and Andrew came over to tell me and Pastor about your plans were right. Deep inside, a part of me took personal pride in being First Lady and in all the trappings that went with it. I was a little threatened when you and Andrew decided to go out on your own. I guess I knew deep down inside that what you two would accomplish would overshadow what Pastor and I had accomplished. I'm ashamed of that now. I am happy that you and Andrew are achieving more. You should be. Pastor and I count you as fruit from our ministry and celebrate that the fruit is better than the tree. I wasn't looking at it that way back then, and I'm sorry. Can you ever forgive me?"

Sandra was so surprised by Vickie's candor that she didn't immediately answer.

"I'll understand if you can't forgive me right now," Vickie said, misreading her silence, "and pray that one day you'll be able to. I also want you to know that this is about me, not Pastor. He really felt that the time wasn't right for you and Andrew to go out on your own. Now I'm wondering if that was because I wasn't ready for it, rather than you two not being ready."

"You're a wise woman, Vickie McCorry," Sandra said. "I've always known that. But you're also a humble woman because it took a humble woman to admit what you just admitted. You're my role model. I accept your apology."

"Let's not get carried away," Vickie said. "Let's just try to rebuild our friendship." She reached over and squeezed Sandra's hand. "I miss you."

Sandra squeezed her hand back. "And you have to forgive me. I invited you here to show off what Andrew and I have. That was wrongheaded and wronghearted of me, and I'm ashamed."

Vickie laughed. "We First Ladies are a competitive bunch," she said. "So you fit right in. Just don't let the competition get the better of you. Compete in the important things like doing the will of God and helping people, not the trivial things like cars and houses. That'll mess up you, your marriage, and your ministry. In the hustle and bustle of ministry, sometimes we lose sight of that. Don't let it happen to you and Andrew, because if you lose that then you have nothing."

Sandra soaked up Vickie's words, knowing they were God's message to her and Andrew. They had some changes to make. She prayed they'd be up to them.

Chapter 19

Sandra felt better after her brunch with Vickie. Her friend's honesty and openness had been the balm her spirit needed. So instead of being in bed now with the covers drawn over her head, she was headed toward her husband's office ready to have the second part of the discussion that could determine her destiny.

"Good afternoon, First Lady," Andrew's secretary said when she reached his office. "Don't you look pretty today?"

"Thank you, Doris," she said. "Is that a new outfit you're sporting?"

Doris tugged on the jacket of her two-piece suit. "I got it on sale at Macy's."

"It looks good on you," she said, watching the woman beam at her words. The power she wielded as First Lady to make or break somebody's day still left her in awe. She didn't think she'd ever get used to it. "Is Pastor free?"

She nodded. "You can go on in," she said. "He just got back from lunch."

Sandra took a deep breath, and then she knocked on the door and opened it at the same time. "Andrew," she called, entering the room. She glanced toward his desk, and not seeing him there, turned to the sitting area. He was rising from a reclining position on the leather couch. "You're taking a nap in the middle of the day? Now that's something new."

"Just resting." He sat up, his eyes sad. "A lot on my mind."

Her heart turned over. Despite her anger and disappointment, she loved this man. He was far from perfect, far even from the man she'd thought he was, but he was still the man she'd married. She walked over and sat next to him. "We have to talk," she said.

He wiped his hand down his face. "I thought you were all talked out."

She knew he was referring to the way she'd gone to the guest room last night and left him standing in the master bedroom. "Last night I was running on raw emotion. Learning that you were gambling again hurt me so much, Andrew. It took everything out of me to deal with that news."

"I'm sorry, Sandra," he said. "I'm so sorry."

She took a deep breath. "When did it start?"

He looked away. "It doesn't matter."

She put her hand on his chin and turned his face back to hers. "It matters to me. When did it start? Was it in Hawaii with the casinos?"

He shook his head. "Horses," he mumbled. "It started when we were looking for a horse farm for your father. I started betting on horses." He took a deep breath. "I did sneak away a few times to go to the casino when we were in Hawaii."

She felt her heart grow cold. "So you never really stopped, did you? Despite your promises to me, you never really stopped."

He met her eyes. "I tried," he said. "I really did."

She got up and walked to the windows. "You need help, Andrew. We can't keep pretending you don't."

He came and stood behind her. "I'll get help," he said. "Whatever you want me to do, I'll do."

She turned and faced him. "How much trouble are we in?" she asked, even though she didn't really want to know.

He turned away, began pacing in front of her. "It's bad," he said. "But I'm managing."

"How bad?" she asked, her stomach tight. "Are we going to lose everything?"

He stopped pacing, shook his head. "We still have the kids' trusts and I have my salary here at the church."

He sucked in a deep breath. "That's all? Everything else is gone?"

He shrugged. "Not gone exactly. There's a big mortgage on the farm, and the bank owns more of our house than we do. I didn't put down as much as you thought I did."

Sandra dropped down in the nearest chair. "You gambled away all of the lottery money?"

He shook his head. "You know we spent a lot of that money on the church, getting it going and keeping it going. Not to mention buying the building. We have a lot of money tied up in the ministry."

They obviously couldn't continue funding the ministry the way they had been doing. "We have to let the leadership team know of the change in our circumstances. Maybe the church can begin to pay back some of the money we've invested."

"We can't do that," he said.

She frowned at him. "Now is not the time for pride, Andrew. We have to tell them."

When he looked away and didn't say anything, she asked, "Is there something you're not telling me?"

He stood and walked away from her.

"What is it, Andrew?"

"I sorta borrowed some money from the church discretionary fund without telling anyone."

Tears began to roll down Sandra's cheeks. "You stole from the church?"

"It wasn't stealing," he said. "My bookie was breathing

down my neck. I had to give him something as a show of good faith. I'm going to repay the money. Besides, it was ours anyway."

Sandra couldn't believe what she was hearing. "It wasn't our money, Andrew. Are you so blind you can't see that? How much do you owe this bookie?"

"Three hundred thousand."

"What?"

"You heard me."

Sandra felt as though she'd worked an eight-hour shift at a factory. "We don't have that kind of money."

"Yes, we do," he said. "In the boys' trust accounts."

Sandra felt her heart grow cold. "I won't let you touch a dime of the boys' money. I can't believe you'd even suggest it."

"I'd replace it, Sandra. I just need it for the short term. My luck is bound to change. Remember the last time we needed a miracle and God came through for us? He'll come through again."

"How? Are you going to ask for the winning horse in tomorrow's race?" she asked, her voice full of sarcasm. "I'm not going down this road with you again, Andrew. We can start liquidating."

"That's not necessary."

She cast him a cutting glance. "And you have to tell the leadership team what you've done. You have to tell them about your gambling addiction. You have to step down as pastor of Showers of Blessings." And she'd have to step down as First Lady. It hurt to even think about it, but this was where Andrew's gambling had brought them.

"You can't be serious," Andrew said. "I built this ministry from nothing. I'm not stepping down and I'm not telling the leadership team anything. Who are they to judge me, anyway?" He poked his chest with his finger. "I picked them, they didn't pick me."

"Do you hear yourself, Andrew? You don't sound like a

preacher to me. You sound like a businessman about to lose his business. Is that what this ministry has become to you?"

"You're putting words in my mouth," he said.

She shook her head. "No, I'm hearing the words on your heart. And what I'm hearing scares me."

He reached for her, but she evaded his touch. "You said you'd do anything to make this right. Well, this is what you have to do. The kids and I will move out to the farm with my parents. You can sell the house and everything in it to get the money you need. But you can't continue on as pastor like none of this happened. It would be an abomination."

"I can fix this," he said doggedly.

She shook her head at his stubborn selfishness. "I wish you could, but you can't." With those words, she stepped around him and left him standing in his office, their dreams of a shared ministry in shreds around his feet.

Chapter 20

Andrew stood in the fellowship hall chatting with a small circle of his members and guests, as he normally did after a Sunday service. The only difference was this time he couldn't lift his head, see his wife across the room doing the same thing, and share a smile with her. Amazing the small things he missed, things he had taken for granted.

"She and the boys are still out at the farm with her parents," he said, repeating the words he'd spoken more times than he could count since Sandra's first absence from Sunday service. Not only had she left him and taken the boys with her, she'd stopped attending church. He wasn't sure what he'd expected, but it surely wasn't her absence from service. She had to know how awkward that made things for him. "You know," he continued, "she hasn't really spent much time with her folks since we started the church. We felt it was time. She'll be back in a couple of weeks." At least, he prayed she would. His wife was being pretty stubborn. Well, he could be stubborn, too. Sandra just needed some time to get over her anger and hurt. Then she would see what she was asking him, them, to give up when they really didn't have to. They could weather this storm just as they had weathered the previous ones. She just needed to have faith.

"Pastor."

Andrew turned at the sound of his name.

"I hate to pull you away," Rob Moore said, bestowing a smile of apology on the small group around him. "There's a matter that needs your immediate attention."

Andrew smiled at his little group. "Work calls," he said. "You all have a blessed week now."

With those words, he turned and followed Rob down the hallway. "What's the problem?" he asked.

"It's better if we discuss this behind closed doors," Rob said.

Rob entered the conference room, and Andrew followed him in. He was surprised to see all the male members of the leadership team seated and waiting for him. "This must be something big," Andrew said, taking his normal chair at the head of the table. "Let's have it."

Rob cleared his throat. "You're our pastor, and you've always been there for us. We want you to know that we're here for you. If there's anything you want to talk about or pray about, we're here to support you."

Andrew relaxed a bit. "That means a lot," he said. "But things are good."

Rob cleared his throat again. "We've all gone through rough patches in our marriages, Pastor. We know how hard it can be. If you and First Lady Sandra are going through something, let us help you. Let the church help you."

Andrew grew a bit tense but decided to go with his standard story. "Sandra and I are fine. Like I told you, she and the boys are spending time with her parents. They'll be back soon."

Rob looked at Jacob.

Jacob said, "Pastor, we know that your wife and kids have been at Praise City the last few Sundays. We need to know if you two are separated. It affects the church."

Andrew sank back in his chair, unable to hide his surprise. Sandra and the boys had been going to Praise City? Was she trying to ruin him?

"You didn't know, did you?" Jacob asked.

Andrew could do nothing but shake his head. "I'm sure there's an explanation," he said. And from the looks on the faces of the brethren seated before him, that explanation was clear.

Rob cleared his throat again. Obviously, the man was uneasy being the spokesman for the group. "We think the best way to handle this situation is for you to come clean with the congregation. Tell them that you and the First Lady are having problems and ask for their prayer."

Andrew began shaking his head. He didn't want to start confessing in the pulpit. Who knew where that would lead?

"You don't have a choice," Jacob said. "People are already talking. How do you think we found out she and the boys were attending Praise City? We have to get in front of this, stop the speculation before it gets out of hand."

"The rumors about the cause for the breakup are already out there," Rob added, "everything from you having an affair to you having a gambling addiction. Who knows what the next one will be?"

Andrew pushed away from the conference table and got out of his chair. "These rumors are ridiculous."

"We know that, Pastor," Rob said. "But people are going to come up with their own reasons, especially when you're in the pulpit saying one thing and they know something else to be true. You can't lie to the congregation from the pulpit. You destroy your credibility and give weight to the rumors every time you do."

Andrew knew they were right. What he didn't know was what to do about it. He needed time.

"We think you should make a special announcement from the pulpit next week," Jacob said. "If possible, First Lady needs to be there as well. Together, the two of you can admit your problems and shoot down the rumors."

They had a good point, but he wasn't sure Sandra would

come. And if she did come, he wasn't sure what she would say. At one time, he could count on her to have his back and keep his secrets, but no more. "I'm not sure I can get her to come," he finally admitted.

"We sort of expected that," Jacob said.

Andrew lifted a brow.

"Our wives have been trying to schedule a lunch with her, anything," Jacob explained, "but she hasn't been receptive. She's cut us all off."

Andrew took Sandra's unwillingness to meet with the ladies from the leadership team as a sign of her reluctance to say anything negative about him. That could be the opening he needed to win her back. "Let me trying talking to my wife again. She loves this ministry as much as I do. She'll want to do what she can to make sure it's not harmed."

The men nodded their acceptance of his plan.

"I know coming here talking to me this way was hard," Andrew said, "but you did the right thing, and I appreciate it. You're right about me making a statement to the congregation, too. I'll do it next Sunday, I hope with Sandra by my side. I just ask that you all pray for us and our boys."

"We'll start now," Jacob said. And they did.

Chapter 21

Sandra sat in the passenger seat of her mom's Hyundai Santa Fe. Her kids played quietly in the backseat with their Nintendo DS Systems. She looked toward the front door of the McCorry home. "I don't think I can do this, Mom."

Her mom reached for her hand, squeezed it. "Yes, you can. Deciding to come here was the hardest step. These people have been your spiritual leaders and friends for all your married life. They were the ones who first recognized God's plans for you and Andrew. It's right that you go to them now in your time of need."

She met her mother's eyes. "If only we'd listened to their counsel."

Her mom shook her head. "Don't play the 'what if' game, Sandra. You are where you are. You've learned and grown from it. I'm proud of you."

Sandra wiped away a tear. She was a regular waterfall these days. "That's a bit of stretch, Mom."

"Not at all. When the time came to make the hard decision, you made it. And you're going to see it through to the end. You just need some help, which is why you're here today."

"How did I forget how smart you were?"

Ida inclined her head to the boys in the backseat. "You'll get your payback as those two back there grow up."

Sandra laughed, surprised she could do so. "I love you, Mom," she said.

"I know you do, baby. I love you, too."

She lifted the door handle. "It's time," she said.

"Call me when you're ready and we'll come back and pick you up."

Sandra nodded. "Bye, boys," she said as she stepped out of the car. "Have fun with Grandma."

"We will," the boys chimed.

Sandra stood waving while her mother pulled away from the McCorry home. When her mom was out of sight, she turned toward the house. Vickie opened the front door and met her on the walkway. When she gave her a big hug, Sandra began to weep.

"There, there," Vickie said, keeping her close as she walked her into the house. "Everything is going to be all right."

By the time Sandra pulled herself together, she was seated on the couch in the McCorry living room with Vickie sitting next to her and Pastor in a chair facing her. "I'm sorry," she said. "I didn't mean to cry all over you."

"No need to be sorry," Vickie said. "We're family."

Sandra wiped at her nose with a handkerchief Vickie had given her. "Are we?"

"I can't believe you're asking," Pastor said. "I thought we had cleared the air more than six months ago when we met at the TV studio. We've never been against you and Andrew, Sandra. We just thought you were moving in the wrong time. But we came to accept it and to pray for your ministry."

"I know," she said. "But things have gone so wrong. If only we had listened to you."

"Don't beat yourself up about the past, Sandra," Vickie said. "You can't change it, but you can correct course for the future."

Sandra nodded, accepting their compassion. "I don't know where to start."

Pastor leaned forward. "Since you and the boys have been coming to Praise City services for the last month or so, we've gathered that all is not well with you and Andrew. Why don't you start there?"

Sandra took comfort in his forthrightness. This was the pastor she knew and loved. She took a deep breath. "Andrew's a compulsive gambler," she said, pushing the words out quickly before she lost her courage. "He has been since before we were married."

Vickie sat back on the couch. "I had no idea." She glanced at her husband. "Did you?"

He shook his head. "Not a clue. I can't believe we were as close as we were and I didn't know."

Sandra laughed a dry laugh. "Don't feel badly. We worked hard to keep it a secret from you, from everybody. I didn't find out until a few years after we were married. The only reason I did was that the gambling got so out of hand that we were on the verge of losing everything—the house, the cars, everything. It was an awful time, but somehow Andrew got us through it. When he did, he promised his gambling days were over."

"And of course they weren't," Pastor said. "I know he didn't come to me, but did he go to anyone for help? Did you?"

She shook her head. "He said he could manage on his own, and I was too ashamed to tell anyone. I didn't want people to think less of us. Andrew was a deacon then. I feared for his status."

Vickie rubbed her shoulder. "Oh, Sandra, that was the least of your worries. We would have helped. We love you and Andrew."

"Our world seemed to be falling down all around us, and it was hard to believe anyone loved us. I even doubted God's love for a while."

"Oh, no,"Vickie said, her voice full of compassion. "God's love never waned. Never."

"Has Andrew started gambling again?" Pastor asked. "Is that the problem?"

Sandra nodded. "That's part of the problem. This is Andrew's third lapse. His second one was right before we got his inheritance, which really wasn't an inheritance. Andrew had taken us to the brink again. As he had done the first time, he used gambling to get us out of trouble. This time he played the lottery and won."

Vickie gasped.

Pastor sank back in his chair. "All this inheritance talk was a lie?"

Sandra hated the disappointment she saw on their faces. "Even though we considered the winnings a blessing, we knew others, especially you and Vickie, wouldn't think so. We couldn't tell you the truth, so we made up a lie."

Pastor began shaking his head. "I fear I haven't been a good pastor to you and Andrew, and I'm sorry for it. I should have known something was off. I did know, but I thought it was Andrew's overeagerness to have his own church."

"So did I,"Vickie said. "And I'm sorry you and Andrew felt you couldn't come to us with the truth. Did you think we'd turn you away?"

Sandra nodded. "By this time, Andrew was an associate pastor. Praise City couldn't have a gambling addict on its pastoral staff."

"You've got that wrong, Sandra. We couldn't have let him continue in the role unless he was getting help for his problem. Andrew's not the only one in the congregation with a gambling problem. God could have used your situation for good if you two had been honest. I'm just sorry you felt we'd judge you and cast you out."

Sandra was sorry, too. "I believe that now, but I didn't believe it then. My mother told me more than once that the lie to cover up the gambling only compounded the problem. I didn't want to hear it. All I saw was the money and the opportunity to have our own church. And I saw you and Vickie as trying to hold us back."

They all three sat quietly. "So where are you two now?" Pastor asked.

"Andrew's gambling again, and we're back at the brink again. And this time we've brought the church into it. I finally see that we have to get off this roller coaster. Andrew can't fix this problem in secret. He needs help. We need help."

"And we're here to help you."

Sandra accepted the truth of the pastor's words. She'd been lost since she and the kids moved to the farm, not seeing how she and Andrew could overcome their problems. For the first time since she left him, she felt hope for their future.

Chapter 22

Andrew's excitement grew as he made his way through traffic and got closer to home. For the first time in a long time, his wife would be waiting for him when he walked through the door. He turned up the CD and allowed Luther Vandross to fill his heart and mind. He felt a reconciliation coming on tonight. And he had seduction in mind, too. He'd enlisted Mr. Vandross and Mrs. Willis to help him accomplish his goals. He had instructed Mrs. Willis to prepare a romantic dinner, complete with soft lights, soft music, and food for love. He was taking no chances. He'd even had the cook prepare an oyster dish.

He was practically giddy when he pulled his 7 Series BMW into the garage and saw Sandra's Mercedes SUV already there. She'd told him she was coming early so she could pick up a few more of the boys' things. If everything went according to plan, she wouldn't be taking another piece of clothing out of their home.

He hummed the lyrics to Luther's "A House Is Not A Home" as he made his way into the house. He knew he should shower and get refreshed before he saw Sandra, but he couldn't wait to set his eyes on her. He greeted Mrs. Willis, who told him his wife was in the family room. He fought for composure, but he was too excited about the possibilities. He practically ran to the family room.

He stopped short when he entered the doorway and saw not only Sandra, but her parents, the McCorrys, and the members of his leadership team seated in his family room. "I didn't know this was going to be a party," he said to cover his disappointment and anxiety. *Why are they all gathered here?*

Sandra stood and met him at the doorway. "I invited them, Andrew," she said. "Come and sit with us."

Andrew had no choice but to obey his wife. To do otherwise would only cause a scene. Knowing his plans for the evening with Sandra were now moot, he prepared himself for the turn of events. "It's my house," he said, with a bit of levity, "but I'm feeling like the guest here. What's going on?"

"I guess you could call this an intervention, Andrew," Pastor McCorry said, making Andrew think he was the leader of this gang. "We're here because we love you and Sandra and want to see you both on the right road."

Andrew glanced at his wife. Then he turned back to the pastor. "If that's true, you would have done better to let my wife and me have some private time rather than turn our evening together into a group meeting."

"I invited them, Andrew," Sandra said again. "Too much between us has been kept private. It's time to bring it all out into the open."

Andrew just stared at her. She couldn't be about to do what he thought she was about to do. "Some things need to remain between a man and his wife," he said.

"Some things," Pastor McCorry said, "but not all things."

Sandra put her hand on his arm, and he turned to her. "They all know, Andrew. I've told them everything."

Andrew shook off her hand. "What do you mean everything?"

"It means we all know about the gambling, Andrew," Jacob

said. "We know about the lottery money, and we know about you borrowing money from the church without approval."

Andrew sucked in a deep breath, feeling as though he'd been gut punched. He shot Sandra a hot look. "How could you?" he demanded.

She didn't waver. "Everything I've done has been out of love. You may not see it now, but I hope you will someday."

"I don't have to listen to this," Andrew said, getting up.

"Yes, you do," his father-in-law said. "If you care anything about your wife and children, you'll sit there and listen."

Andrew sank down in his chair, unable to defy Grady. "I'm staying," he said. "Let's get on with it."

Ignoring Andrew's petulance, Pastor McCorry said, "There are three phases to an intervention. The first is where the loved ones share how the addiction has affected them. The second is where the options for help and recovery are presented. And the third is where a decision is made. We'll go in order."

Rob took a deep breath. "You lied to us, Pastor. You lied to us when you asked us to join you and Sandra at Showers of Blessings, and you lied when we came to you last week and told you about the rumors. We trusted you, and you lied to us. It hurts. And it makes us angry. Why couldn't you tell us the truth? If not in the beginning, then why didn't you come clean last week when we met with you? It was the perfect opportunity."

Jacob chimed in. "Our anger is not just for us. It's for all the members of Showers of Blessings. A scandal like this can make folks lose faith in church and in God. What pains me most is that you've been thinking more about yourself than the souls you were entrusted with. How could you forget them?"

Andrew sat up straighter. "Nobody here cares more about Showers of Blessings than I do. Nobody here has given more to that ministry than I have, not financially, not emotionally.

Say what you will about my gambling, but it has not affected the church."

"How can you say that, Andrew?" Sandra said. "You stole money from the church to repay a gambling debt. You stood in the pulpit and lied about the status of our relationship. How can you say your gambling hasn't affected the church?"

"I borrowed that money," Andrew said, "and I'll pay it all back."

"We're getting off track here," Pastor McCorry said. "Does anyone else want to speak to how Andrew's gambling has affected them?"

Grady cleared his throat. "It's no secret, Andrew, that I didn't think you were the man for my daughter when I first met you. I'm saddened to find out I was right. She's had to deal with the stress of living with a gambler. I can only imagine how insecure that's made her feel over the years. Stress and shame are what you've given my daughter, and I'm not sure I'll ever be able to forgive you for it." He glanced at Sandra. "I'm willing to try, though, for her sake."

Andrew loved his father-in-law, but he couldn't deal with his hypocrisy. Not now when his whole life was on the line. "I don't know how you can be so judgmental, Grady. It's not like you haven't dealt with addiction yourself."

"You're right," Grady said. "That's why I wanted Sandra to find a man better than I was. I wanted her to know the security that comes with a spouse you can lean on. Her mother tried to provide stability for her when she was growing up, but she could only do so much because my very presence made life for both of them unstable. I wanted more than that for Sandra in her marriage. Right now, I wish I had done more to end your relationship back then."

"Dad!" Sandra said. "You don't mean that."

"Yes, I do, Sandra. Pastor McCorry said we were supposed to be honest, and I'm just being honest."

Andrew had no response to his father-in-law's truth. Sorrow began to gnaw in his belly. He wanted to provide stability for Sandra and his kids. He wanted nothing more than that.

Nothing but the gambling, a voice said in his mind.

"I hate to say this," Jacob's wife, Pam, said, "but I'm disappointed with both of you. I know it's wrong, but I'm angry, too. More angry with First Lady than with Pastor."

"You can't blame Sandra for any of this," Andrew said, defending his wife. "She's an innocent in all of it."

"No, she's not," Rob's wife, Gloria, said. "She's as much to blame for the situation we're in as you, if not more. In a way, you have an excuse because you have an addiction. She doesn't have that excuse. She knew your problem and kept quiet. If she had spoken up, we wouldn't be here today."

"That's not fair—" Andrew began.

Sandra put her hand on his arm again. "I appreciate your coming to my defense, but Gloria is right. You needed help, Andrew, but instead of forcing you to get that help, I covered for you. Things couldn't have gotten this far out of hand without my compliance."

"You can't blame yourself," he said.

"It's not about blame," Sandra said. "It's about learning from our mistakes and not repeating them. My mistake was not to love you enough to force the issue before now. I'm sorry for that."

"I want to say something," Vickie said, causing all eyes to turn to her. "I'm hurt and disappointed that you and Sandra didn't feel comfortable enough to come to me and Pastor with your problem. We accept some of the blame for that. We should have done a better job of making you feel welcome and accepted. We failed at that, and we're eternally sorry."

"We also should have done a better job of explaining why we raged against the lottery so often," Pastor McCorry said. "It's not the lottery that's the sin. The sin comes when we look to the lottery instead of looking to God. The sin comes when the lottery brings harm to us and our families. We should have made that clear."

Andrew felt the sincerity of the McCorrys, and it was a balm to his aching heart. Unfortunately, he couldn't find the words to express to them what he had been thinking back then and why he'd come to the conclusions he had.

"We'll let that wrap up phase one," Pastor McCorry said. "Now let's move to phase two. It's pretty clear that you need help, Andrew. At least, it's clear to us, and we hope it's clear to you."

"I'm handling things," Andrew said. "They just got out of hand for a minute."

"Oh, Andrew," Sandra said. "It so much more than that. Can't you see?"

"You have to take a sabbatical from Showers of Blessings," Jacob said. "You need to make a statement to the church, an honest statement telling them what's happened and that you need the time to get well."

"I'm not stepping down," Andrew said. "I built Showers of Blessings. It wouldn't exist were it not for me."

Jacob shook his head. "We built Showers of Blessings, and it'll withstand this scandal. It'll thrive, too, but how much and how long it will take will depend on you. You can resist stepping down, make folks in the congregation choose. But what would you have left? A split church and a lot of wounded souls. I don't believe you want that, Andrew."

"If the church splits, it won't be because of me," Andrew said.

"Yes, it will, Andrew," Sandra said. "We're the ones who lied and stole. A wise woman"—she glanced at her mother—"told me that you couldn't build a firm foundation with lies. Well, we didn't start Showers of Blessings with a firm foundation, but we can leave it with one."

"We've put everything into that ministry, Sandra," he pleaded. "We can't walk away."

She smiled sadly. "I don't want to walk away, Andrew. It breaks my heart to even think about it, but we have no other choice."

"Nobody denies how much you put into the church, Andrew," Jacob said, "and we're willing to keep paying your salary for as long as needed, but you cannot continue as the spiritual leader of the church until you get your house in order."

To Andrew, it sounded as though they were giving him room to return to Showers of Blessings once he'd overcome his addiction, but his pride wouldn't let him ask. He hadn't decided he was stepping down yet.

"Sandra has already come back to Praise City," Pastor McCorry said. "We'd like you both to come back. Home is where you go to heal, and Praise City is your home."

"We need to get back to basics, Andrew," Sandra added, "you, me, and the boys. We've gotten off-track and we need to get back on. I think going back to Praise City is the way to do it."

Andrew looked around the room. The sad faces looking back at him made him want to scream. He hadn't wanted things to come to this. All he'd wanted was to follow the path God had for him, be a good husband, father, and minister. These folks were telling him he'd failed at all three. He wasn't sure he believed them.

Chapter 23

Even though Sandra felt extremely conspicuous when she entered the Showers of Blessings sanctuary on the following Sunday, she wore her best smile and greeted everyone she saw.

"We're so happy to have you back, First Lady."

"We've missed you. I hope you enjoyed your time with your parents."

"Don't stay gone so long next time."

All the warm welcomes had Sandra tearing up. They made up for the behind-the-hand whispers she saw and the smirks that were sent her way. With her parents and the McCorrys by her side, she made her way to her usual seat in the second pew from the front on the left of the aisle. She tried to enjoy the service, but her anxiety got the best of her. The intervention hadn't gone as planned. Andrew had listened, but he hadn't agreed to anything. She didn't know if his statement this morning would be one of defiance and fight or one of apology and repentance. She prayed for the latter.

A collective sigh went up from her little group when Andrew stepped into the pulpit and up to the podium. She guessed they were as anxious as she was about what Andrew would do.

As she looked at him standing there, a mosaic of their life together flashed in front of her. She recalled all the times she'd stood with him and stood up for him. She despaired that this might be the day she'd publicly defy him. But that's where they were. If Andrew refused to do the right thing, she'd have to do it for him. Her mother squeezed her hand in support, and she smiled down at her. One wonderful thing to come of this disastrous situation was her renewed relationships with her parents and the McCorrys.

"Good morning, church," Andrew said. After the returned greetings, he continued. "It's a brighter day at Showers of Blessings this morning because First Lady Sandra is back with us. Why don't you stand up, sweetheart, so everybody can see you? The way folks have been asking about you, I think they get more from seeing you than they do from hearing me."

Sandra stood and waved as the congregation laughed at her husband's comment. She watched as Andrew instructed one of the ushers to hand her a microphone. She took it and said, "It's good to be back at Showers of Blessings. But sometimes you have to go away to see things clearly. And today, church, I see more clearly than I've seen in a long time. I see a long and prosperous future for Showers of Blessings and each of us here. The pastor is going to set us on a new path today. We have to trust God and walk in it. God bless you all." Amid a round of applause, she handed the microphone back to the usher and sat down.

"Now that's a First Lady, y'all. Believe it or not, her job is harder than mine. You know why? Because she has to put up with me." He paused while he waited for everybody to stop laughing. "Not only does she have to put up with me, she has to keep me in line. That's the hard part. We preachers can get a big head sometimes. A good First Lady knows how to deflate that big head without killing the spirit." He paused again, and this time he turned to her, his heart in his eyes, and smiled. "This morning, church," he continued, "I want to tell you a story about a hardheaded preacher with a gambling problem and the softhearted first lady who refused to give up on him."

Sandra's heart grew warm as her anxiety eased. Andrew was going to do the right thing. They were going to make it. God had given them another miracle just as Andrew had said He would. How could she have ever doubted him?

Second Chance Blessings

MARILYNN GRIFFITH

Chapter 1

"Don't do this, Bri," Craig said to his wife in an even voice. "You don't mean it."

"Get this end, Tenisha," Brianna said just as calmly, encouraging her girlfriends to lift the head of the bed her husband was sleeping in. A week before, they'd made love in that bed for what Brianna vowed would be the last time if he didn't make something happen. Evidently his time was up.

Craig gave his wife's friends a stern look as they approached the four corners of the bed. "Can you ladies leave us alone for a minute?"

The redhead, who'd never liked him, spoke first. "Time's up, Craig. She's done with all your games. We've been the ones here with her while you're on the road with your girlfriends. Now you blow your knee and want to give up—"

"I got hurt, Tina—"

"You and my grandmother. What do you want, a cookie? You know how this works. If you want a certain kind of woman, you have to be able to take care of her."

Craig wrapped the sheet around himself and got out of the bed, but not before noticing how Asia took him in with her eyes. Brianna was so busy trying to dog her husband that she didn't even notice the look her girlfriend was giving him.

A month ago, Craig would have been a raving idiot right now, cursing and breaking things until all these women ran out of his house crying. Instead, he watched as Brianna and three of her friends—one who'd flown in from Tampa for the evil deed—packed seven years of their life together into a U-Haul truck.

A few months ago, he'd considered doing the same thing. He'd even gone as far as telling his best friend Dante that he was going to leave, but God had other plans. The one thing Craig was sure he'd heard from God was that he shouldn't leave his wife. Now she was leaving him.

"Girls, wait by the truck. Let us talk for a minute." Only when the crazy crew had gone outside did Craig try one last time to stop her.

"I thought you loved me. Forgave me. We were going to make a go of this."

"Maybe I was in love with who I thought you were, Craig. And now with your knee . . . Who knows if you'll get another contract. You're certainly not too worried about it. The money is going fast. I need to get out while there's still something to get."

She might be disappointed then. "About that . . ."

Brianna spun around like Wonder Woman. "What? What did you do?"

Craig shrugged. There was no use trying to hide it. "There's not much left. I made some investments. The bank failed and . . ."

She slapped him.

Hard.

Before she could do it again, Craig caught her wrist. She was crying now, the sloppy kind of crying that she never let him see. He'd only heard it from the other side of locked doors. Until now.

She beat his chest with her fists. "I gave up everything for you. Everything. And for what? For you to give everything away? You're always giving somebody something, taking somebody's advice. Didn't you tell me that those who really love you don't care about your money?"

Except for you, of course. "They don't."

"Then why? Why do you always have to give people things?"

It was a good question. Nobody had asked Craig for anything. Maybe he couldn't take being just like everybody else. It scared him. Maybe he needed to do something big to feel good. It didn't matter now. It was done.

Craig held Brianna, even though she fought him. He kissed her hair. "I guess it's the same reason you're always buying something. We're messed up, both of us. But you'll always be my angel. Always."

She looked at him with empty eyes, then pushed his arms open and walked away.

Craig swallowed hard and turned to the window, knowing that watching her go was a waste of time. She wouldn't be turning back.

> *The bonds of matrimony now existing between the Plaintiff and the Defendant are dissolved on the grounds of irreconcilable differences, and the Plaintiff is awarded an absolute decree of divorce from the Defendant.*

If it weren't for the pain shooting through his knee and Dante snatching the paper away, Craig might have spent another week sitting on the floor in his empty house reading his divorce decree.

"Come on, man. Put that down." Dante was the only one to come and help Craig move out. Nobody wanted to be around a loser. Craig got that. When other guys had gotten injured and lost their deals, lost their lives, Craig had shaken his head and gone on to the next game. The last time he'd cared enough about a guy to go check on him was when Dante got cut years ago. Now his old friend was here to return the favor. All Craig had left were his Super Bowl rings, and the way Brianna was acting, they'd be on eBay pretty soon.

"She's changing her name, too. Back to Davis. Can you believe that?"

Dante shot Craig a look. He and Brianna had never quite gotten along, but both were careful not to disrespect the other.

"Actually, I can believe it. Now come on. The divorce papers state that you've got until today to get out. Let's go. I don't want to get into it with her."

Craig shook his head, fumbling through the stack of papers Brianna had been so kind to have hand-delivered from the Surrey County Courthouse. As if a career-ending knee injury and the announcement that he was being let go from the Atlanta Falcons wasn't enough. It was raining good news.

Dante dragged his friend toward the door. "Not that I can blame her much, though. You treated that woman bad, Craig. Y'all two deserve each other. Looking at the two of you, I'm glad that I got cut back in the day. I know you think my life is little, but I'm loving my little life right about now. This is madness."

Craig was inclined to agree. In the past month, Brianna had slashed his tires twice; filed for divorce; pretty much sold everything in the house out from under him, except for the clothes on his back; and made passionate love to him. Twice. It was past crazy. When he complained to a teammate, the guy had laughed and said that Craig should be happy Brianna hadn't burned the house down.

Craig didn't laugh. In a way, burning the house down might have been better. Things would look the way he felt, like everything was ruined. Destroyed.

With God, nothing is impossible.

The verse, fresh from his aunt's mouth on the phone this morning, had once been Craig's inspiration. It mocked him now. Sure, nothing was impossible. He was living proof of that. It was the "with God" part that worried him. For a long time, Craig's only church had been a prayer in the end zone. How could he go back and find God now?

Dante opened the front door. Craig slung his duffel bag over one shoulder and looked around the mansion he and Brianna had shared: eight bedrooms, a home movie theater, formal dining room, and a library. Almost twenty thousand square feet. He'd told Brianna it was too much, but she said they needed it to entertain. True enough, it was what people expected, but he wished they'd just kept what they had before, what they needed.

He'd thought it would have been full of children by now, but it had never been the right time, not for Brianna and, honestly, not for him. He wished now that they had made the time, that he had a piece of their love, their life, to remain in the world.

"Is that it? That bag? That's all you've got?" Dante was looking back, too, probably remembering the parties held there. All those people. Where were they now?

Reluctantly, Craig grabbed at the cane his doctor had recommended. He hated to use it, but he had to start somewhere, and walking without it was almost impossible.

Almost.

With great effort, Craig stepped to the door. "This is it. All I've got left."

Craig took a deep breath and considered how fragile life could really be. He'd had everything: a trophy wife, a showcase house, and a pro football career on the rise. Then his knee snapped and so did his life. Cut from the team, divorced by his wife, and abandoned by most of his friends, here he stood with a duffel bag and a cane, forced to go back to his aunt's house in Tampa. Forced to concede that no matter how hard he'd tried, Craig Richards had failed.

"You ready, man? We don't want to miss the plane," Dante said.

"Actually, I'd love to miss it," Craig said. "Heroes only get one-way tickets."

Dante gave his friend a weary smile. "And losers come back home?"

Craig shook his head. "I didn't mean—"

"It's okay, man. Your head will deflate soon enough. Let's get you home."

Craig almost fell off the plane.

There were people, hundreds of them, waiting. They had signs that said, WELCOME HOME, CRAIG! or WE LOVE YOU, RICHARDS!

"What's going on?" he whispered to Dante.

His friend laughed. "You're going on, man. You have no idea. Come on."

Craig went, waving to the crowd in confusion, but happy and angry at the same time. Didn't they get it? He'd lost everything. Gone were the days when he could come home bearing gifts or leave the pastor a fat offering, so they could stop cheering. This wasn't the Super Bowl. It was a disaster. So why didn't anyone seem to notice but him?

He saw his aunt in the center of the crowd. She'd been a mother to him when his own mother worked three jobs, a family when there was none when his mother died. She grabbed him as if he were a little boy instead of a broken man.

"Auntie, what is all this? Why are these people here?"

"We're here because we love you, baby. Because God loves you. Did you forget that up there in Atlanta in that fancy house?"

Craig sighed and hugged his aunt, feeling all her years bony to his touch. He'd been gone too long. "Yes, ma'am. I think I forgot a lot of things."

Craig could barely walk, but young men followed him everywhere, offering to carry his bag, give him a ride home.

One young man, clean-cut with glasses and a full beard, silenced the others and extended his hand.

"You don't know me, but I'm a big fan. My sports clinic would like to offer you free rehabilitation and therapy for your knee for as long as you're in Tampa."

Before Craig could turn it down, his aunt reached across him and shook the young man's hand. "Thank you so much, son. He'll be down there. I'll bring him myself. We appreciate you, baby."

Craig forced a smile as the guy extended a business card to him with an initial appointment time scrawled on the back. He knew how much therapy and rehab cost, and no business would make it giving that kind of service away for free. Not that it was going to help him play again, if that's what they were hoping for. Craig would be content just to walk without a cane.

"Thanks, man. I'll do one appointment, but I can't accept more. You can't afford not to charge for that. I appreciate your kindness, but I want to be clear—I've got nothing. I'm not even going to be playing anymore."

The young man smiled. "I know. I hate that I won't see you running the ball again, but this has nothing to do with that. I just wanted to say thank you. You know, for all you did for me. If it wasn't for you, there wouldn't be an Agape Sports Medicine at all. I think you paid for every one of us to get through community college."

Craig pulled up short, ignoring the pain that shot through his knee. "I don't understand. How could I have paid your way to school? I've never even met you."

His aunt giggled while Dante opened the car door for her. "Well, now, you know I could never spend all that money you sent on me."

Craig closed his eyes. Women. They were unbelievable. "I told you to invest it, for you to have in case something ever happened and I couldn't play. Something like now!"

His aunt smiled, totally ignoring his rising tone of voice except for a squeeze on the wrist that had always meant that he should watch his mouth. "I did invest it, son. I just invested it in people. I think you'll be amazed to see how some of those 'securities' have turned out."

As the day went on, his aunt's house filled with people and hickory smoke funneled from the grills lined up across the backyard. In fits and starts of introductions and watching pots on the stove, his aunt told him about the Craig Richards Foundation, something he'd always thought was a joke when his aunt had mentioned it.

Aunt Tee had been using Craig's money to help people for years while he and Brianna were burning through it. After his fourth invitation to dinner by a family who'd been helped by the Foundation, Craig felt something inside him break. Mortgages, medical bills, college tuition, home renovations, even the church day care center was bankrolled by his money. All the investments he and Brianna had made: a house that now wouldn't sell, funds that had gone bust, more cars than they could drive—none of it compared to what his aunt had done by seeding into people instead of just things.

"Are you coming to church tomorrow?" asked a little girl with a red tongue from her melting Popsicle. "They gonna pray for you, since you poor now."

Craig closed his eyes. The little girl was right. He was poor, and in more ways than one.

Blessed are the poor in spirit.

He gave the little girl his best smile. "Yes, sweetheart. I'll be there."

Chapter 2

Winning the house in the divorce was a hollow victory for Brianna. She'd insisted they buy it even though Craig's contract was ending. He'd been cautious, but Brianna had pushed and gotten her way. He owed her. And besides, he always got a contract. Until now, anyway.

Now she'd been served with foreclosure papers—by the same messenger who'd served Craig his divorce papers—and her only way out of this was to convince Craig to stop playing crazy and rehab his knee. He'd been injured before, but this time he seemed frozen, as if he just didn't have the will to recover. Her father said it was because she'd divorced him, ripped his heart out for the world to see. Well, she thought as she stepped into Soul Harvest Worship Center where she and Craig had grown up together, she was just getting started.

She was late, but not too late to hear the burning—no, scathing—message from the pastor. If she'd been a weaker woman, she might have walked the aisle herself. Craig, who was seated next to his aunt with all eyes on him all service, looked as though he might jump up and limp down the aisle himself.

As if.

Brianna settled back into the plush balcony pew, sick of

looking down on so many people whose lives hadn't changed since high school. She sat back, but not before seeing Craig be the first one to respond to the pastor's altar call. He'd walked stiffly without his cane, but Craig made it to the front. There, he did something that made Brianna cringe. He went down on one knee. His bad one.

She'd heard his screams in therapy sessions when they'd bent his knee like that, but Craig looked as though he were somewhere else, somewhere bigger than his pain. Brianna made a mental note to encourage Craig in his church attendance. All this shouting and carrying on might be just the thing to help Craig get his mojo back. God knows he needed it. So did she.

Craig's aunt Theresa, always one for the dramatic, went down and took the microphone and stood over Craig. "I've prayed for you since you breathed your first. And God let me see you get in before I take my last. I'm mighty glad about it, too."

And she isn't the only one. The whole church started clapping and rejoicing like crazy All except for one visitor, who wasn't impressed.

Just when Brianna decided she'd had enough and got up to leave, the pastor pointed her out to the crowd.

"And this is Craig's wife, Brianna Richards. She was once a junior usher here. You all know her daddy, too. Come on down, Brianna. Everyone wants to meet Craig's wife."

"Ex-wife," she corrected the pastor when someone shoved a microphone up to her mouth.

There was silence for a moment, then a booming laughter that unnerved Brianna. She didn't want to know what their laughter was supposed to mean, but she had a copy of the divorce decree in her purse, for times just like this.

"Don't mind us, Sister Richards. God has a sense of humor. He always gets the last laugh," the pastor said before dismissing service. "May God bless you and shine His face upon you. You are dismissed."

As the women from the Ladies Hospitality Committee

whisked her downstairs for a "light repast," Brianna conceded. God might be getting the last laugh after all. For today, anyway. No doubt she wouldn't be able to eat any of the food. Things weren't that bad yet for her to start letting herself go.

Once downstairs, Brianna held her breath as the women helped her to her chair, the seat next to Craig's. The women and families who came to hug her and thank her for what they received from the Craig Richards Foundation kept Brianna from lighting into Craig about his Jesus act. It was a nice try, but she wasn't buying it.

Just as she was about to give Craig a piece of her mind and flee the scene, an older woman grabbed Briana's hand and whispered in her ear.

"My son wouldn't be alive today if y'all hadn't paid for that medicine. Look at him now. He's about to graduate. First one to go to college. Give her a hug, Montez."

Moved by the moment, Brianna hugged the boy and leaned into Craig and laughed. Craig hugged her and continued talking to the mayor. She laced her fingers in his and squeezed. A few seats away, her father, the church janitor, beamed. For a moment, they were Craig and Brianna again, the power couple, the forever lovers.

It wasn't long before Brianna pulled away. Love was for fairy tales, and Brianna was done trying to play Cinderella. She had to get out of this town. And quick.

Craig didn't know what to make of Brianna. One minute she was screaming across the sanctuary, telling everyone she was his ex-wife, and the next minute she was reclined against him at the dinner table, laughing.

He'd been holding steady, disregarding the strawberry scent of her hair, the intoxicating closeness of her body, but her laughter disarmed him completely. It had been years since she'd laughed like this, talking fast and loud with food still in her mouth. Money had made Brianna too cultured. Too careful.

Against his better judgment and the advice of his attorney, Craig had reached out and grabbed Brianna's hand. He'd braced himself for a slap, but he'd gotten a squeeze before Brianna caught herself and let go. She was good at that, letting go.

You're not too bad yourself.

"Where's she going?" Aunt Theresa asked when Brianna got up to make her escape from the church.

Far away, I hope. "I have no idea," I said, watching in horror as my aunt ran after Brianna. I didn't move, and it wasn't just because of my knee. I'd chased enough women to last a lifetime, especially this woman.

"Aunt Tee! Let her go. I think Bri has somewhere to be—"

Brianna stopped and walked back to the table with Craig's aunt. "Actually, I don't know what I'm going to do. I was supposed to stay with Asia, my friend, but I guess she must have gone out last night and hasn't made it home—"

"Uh-huh. Well, you just forget about that. You're family. Come on home with us. Right, Craig?"

Hmph. "Yeah. Right."

Brianna looked up at Craig with questions in her eyes as Aunt Theresa took her hand and led her out of the church. Having no answers, he looked away. It was bad enough that he'd had to come home, but the two of them under one roof again? He wasn't so sure if even Aunt Theresa could handle that.

She looked back. "Craig, you don't have to—"

He raised a hand, thankful for the ringing phone in his pocket.

"Hello?"

"I tried to talk to you after service, but you and Brianna were so busy playing king and queen in the basement that I couldn't get to you." Dante sounded agitated. Craig couldn't blame him. He felt like an addict heading home with his worst drug, only Brianna was more addicting than anything Craig had ever tried.

"About the king and queen thing. I never planned to—"

"Whatever, man. Look, when I got home there was a message from the principal. I told him I doubted you'd take it, but I've been instructed to offer you a coaching job. It'd be you, me, and Butler. Tim Butler. Remember him?"

Craig remembered. Butler had been his nemesis in high school, his second. They'd battled for first-string position all four years. He wasn't about to battle him again for some high school coaching job.

Face reality. This is it. The end for you.

His friends from the NFL would never let him live it down. "I don't know, man. I'm starting rehab tomorrow. . . ."

"So you're still trying to get picked up? I thought you were over that."

Craig watched Brianna disappear out of the church on his aunt's arm. "I thought so, too. I don't mean to be ungrateful. I just don't know. I'll be glad to come and help while I'm here, though. I'm just not sure about something permanent."

"Let it go, man. That's all I'm going to say. Later."

"Later."

Rehab was going well. Almost too well. With Brianna around, Craig had to do all he could to stay away. His days seemed like one long workout interspersed with lots of cold showers.

After a particularly long lukewarm one, Craig wrapped a towel around his waist and started to shave. He'd been doing the caveman beard since arriving here, but it was time for that to go. He might not be playing ball anymore, but the scruffy look was played out. For Craig, anyway. Dante's beard and locks looked quite professional on him.

He mixed the soap in the mug his aunt had bought him

when he turned thirteen and dabbed at his chin. He lifted the razor and started in. This was going to be a big job.

"Let me help you with that."

Craig jerked and nicked his chin. The soap stung, but only for a second as Brianna took the razor from his hands and started shaving. She knew how to do it just right so that he didn't get ingrown hairs. Even the barbers on the road couldn't compare.

Though his head was tilted up at the ceiling, Craig tried to meet her eyes. "I didn't hear you come in. You don't have to—I could go so you can have your privacy."

He could hear her breathing against him, slowly and evenly. She was nervous, too.

"I wasn't paying attention. I just sort of came on in, and you were so intent on shaving that you barely noticed me."

That was hard to believe. It was more like he was so busy thinking about her already that he hadn't differentiated the real Brianna from the one who was always with him: in his dreams, in his heart. "Oh, I'm noticing you. Lift up that towel and you'll see just how much."

She curved in, next to his mouth. "Craig . . ."

He shrugged. "I'm just keeping it real. Some of my body doesn't know we're divorced."

Some of my mind doesn't, either.

Brianna made quick work of her ex-husband's face. She reached down into a bag she kept under the sink. "I've got something that will be really good for your face. Hold on."

"Take your time," Craig said, his eyes on the slip of Brianna's back that refused to stay in the towel. He'd spent a lot of time curled around that back in his lifetime. It was hard to believe that he'd never do it again. Even harder to consider Brianna in the arms of someone else.

She stood and shook her head. "This was a bad idea. Take this and put it on your—"

"I think I've got an idea of my own," Craig said, pulling

Brianna against him. The state of Georgia might not consider them married, but to Craig, Brianna was still his wife. Till death do us part, he'd once said. Though many of their vows had been broken, that one stood out, even in the small bathroom clouded with steam.

He lifted her into his arms and stepped toward the shower, dropping his towel on the way.

"Wait . . . your knee . . ." Brianna said in a half whisper as she wrapped her legs around his waist.

"Will be fine," Craig answered, turning on the warm water with one hand. "Just like you."

The water rained down, drowning out the sounds of their reunion, washing away both their tears.

Chapter 3

He felt as if a car had run over his knee . . . and he'd never been happier. Brianna, however, was not happy. She was scared to death. And for that, and that alone, Craig was sorry.

"About the other morning—"

"Let's not talk about it, okay? We got caught up in the moment. It happens. The trick is to make sure that it doesn't happen again."

Okay, so she's got tricks.

"And how does that work exactly?" It was a rhetorical question. The Louis Vuitton bag on her bed said it all. He could see it and the rest of the things she was packing from where he stood in the hall.

"By leaving. I never should have come here. We both know that. I just couldn't say no to your aunt. She was like a mother to me. She still is. And now I'm afraid that the Richards family will be disappointed in me once again."

He wanted to reach for her, to touch her, but he didn't. Once Brianna got like this, there was no stopping her. Not with human hands, anyway. Not that he could chase her, anyway. As it was, he was minutes away from his legs buckling beneath him. He wanted to give Brianna's exit speech the proper attention, but the pain was almost as blinding as the pleasure that had caused it.

He took a deep breath and started for his room with a bit of a limp.

Brianna put down her purse. "Is it your knee? Oh no. I knew we shouldn't have . . . Craig, I'm so sorry. Is there anything I can do?"

Yes, head back to the bathroom. "No. I'll be fine. You just do what you think you need to. Are you going to Asia's? Your dad's?"

Brianna's eyes narrowed. "Not that it's any of your business, but I'm going back home. Atlanta."

"Atlanta?" That wasn't Brianna's home, or at least he hadn't realized she thought of it that way. But what would he know? Most of the year, he just got off a plane and hugged his way through the crowd until he got to her.

He stared at her, really looked at his ex-wife. She could be so powerful at times, but now she looked like a little girl afraid of being hurt, afraid of falling in love. She looked like his angel.

"You don't have to leave, you know."

She pulled out the vial of oil that she'd had in the bathroom and rubbed it across Craig's cheeks, over his chin, his lips . . . "This is kissi oil. It's Asian. It'll make your skin feel wonderful."

Craig reached up and placed his hand over hers against his face. "My skin already feels wonderful, but a little kissi can't hurt." He started to kiss her, but—

Let her go.

Craig had been praying for God to speak to his heart, but this didn't seem to be the best timing. And yet, he obeyed.

"Good-bye, Brianna. Be safe." It took all he had to keep from kissing her hand, but Craig let things drop once he'd given her a deep bow.

She didn't curtsy back. She made a run for it. All the way to her car.

Craig didn't laugh as he tumbled into his bed with pain shooting up both sides of his legs. Love was no laughing matter.

"I still think you should be careful, Brianna. I mean, he's a football player, for goodness sake. Just because he let you walk out of his house doesn't mean it's over. It's never over with Craig. You know how he is."

Brianna shifted gears and turned back onto I-75. ATL or bust. She was headed back to Georgia, and as always, Asia was along for the ride. "That's just it. I don't know how he is. This Craig isn't someone I know at all."

For that matter, I don't know this Brianna.

Brianna braked to yield to the flow of traffic and for a moment held her latte with both hands, even though it burned her palms. She needed to feel something, to know that north was still up and Starbucks was still hot as hell. One thing hadn't changed—Asia wouldn't shut up.

"See, he has you fooled with all this Jesus bit, but I ain't going for it. He was playing church when we came to move you out. Bible all up in the bed and foolishness. Like that means anything?"

What did mean something was that Asia had scoped out Brianna's bed hard enough to know what was in it. Brianna hadn't even caught that little tidbit. Having her and the girls come with her to move Craig out was a mistake. She'd disrespected Craig in the worst way, Brianna realized. If he'd gone off on her like she'd expected, she would have felt like it was warranted, but he'd been so calm, like he'd seen it all coming. Like it was a movie and only he knew the ending. Well, he and Asia. She seemed to think she knew everything about their marriage. And Brianna was sick of it.

"Look, let it go, okay? I don't want to talk about Craig. He's still my husband—"

Asia threw up her hands like a kid on the playground. "Umm, not the last time I checked. He's your ex-husband, hello? I heard how you played him at church. And remember how you schemed to get the papers delivered? Bam! You got served, baby! I wish I could have been there."

I bet you do.

Brianna put her latte in the drink holder and ran a hand through her hair. She was glad that she hadn't been there when Craig got the divorce papers. Craig had a thing about divorce. Even though both their parents had split up, he hadn't wanted that for himself. They'd both agreed that they'd never split up, that they were forever. One day, Brianna woke up and realized just how long forever really is.

Turn around, Bright Eyes . . .

A song Craig used to sing to her popped into Brianna's head. Turn around. Was it possible? Was it too late to admit that maybe she'd made a mistake? To tell Asia and everybody that she was mad and confused but still wanted Craig?

"All those girls. The drinking. Everything he did to you. He had it coming. It's a good thing he found God. He's going to need Him."

Something in Brianna turned crisp and hard. Asia was right. Craig had this coming to him, all of it. She didn't dare tell her friend about the money, though. Craig was rehabbing his knee. Brianna had called the trainer in Tampa. He said it was bad, but there was always a chance that some team might take him for one last season. She'd once been willing to be a starter wife, but those days were long gone. She'd paid her dues. She couldn't be like Tenisha and move back to Tampa and be the wife of the local has-been . . . no matter how cute he was.

That's all Brianna needed, a chance. And when it came,

she'd be there, waiting to get everything what was hers, to reclaim everything Craig had given away.

Asia reached across Brianna for her latte. "Are you going to drink that?"

Brianna shook her head. "No. I don't feel so good all of a sudden. Take it."

With a shrug, Asia chugged down her friend's drink without a thought. Craig wasn't the only one who had changed. Asia would have never drunk after Brianna a year ago, but that was when she had a husband keeping her in style. These days, the most interesting man in Asia's life was . . . Craig.

Brianna pressed her foot on the gas. Divorce or not, she was going to have to keep an eye on her ex-husband . . . and her friend.

Chapter 4

The timing couldn't have been worse.

Craig buttoned his suit coat with regret as he headed toward his first speaking engagement, an invitation to give his testimony to some professional athletes in the area. Some of the men who once coached him would be there, too, since the event was to raise funds for the Fellowship of Christian Athletes.

In high school and college, Craig had attended those events, always amazed by the steadfast faith of the players and coaches who came to share. And now he, a divorced and damaged ex-player, would be the evening's attraction. Even as he reached for the keys to his aunt's car, he considered backing out.

The phone rang before he could dial. He smiled as he recognized the number. Pastor Green.

"Hello, Pastor." He'd known. Even when Craig was a kid, that man always seemed to know what people were feeling.

"Hello. Now look here, son. There's nothing to be nervous about, hear? We overcome the enemy by the blood of the Lamb and the word of our testimony. And you've got a testimony, so just tell it, a'ight? God'll do the rest."

Craig blew out a breath. "I guess. I just don't know what to say. I'm not one of those guys always trying to give speeches and perpetrate. I just played ball. And now even that's messed up."

The pastor laughed. "So tell 'em that, son. You'd be surprised what folks need to hear. Just keep it real and let God do the rest. Now, go on. The whole men's ministry is over there waiting on you. Don't make me come and get you."

"No, sir," Craig said, laughing to himself and heading toward the Emerald Greens Country Club where the fund-raiser was being held. He had to laugh at pulling up there in his aunt's Mercury Grand Marquis instead of one of his sports cars. He'd sold most of them and split the money with Brianna in the divorce, but as evidenced by her trip to Tampa, she'd probably burned through that money by now. Aunt Tee's ride was comfortable, though, even if it did feel like driving a flotation device. As big as Craig was, the car still seemed huge.

Once he arrived, Craig was thankful for the easy ride. He quickly found himself facing men who he hadn't seen in years. Men who had prayed for him, trained him, and now felt sorry for him. He could see it in their eyes.

The evening went quickly, and soon Craig found himself at the podium with a microphone in front of him. His talk was short but powerful as he bore his heart about many of the parts of his journey, including the heights of winning his first Super Bowl to the low of losing his wife.

"She was just something else that I had to have, and then when I got her, she was just something else to keep. I loved her once, but in all the running to nowhere, I forgot that. Don't let that happen to you. Keep the main thing the main thing. God, family, then football."

There was the giving, too, the Craig Richards Foundation. Giving that he hadn't planned for but had reaped the benefits of.

"Invest in people. At the end of the day, that's what matters. My cars aren't rehabbing my knee, the kid I helped put through college is. My house isn't praying for me, my pastor is. There will always be something more to buy, but God said it best—store up your treasures in heaven."

Craig didn't think that what he'd said was anything particularly insightful, but when he was finished, every guy in the room came to tell him something about how his story related to their lives, even the coaches and high school kids from FCA. When he'd shaken the last hand, Craig found Dante in a middle of a crowd calling for order.

"Who's next?" his friend shouted as he scribbled down something on the notepad he always kept in his pocket.

"What are you doing, man? Taking bets on me?"

Dante laughed. "Even better. I'm booking your speaking engagements." He flipped through several pages of his notebook with dates and times.

Craig took a step back, glancing at one of the dates, several months in advance. The next month looked booked solid, with Craig speaking every few days. That would cut into his rehab time, not to mention his helping Dante out after school with the team.

He'd wanted to be honest and encouraging, not become some goofy guru, going around spouting things at people. What was God trying to do?

Life back in Atlanta wasn't as wonderful as Brianna had thought it would be. The word was definitely out about her breakup with Craig as her phone had started blowing up with messages inviting her on dates as soon as she crossed the Georgia border. The problem was, the only man on Brianna's mind was her ex-husband—or the church boy pretending to be him.

Try as she might, she couldn't shake the image of Craig bowed on his hurt knee before the cross. She'd married him after he'd bowed before her like that, only to become a wild thing who often left her crying on his whirlwind trips in and out of town. And in just a few days, the church had done what she could not—tame her husband.

It was what Brianna always thought she wanted, but now she wasn't sure. The fighting and games were all she knew, and now Craig refused to fight back. A year ago, if she'd left him like this, he'd have taken a red-eye flight and been waiting to pick her up and carry her home. Now, he was Mr. Nice Guy, and life with her own father had taught her that nice guys never win.

"Hey, do you have some unmentionables?" It was Asia, annoying and unwilling to go home. She was on the make, too. It was so obvious that some of the guys who came to see Brianna avoided her.

"What?"

"Unmentionables. You know, the monthly rations. Goodness, girl. Where do you keep your tampons!"

Brianna closed her eyes. If Asia hadn't been her girl from back in the day . . . She got up and went to the bathroom, shoving things aside until she found what her friend wanted.

A whole box of them.

"Are these the same ones you had when I was up here last, when we were planning Craig's demise? You ain't had a cycle since then? Don't tell me you pregnant, 'cause that would just be stupid. . . .

Brianna dropped the box and fell back against the bathroom wall. Though she'd been with Craig a few weeks before the breakup, she'd been safe. She'd made sure of it. But she hadn't planned on staying so long in Tampa, hadn't brought her birth control along. There'd been no reason to.

"I'm not pregnant," Brianna said softly. "I can't be." She promised herself that it would never happen. Not with Craig. Not ever.

"I mean, out of anybody I know, you are the most careful. I thought you would have been done gave that man a son. But now? I mean, for real, sis. I should have known when you said that you were staying over there, that wasn't a good idea. Is that why you running home? You divorced the man and then got knocked up? Now that is a ridiculous plan, but I'm gonna trust you on it. We should do something. Get you vitamins or something. That's what we did last time, right?"

"Don't go there, Asia."

Her friend's face softened. "My bad. Seriously, though, what do you want me to do?"

"Nothing. Just leave me alone."

Sunday couldn't come fast enough, not for Craig and not for Dante, especially since Craig had made the mistake of telling Dante what had happened between him and Brianna. It was all Craig could do to keep from hopping a plane to ATL. By now, fools would be swarming, especially the dudes who'd been jealous of him. He'd seen the looks in their eyes when he and Brianna had had parties, the same look he'd had when Bri was on the arm of Terrell Rue. And now, there was nothing Craig could do or say about it. According to Dante, he shouldn't care.

"Snap out of it, bruh. You can't let her do you like this, man. I'm for real. You're making it bad for brothers everywhere. If Craig Richards can get rolled up out of his bed, what chance does the next man have to hold it down with his woman? No. You can't let her play with your head. She chose the divorce. You can't run after her this time."

Though Dante was usually the one to take Brianna's side when Craig did something stupid, there was no love lost between the two of them, especially since his own wife, Tenisha, had taken part in rolling Craig out of his bed. Craig wanted to tell Dante that he didn't have to worry. The sistah squad wouldn't be rolling up in his bedroom anytime soon.

"She's your wife, man." Dante would always tell Craig when he was saying or doing something stupid. Sometimes Dante would even remind Craig of how he'd acted such a fool to get Brianna, how he'd done everything in those first few years of his career to be worthy of her.

Now, though, it seemed as though Dante was sick of both of them.

"I'm not saying you're a saint or anything. One trip down the aisle doesn't change the facts. You've done some dirt, but Bri wasn't trying to go anywhere then, because that money was flowing. Now a man gets hurt, and you bring your girls and clean out the house? Naw, man. That ain't right. You gave that girl everything you had."

Everything but what she needed.

"Man, I don't want to talk about it, okay? You didn't trip like this when it happened. I just called to see if you're coming to church this morning or if you're attending Bedside Baptist."

"Oh, I see. You got jokes now? Huh? Let a brothah go to the altar one time and now he's the church secretary, taking attendance."

"Naw. For real, though. I was just asking . . ."

There was a lengthy pause on the line. Dante had joined Soul Harvest Worship Church years ago and made his respectable appearances on Christmas, Easter, and the occasional Sunday that Tenisha dragged him there.

Dante cleared his throat. "Look, don't start, okay? I know you got the peace that passes understanding down in your heart and all that, but I'm not up for a Sunday School class right now. Tenisha's mama is here."

Craig swallowed hard and prayed for his friend. That woman was insane. Certifiable. "Now? As in right now?"

"This second, dog. She's in the kitchen fighting with 'Nisha. I'm about to cut out to run a few miles, but she'll be waiting for me with something to say. Even the kids have been dreading it. Man, if I mention going to church this morning, she'll have Tenisha out the next hour buying matching suits for the kids or some foolishness. She tries to be so saddity when she knows good and well I bought the first St. John suit she ever wore."

Now, that was the truth. Tenisha was a sweet girl and Dante's kids were too cute, but Tenisha's mama? Even Bri couldn't hang with her. She was something else. Couldn't stand anybody, even her own daughter. Except Craig, that is.

"Want me to take her off your hands for a few hours? I can take her to church with me while you spend some time with T and the kids."

"Would you? I wouldn't ask, but you know she loves your tired behind. When I told her you got saved, she had a fit. Ran all around the room. She acts like you're her son-in-law instead of me."

At least somebody loves me.

"Yeah, well. I'll pick her up around eight. Anything I should know?" Craig felt as if he were agreeing to babysit a child.

"Just one thing."

Here we go. "What?"

"A lottery ticket. She buys one every Sunday. Bring it with you and give it to her or she's going to have you stopping at twenty hundred stores on the way. You know the Georgia jackpot is booming right now, so she's going to be all over it."

Craig had to laugh then. Or at least he tried. "A lottery ticket? On Sunday? Man, that has to be about the craziest thing I ever heard, but I'm going to trust you on it. How do I know what numbers to play?"

"It doesn't matter. It's not like she's going to win. Just pick something. Pick an old play or something. And for real, do something about Brianna. Tenisha is over here talking trash to me already. And if them heifers think they're ever going to turn me up out of my bed—"

"They won't. Later, man."

Dante took a deep breath. "Later."

* * *

Craig showed up at Dante's at eight o'clock on the dot with lottery ticket in hand. He'd felt like a fool buying it. One person in the store had recognized him and commented that things were really bad if Craig Richards was playing Lotto. Craig didn't bother to explain. Truth be told, things were pretty bad. He'd gotten a call from his accountant and between the divorce, the new house, and his bad investments, the money wasn't adding up. By the time Craig paid his taxes, he'd be screwed for real.

"You've got to get Brianna to agree to sell the house. I know that it didn't sell before, but she's going to lose it anyway. Call her and see what you two can work out," his accountant had said. Craig hadn't bother to explain to him, either. He and Brianna didn't have rational discussions. Wild, passionate sex? Absolutely. But normal communication? Rarely.

It was Sunday, though, and Craig had decided to leave his burdens at home. Or at least he'd thought so until Tenisha's mother, Mrs. Wright, got into his car.

She started by pinching his cheek. Hard. Craig overcame the impulse to swing his fist and settled back into his seat, waiting for her to let go.

Eventually she did. "How are you, baby? What's this you bringing me? A lottery ticket? Now, you now I'm a woman of God and I don't gamble, but I'm going to let you off the hook 'cause you just got saved. Put that thing away. You might need it once that woman gets through with you. Yes, I heard all about it. . . ."

It was probably more like overheard, but there was no use in finessing that point. Craig listened to Mrs. Wright's recommendations on how to get Brianna back all the way to church. When they pulled into the parking lot at Soul Harvest and got out, a slender white man with a ponytail approached. By now, Craig knew him well enough to recognize him for what he was—a bearer of bad news.

"Are you Craig Richards?"

"C'mon, man. Let's not play this game. You know who I am. What do you want?" Craig said, holding back Dante's mother-in-law as she hurled insults at the man.

"This is for you. Please sign here," the man said, handing Craig a slim package and his clipboard.

Craig scribbled his signature, wondering what Brianna had drummed up now that was important enough to have him served at church.

"Just a crying shame. That girl is as trifling as she ever was, but nobody listens to me. I told your mama back then to get you away from her. Them Davises ain't nothing but—"

"Juanita, it's good to have you in God's house this morning. How was your trip?" Pastor Green cut through the tension like butter as he took Dante's mother-in-law by the arm and led her away. He turned back to Craig with a smile. "It ain't a testimony without a test, brother. Stand. Just stand."

Stand.

As one of the deacons hustled the messenger out a side entrance, it was all Craig could do to obey his pastor and keep his feet underneath him. He should have waited until after service to look at the contents of the package, but curiosity got the best of him. He ripped the package open, only to be surprised when a stack of photos littered to the floor instead of the stack of legal documents announcing some other proceedings he'd been expecting.

He knelt and picked up one of the pictures but didn't rise as he realized what he was seeing: Brianna, in her angel dress, laughing as she danced with Terrell Rue. The photo was dated from the day before.

Probably the night before.

Only when Pastor Green returned and put his hand on Craig's back did he start walking, and even then his feet felt like lead.

"Sometimes the enemy tries to steal away the word before it can take root, son. Stand strong and see the salvation of the Lord, brother. It's coming."

For the first time since walking the aisle at Soul Harvest a few weeks ago, Craig was starting to wonder. "When is it coming? I don't see it. First my knee, now this. It seems like the closer I get to God, the worse things get."

The pastor smiled. "Exactly. Think about that, brother. Why do you think that might be? The enemy doesn't like losing souls from his kingdom. He can't take you to hell anymore, but he sure doesn't want you sharing your faith or doing anything real for the kingdom. He wants to shake you before you get rooted good, but God's got you. We've got you too. Hold on, Brother Craig. Just hold on."

And though that man was a foot shorter than him and fifty pounds lighter, Craig did just what Pastor Green said—he held on. For today at least, his life seemed to depend on it.

Chapter 5

Word got around fast about Brianna's pictures. Craig went on running, rehabbing, and speaking, growing closer to God each day while trying to dodge all the women who were coming after him.

"They think y'all are truly over now," his aunt said. "A single man going to church with a job—"

"I work for the high school, Aunt Tee. My money is almost all gone. I'm hardly a catch."

The old woman shook her head and untied her apron. "You just don't get it, do you? You have no idea who you are. Even now with Christ inside you. Well, they see, baby, and guess what? They're not going to go away quietly. So get ready because the word is out that you're home tonight, and the last time I looked outside, them hussies were winding around the block."

In disbelief, Craig peeked out the window. He could hardly believe his eyes. What looked like an army of women were coming his way, and not one of them looked like she was taking any prisoners.

"What am I supposed to do?"

His aunt laughed. "You'll figure it out. I would stay, but

I'm embarrassed for these sisters. I don't want to have to look at one of them in the face at church, knowing how they came over here and showed out like this."

Craig wouldn't take it that far.

They did look like the welcoming committee for a nation of angry females, but beyond that, Craig figured they were just trying to be nice. The doorbell rang, giving him a chance to test his theory.

"I'm out," his aunt said, easing past him toward her bedroom. Her home wasn't as big as the one he'd had with Brianna, but it wasn't small, either. It had been his first purchase as a pro player, and now faced with so many women at once, Craig was glad that they'd all have somewhere to sit down, far from him, he hoped.

As he opened the door, they flooded in: tall women, fat women, old women, young women . . . Each with a dish of food and their best outfit, though some of them should have gone shopping or stayed home. Seriously.

"What are you doing here? You said you had choir practice."

"You said you were working late."

Goodness.

"Ladies, thank you so much for coming to welcome me to the church. I do appreciate it, and I'm sure that my aunt Theresa does, too. She's always telling me about the beautiful, godly women at Soul Harvest, and now I see that she was right—"

"See! He's talking about me."

"Girl, please. You look like you've been squeezed into those jeans with some forceps. That man ain't paying you no mind. Did you see his ex-wife? That's his type. He's looking at me—"

Craig blew out a breath. The only thing that topped this was putting up the lottery ticket he'd bought for Dante's mother-in-law and discovering that she'd written her number on the back of it . . . in lipstick.

"Anyway, thanks to all of you for stopping by. . . ."

Just as Craig was about to be swallowed up in a circle of desperate women, Dante came shoving through the crowd. With his notebook, of course.

"Excuse me. Step aside. Excuse me! All right, ladies, please approach me one at a time with your contact information and availability. I have Mr. Richards's schedule, and I'll be booking his dates as well. We'll go alphabetically. If your last name starts with A, meet me in the kitchen. Everyone else into the family room. Mr. Richards has an appointment. . . ."

Craig didn't have to be told twice. He grabbed his keys and headed for the door. As he went, each of the women made a point to parade past him, but Craig barely bothered to look. He already knew that none of them would smell right or laugh at his jokes in the right places. None of them had the power to hurt him like no one else could.

None of them was Brianna.

Dante had been after Craig for weeks to admit the truth—that he was in love with the only woman he could never have. His ex-wife.

"Lord, help me," he prayed, going out the door. "I love her again, but it's too late."

"I don't have a lot of time, but I need to talk to you."

Brianna was irritated and intrigued. This was the Craig she knew. "About what? Talk to my lawyer, Craig. I don't want to fight."

"Don't you mean my lawyer? I'm paying for him, too, right?"

She didn't like the edge in his voice. "What's the problem?"

"Don't have anything else sent to me, especially not at

church. You said to let you go, and I did, but don't disrespect me. And be careful with Terrell. I wouldn't want to have to come up there and hurt anybody."

Brianna sat down on the corner of her bed. Terrell? She'd seen him the other night at a fund-raiser. Danced with him once. How did Craig know, and what did he mean about sending him things at church? "I haven't sent you anything, Craig, and as for Terrell, I saw him once at a party and danced with him for a few minutes. We barely talked. I'm touched that you're jealous, though." She put a hand across her belly, and her stomach started to turn. Asia was convinced that Brianna was pregnant, but she knew otherwise. It was just stress.

"Someone had a stack of photos of you and Terrell delivered to me at Soul Harvest last Sunday. And they were delivered by the same guy who served me the divorce papers."

Foreclosure boy? He was so tired. "Okay, that wasn't me. I'd be interested in knowing who it was, though. I don't appreciate anybody sending my husband—"

"Ex-husband."

Touché.

"Whatever. I don't like people getting in my business."

"The accountant says that we should sell the house—"

"Out of the question. Where would I live?"

"Here. You could live here. We can get our own place. There won't be a pool or a chef, but we could make it."

"We? What are you talking about, Craig? We're divorced."

He cleared his throat. "I know that. I didn't mean that kind of we. I just meant to get us through this. Financially. You know."

She thought back to that morning in the shower and how quickly and thoroughly Craig had melted her resolve. "I know all right. I know that within a week of staying at your place we were all up in the shower sweating. It seems like that's all we're good at these days. It takes more than that to . . . live together."

"It worked for us for seven years. Longer if you count—"

Brianna wasn't counting. She didn't want to. "Look, is there anything else you want? I need to go."

"Tell the chef I said hello. I love Aunt Tee's food, but she's trying to fatten me up. I don't know how Dante still affords his chef. I miss that brother dearly."

"More than you miss me?" She gasped. That wasn't meant to be said out loud. She could almost see Craig smiling through the phone.

"I think you just agreed that it'd be best if we didn't go there. I never wanted that house, but I hate to see you lose it." He seemed sincere.

It was Brianna's turn to get real, too. "Okay, I admit it. You were right about the house. I should have waited until you got your new contract. It just seemed so . . . perfect. I couldn't let it go. I should have, though. I see that now. It was a mistake."

"I know just how you feel." Craig said, strong and firm, like the man she'd known.

Brianna regretted her words as soon as she'd said them.

"Speaking of mistakes, Craig, I think this conversation was one. Let's stick to talking through the lawyers until everything is resolved."

"It doesn't have to be like this, but if that's what you want. You can always call me. You know that. No matter what."

Brianna looked down at her stomach, curved a little from its usual flatness. How she wished she could believe Craig, but she'd tried that once and lost everything. . . .

"I've got to go, Craig."

"Hot date, huh?"

She didn't bother to answer. Instead, she hung up the phone and ran to the bathroom. Brianna had a hot date all right . . . with her toilet.

Things were spinning out of control, but everyone else thought life was great.

"I'm so proud of you," his aunt said every time he left the house for a speaking engagement.

Dante spent the time after every practice to drill Craig about a possible book deal.

"My boy's cousin's friend's brother lives next to Oprah's assistant. All we have to do is get you on once and *cha-ching!* Now let's go through the titles again: "Every Knee Shall Bow," "Bruised but not Broken". . . Are you listening? Craig?"

The phone rang now almost as much as it had when he was playing for the Falcons, only now Craig was on God's team. This time, though, he didn't know the plays. He often felt like a fool when offered a seat behind the pulpit when he went to speak. He was a new Christian himself. How could he tell anyone anything about how to live, how to trust God? He could barely get his own ex-wife to talk to him

Still, people came from all over to hear the busted-up ex-NFL player talk about his life with his beautiful ex-wife. Craig felt as if he should go around with a big "X" on his chest, lest anyone think he was currently capable of holding down a job or a relationship. He thought better of it, though. Someone would only copy it and make it the new style.

Tonight, though, something different had happened, something he knew would happen eventually. A heckler had gotten up during Craig's speech and challenged him, and everything he said had been true.

"The guy's a fraud. He just found God because there wasn't anything else to do. If he hadn't given so many of you people money, you wouldn't care about him now."

The truth in the man's words had scared Craig more than the offense of any insult. The man was right. It wouldn't be as easy for Craig to walk in faith if he was playing again. When you're almost broke and your wife leaves you, praying comes easy.

His aunt told him not to worry. "There'll always be something to keep you on your knees. There will be Jesus, and there will be people. God has given you a heart to help folks. They'll be on your mind, too." The other person who'd always be on his mind went unsaid. Craig silently thanked his aunt, but his decision was made: he wouldn't be speaking to anyone else until he got some things straight with himself.

Chapter 6

YOU ARE INVITED TO AN EVENING OF
SISTERHOOD AND STRENGTH,
HOSTED BY THE FIRST WIVES CLUB.
GUESTS BY INVITATION ONLY.

When her marriage ended, Brianna gave up on getting an invite to the most exclusive women's group in the area. Composed of wives of professional athletes, entertainers, and celebrities, the group had pull and class. How she'd gotten an invite now with her life coming down around her ears, Brianna didn't know, but she did know one thing—she was going.

Asia had gone back to Tampa for a modeling stint, and Brianna was glad to be alone and have some time to think. After trying on her tenth outfit, she realized that maybe she was too tired for what might be required for this. Still, she pulled on a black silk babydoll dress and some comfortable heels and headed out.

The ladies did not disappoint. While a valet parked her

car, Brianna took in the sights: ice sculptures, fresh flowers, and an outdoor gazebo. It looked like a wedding instead of a tea.

"Brianna . . . there you are. We were hoping you'd come. What a cute dress—wait you're pregnant? Why didn't you tell us? We could have made this a baby shower, too."

Another woman pranced across the yard. Her bracelets sounded like music. "Baby? What baby—oh my goodness! She's pregnant. Come here, y'all. Craig Richards's wife. She's so cute. . . ."

"Didn't they get divorced?" someone asked.

"I think so, but who cares. He'll take care of the baby. They always do." The woman turned to Brianna with concern. "It is his, right?"

I can't believe this! They hardly know me. "Yes. It's his."

They sighed collectively. "Thank God. There's still a chance for his knee, honey. And if not, don't worry. He'll take of you. God will, too. Is he excited about the baby?"

"Actually, I'm not—"

"Brianna!" Clare Stephens, the only woman in the group who really knew Brianna, came toward her with outstretched arms. "Just keep walking. I love them, but they can be really nosy sometimes. Please excuse them," she said under her breath as she led Brianna into the house.

"I'm not pregnant. Really."

"Of course." Clare just smiled and handed Brianna a lemonade. Each glass had swirls of fresh mango.

"My period is a little late, but it's just stress."

"Of course. Have a seat, sweetie."

Brianna wanted to scream. They were treating her like a second grader, Clare included. She wanted to scream, to tell them all that she couldn't get pregnant that easily, her life is complicated, and she shouldn't be here. And she would have told them all that if the food hadn't been so good.

Shrimp salad with champagne grapes on a bed of spinach,

carved melons, and squash soup. The chef outdid himself, and so did Brianna. She ate more than she ever would have at home, let alone in front of a bunch of beautiful women.

"How far gone are you, honey?" someone was asking. The other women started pulling out Bibles and forming a circle.

Brianna felt as if the walls were going to close her in when someone put a New Testament in her hand and told her to join them.

"What are you doing?" she couldn't help but ask.

"Bible study. Didn't you know? We do it after all the meetings now."

Great.

"I know. That's what I thought, too, but it's really changing me and my marriage. I wish Clare had added the Bible study years ago. We used to just get drunk after."

Sounded like a good plan to Brianna.

"Clare, you start."

The women pulled their chairs closer and grabbed hands. Brianna didn't extend her hands, but the other women reached for her anyway.

". . . and Lord bless Brianna Richards, who we believe you led us to invite here. Now we can see why. Bless her marriage, bless her body and her baby, but most of all bless her heart. Let her know when she leaves here beyond a shadow of a doubt that You love her and have a plan for her life. For all our lives. . . ."

Brianna tried to pull her hands back, but the women held fast. As Clare closed, the next woman began, sharing her heart, her struggles, praying for everyone present, including Brianna. By the time they got to her, she was a mess.

"I guess being pregnant is the least of my worries. You guys were killing me with all that praying."

The woman next to her got up and pulled her chair closer, putting an arm around Brianna.

Don't do this. They will talk about you . . . to everyone.

It was too late. One of the women, whose name she didn't remember, though Brianna had seen her singing on TV, began to hum "Amazing Grace." Whatever was left of Brianna's defenses fell apart.

"We lost everything, and I kicked him out of the house," she whispered as another woman got up and rubbed her back while she threw up their catered lunch into an expensive vase. "And now I'm pregnant. What am I going to do?"

The hostess, whose husband was a golden boy with a string of records since back in his Heisman Trophy days, was first to speak.

"You are not going to do anything, sweetie, but accept that Jesus is in control of your life and give that life over to Him. We are going to do the rest, starting with bringing you and your family before the throne of God. We were just being friendly when we prayed before, but now it's time to get serious. Come on, sistahs. Let's pray."

And pray they did. These women, who Brianna would never have dreamed of telling her secrets to, prayed with her, for her, and before she knew it, Brianna was praying for them, too. The faith she'd left behind as a little girl sprang to life as the ladies opened the scriptures to Brianna.

By the time they got around to asking her if she wanted to rededicate her life to God, Brianna was facedown in the plush carpet being received by Christ. She spent the night there, right on that spot.

"I'm serious, man. I'm not going. I have nothing to say." Craig hung up on Dante, tired of having the same fight. No matter how many times he tried to explain, his friend didn't understand. His aunt didn't, either.

"After all God has done for you, this is how you repay Him?"

Craig hated to hurt her feelings, but the truth is best, he knew that now. "Look, I'm just some guy who lost everything and came home. I didn't plan any of this. I'm not chosen. I didn't go to seminary. If it wasn't for you, I probably wouldn't have ever gone to church. I'm not the right man for the job."

Aunt Theresa balled up her fist and socked Craig in the arm. She spoke with what's left of her energy. "Do you think this is about you? Any of it? God didn't allow you to run that ball or open your mouth because you were qualified. He just blessed you. Now you need to use everything you have to bless Him back. You can go to seminary if you want to, but schooling ain't calling. You need to have the second before the first. And you got it. Always had it. Just ain't had time to notice until now."

Craig stared at the hall mirror across from him, wishing he could see the man his aunt saw. All that stared back at him now was failure. Brianna must have seen it, too. She wasn't answering his calls.

She stayed three days at Clare's house. That's how long it took for them to convince Brianna to take a pregnancy test. She was fine without it, she said, but they said it was always best to be sure. She'd finally agreed. Until she saw those two pink lines, that is. Then she went crazy.

"I can't do this," Brianna said, out of breath.

Clare and the other women exchanged looks. Clare spoke to Brianna first.

"What are you so afraid of, honey? It's just a baby."

Brianna didn't answer. She couldn't. It was much more than just a baby. She'd learned that the hard way. The last time she'd seen two pink lines, everyone in her life, including Craig, had turned against her. How could she risk that again?

The ladies took her home even though she didn't go through with calling Craig to tell him about the baby. Back at home with time to think, Brianna realized that she'd never forgiven herself or her ex-husband for what happened when they were in high school. They're grown now, and whether they were together or not, Craig had a right to know about his child.

Just as she was about to call Craig and tell him, Brianna got a text from Asia:

Check out the happy couple.

A picture came up on the screen next, a picture of Craig looking fine as ever walking arm in arm with a beautiful woman. The high school prom queen to be exact, the good girl that everyone said he should have been with in the first place.

Brianna put the phone down and started praying. Out loud. It was weird but comforting somehow.

"Okay, God. I can't be mad. I pushed him away. He deserves better. I'll wait and tell him about the baby later. If I tell him now, people will think I am trying to trap him. Again."

In the meantime, Brianna needed to make some decisions. She had filed a response to her foreclosure, but time was winding up. She'd been trying to get a job, but nothing she could do would make up the past due mortgage payments. She was going to have to face the truth—her days of living the high life were over. And for the first time, Brianna didn't think that was the end of the world.

These days, Craig sat in the church balcony. It was quiet, and people stayed focused on the message instead of him. He'd taken Rhonda Walker to a party with the mayor as a courtesy, and now the whole church practically had them married off. Thankfully, Rhonda was a friend from way back and knew how to tone things down. Still, if he didn't time his exit just right, somebody would catch him and get some gossip going.

He took the back stairs two at a time, but already there

was a man on his heels. Too late. Probably a reporter or someone trying to book him for an event.

"I'm not speaking anymore, if that's what you want."

"Good," the man said. "You'll have more time to train. How's the knee? I have a team that's interested."

Craig could hardly believe his ears, but the man was serious. "The knee? It's . . . good, actually. I'd say eighty-five percent. Not good enough to play but—"

The man wrote something down. "When it gets to ninety-five percent, call me. I figure we can get a million and a couple more seasons. You might not even play, but it might get that pretty wife of yours back and save your home."

Craig turned away. Was there nothing about his life that everyone didn't know?

You're the one who's been going around telling everybody, fool.

When the stranger left, Craig studied the business card the man gave him, surprised that he didn't instantly recognize Arman Gunter, an agent well-known for his ability to get last-chance guys one last deal. He and his teammates had often joked with each other about giving Gunter a call if someone's play didn't improve. Though Craig didn't like to hear it, the man spoke the truth. Going back to football was the only way to get Brianna back. And God would want that as much as Craig did.

Chapter 7

Aunt Theresa wasn't impressed.

"It's not the kind of money I once made, but now I know what to do with it. Maybe this is God's way of bringing Brianna and me back together."

Craig's aunt didn't give him the reassurance he expected when he told her about the possibility of another offer and the interest of Arman Gunter.

"Sounds like a wrestling match to me," his aunt said, in a tone that drove Craig crazy.

Huh?

"There's a blessing on the way, that's for sure. Sometimes, though, you have to do like Jacob and wrestle God to get it. It might leave you wounded." She touched Craig's knee. "But in the end, you get a new name and sometimes a new nation. Jacob went from a joker to becoming Israel, the nation of the King. Who do you want to be?"

"Brianna's husband," Craig whispered as he walks away. He'd taken his marriage for granted for so many years, trusting that as he and Brianna agreed, they'd always be together, no matter what he did. Now he knew that real love was more than just survival or endurance. It also meant sacrifice.

He checked his e-mail and text in-box. Still nothing from Brianna. It was time to take a ride.

A friend to whom he'd loaned a Porsche and forgotten about it had driven the car down a few days before. He left his aunt a note, loaded up the car, and headed for Atlanta, praying all the way.

Though his knee made the drive a little uncomfortable, Craig still made it to Atlanta in good time. When he pulled onto his old street, though, he noticed a black Mercedes in his drive. He could read the tag from where he was:

T-RUE 52

Terrell Rue. So they were together after all. Craig began to back up, but he couldn't escape Brianna and Terrell coming out of the house hand-in-hand. If seeing his wife on the arm of the former Hall of Famer wasn't enough, what he saw as they ascended the steps stopped Craig cold. He put his foot on the brake and leaned forward to be sure.

She's pregnant. Not very far along, but definitely pregnant.

He could tell from the sway of Brianna's back as she climbed the steps, the subtle fullness of her face. She'd looked this way only once before, when they were both too young to handle it. Craig had let other people influence him then. They'd convinced him to go off to college without her. She lost the baby alone. It had haunted him every day until he saw her that night in Dallas when he'd stolen her from Terrell. Now it seemed that the guy had pulled an interception of his own.

"I was surprised to hear from you, but now I'm glad. I really had a wonderful evening." Brianna pulled her hand back from Terrell's gentle touch. She didn't sense any desire in it, but she wanted to keep things clear just the same. She and Craig might be divorced, but she wasn't about to become one of those groupie wives going from one player to another. At one time, that was all she could see for herself, but now she knew that God had other plans for her—with or without Craig.

"I was surprised to hear from you, too. I got a text from your phone saying you needed to speak to me, but the words were misspelled so I had my doubts. And yet, here you are. It seems someone wanted us to meet up."

Brianna tried to contain herself as it all came together: the pictures that were sent to Craig, the text that was sent to her, and now the message to Terrell. All Asia. She was the worst speller Brianna knew. Could her friend be so desperate as to try to force Brianna and Terrell together in hopes of getting with Craig? Craig could barely stand to be in the same room with her.

"I think it might have been Asia."

Terrell crossed his legs and took a sip of the water with lime Brianna had offered him. "That fits. Now you see why I never wanted her in my house. I don't know why you persist in holding on to her."

Because she held on to me. She was there when nobody else was, when everyone pushed me away.

"Old habits die hard," Brianna said as her stomach did a flip-flop.

"Yes," Terrell agreed. "So true. Did you enjoy church Sunday? I saw you there with Clare and her crew. Did they mention me? I think they knew that we used to date."

Brianna ate a grape and prayed it would stay down. "Don't overestimate yourself, Terrell. I doubt they care much about our past together. Your name didn't come up at all."

He nodded. "They're sweet. That group. Especially that Clare. Some things have come out of late, and I'm afraid your name might have gotten stirred in the soup, as it were."

Brianna was more than confused. "I'm afraid I don't understand."

Terrell smiled, showing all his gold teeth. "You wouldn't. You never did. Let me spell it out for you, baby. The reason I treated you so bad while I was with you is because you were a cover . . . for my homosexuality."

Brianna tried to swallow but couldn't. Terrell had to pat her on the back so that she wouldn't choke on the grape.

Once she caught her breath, Brianna gripped the table. "It was Mark, wasn't it. That guy who was always with you?"

Terrell nodded. "Maybe the princess isn't totally blind after all. God has brought me to a place of total deliverance but it's important for me to be open and honest about who I was and where I've been. I've found that secrecy only places me at risk. It's a hard thing for people to hear, that their hero wasn't exactly who they thought he was, but hey, the truth is the truth. Clare was one of the first people I came out to. I told her about us."

It all made sense now. "I can still hardly believe it, T. You're so . . . fine. Even now. There never was anything sweet about you."

"It's complicated, and don't look at me like that. Whatever we had between us wasn't all a cover. Believe that. Now, tell me your secret. You've got one. I can see it all over you."

"You've got to tell him."

This time it wasn't Terrell or her new girlfriends insisting, but Brianna's new pastor, Dr. Lewiston.

"The rumor mills are already buzzing about you and Terrell, and soon enough they'll figure out that you're pregnant. Don't put the man through that, dear. No matter what happens between the two of you, being a parent means putting yourself second. Put your child first. Tell the truth."

The man spoke the truth. After spending some time staying at Terrell's place to get her head together and focus on God's Word, Brianna knew for sure that many of her marital problems with Craig sprang from what happened to them in high school. Craig going off to college on a football scholarship and leaving her behind carrying his child while the church and community denounced her as having trapped him left

Brianna insecure and determined never to need anyone like that again.

Finally, Brianna forgave herself . . . and Craig. She saw them both for what they were—kids trying to make it. During a Sunday service at her new church, Brianna left her past at the altar once and for all. She stood up feeling different. Free. This time, she may be pregnant, but she would never be alone. God was with her.

Back in Tampa, Craig struggled to hold on to God. His pastor explained that Craig had the wrong problem.

"You don't have to worry so much about holding on to the Lord. He's holding on to you. The thing is, your hands are full of these burdens. Lay your worries down and you'll be able to hold on all you like. You did it before. Just let go of all of it. Even your ex-wife."

That was easier said than done, especially now that he knew Terrell Rue had his hands on her. Craig wanted to confide in Dante about this latest development with Terrell, but some things were too intimate to discuss. When it was all said and done, Terrell didn't matter. Brianna being pregnant didn't matter. What mattered was God and what He wanted Craig to do about all of it.

To make things worse, someone had overheard Aunt Theresa talking on the phone about Craig's possible million-dollar contract. Everyone in the neighborhood was excited at the prospect of Craig helping out as he'd once done. Now they'd be able to finish the church on time, someone said.

Like there's not enough pressure to deal with.

When Craig realized what people expected of him, he trained even harder. Maybe he'd never have the family he dreamed of with Brianna, but at least he could provide for the family of God. It seemed like the right thing to do, so why didn't Craig have any peace about it? Craig shrugged and kept working hard. Going back to the league might not have been the best thing, but it was all Craig knew.

"They're shaping up nicely," Craig said as he watched his high school alma mater's team go through preseason practice. Dante had done a great job with the kids at the school, and Craig had to admit, he enjoyed the work, too.

"Man, I don't know why you don't just commit to coaching. At least for a year. The kids love you. You love them. It would definitely help ticket sales and boosters. Are you still chasing this Arman Gunter thing? You know that guy has driven a lot of cats to the grave trying to juice a few more dollars out of them. I know your knee is feeling good, man, but think about what league play is really like. Nothing you've done here in rehab compares."

Craig turned over the lottery ticket in his pocket. He'd bought it for Tenisha's mother, but it had become sort of a joke, a metaphor for his life right now. On one side was smudged lipstick and on the other the chance—but not a guarantee—of winning millions.

"I don't know, man. I'm praying and getting ready for whatever. That's all I can say. And while I'm here, I'm going to give you and these kids everything I've got. I hope that's enough right now, because it's all I've got."

Dante held out a fist, and Craig pounded it with his own.

"It's enough, man. It's enough. What do you make of that one there?" Dante said, pointing to the fastest boy on the team. He was cocky and sullen with all of the physical skills he would need in the pros, but few of the social ones. He reminded Craig of himself.

"He's good, but he's got a bad attitude. I see that you gave him my number."

Dante laughed. "I thought you'd get a kick out of it. I did. That boy makes me crazy, but he can run like the wind. He likes you, you know. He's always watching you."

"I know, but when I try to talk to him he blows me off. What's his real story, D? What's he so mad about?"

Dante put a hand up to shield his eyes. "Bring the ball to your chest! Protect it! Run that again." He took a deep sigh and turned back to Craig. "He's got your number, man. Figure it out."

It didn't take long for Craig to do just that. "Where is she?"

Dante pointed behind them without turning around. "Back there under that willow or on the bottom row of the bleachers."

Craig turned. She was taller than Brianna but had that same look that dared anybody to come between her and what was hers. She sat on the bleachers with a book propped on her belly, looking straight back at Craig. Straight through him.

"When's she due?"

"Soon," Dante said. "He's not claiming it, though. He's not saying anything. Lots of scouts hanging around him.

"Don't tell me. Your advice?"

Dante shook his head. "Nope. I learned better than to advise from dealing with you. I think he's coming up with this stuff on his own."

"Call him over. I want to talk to him."

Dante blew the whistle. "That's it. Let's break up into special teams. TreShard, go and take a run with Coach Richards and join us in a few."

The boy stopped and stared at Craig for a moment before jogging over to join him. Like most kids these days, he wasn't dumb. He knew what was coming. And by the look on his face, he was prepared to fend off anything Craig had to say.

Craig swallowed hard and flipped the lottery ticket in his pocket one last time before starting to jog beside the boy. A year of football could bring Craig a million dollars, but how much was it worth to make the difference in one boy's life? To make a difference for one family?

They went an entire mile in silence before Craig started the conversation they'd both known was coming.

"So what are you going to name your baby?"

"I ain't got no baby," the boy said, keeping stride with Craig and barely breaking a sweat.

"That's not what I heard, son."

"Look, I'm not your son and it isn't your business, okay? If you must know, I tried to be nice to that girl. When she first told me, I was even happy. Then she started getting all moody and crazy, telling me I can't leave without marrying her and taking her with me. I'm too young for all that. I figure I'll do what you did and just bounce."

Craig forced himself to keep running. "What?"

"Did you think I didn't know? Man, we all know. Your girl got pregnant, too, and you left her so you could get ahead. And it worked, right? You ended up married to her anyway. So I figure I'll do that, too. Maybe my girl will lose her baby, too, and we won't have to worry about it."

Before Craig realized it, he had the boy's shirt gathered in his hand and the kid was two feet in the air.

"Boy, don't you ever say anything like that again, do you hear me?"

"Yes, sir."

"I made a mistake, one I'll always have to live with. You have a chance to have a different life. Now, you weren't saying all this when you were laying down with the girl. It was all good then, wasn't it?" Craig said as he lowered TreShard back to the ground.

"*Hmph.* Better than good. I love that girl, man. She knows it."

"Show her. Do what you have to do. I might not be your daddy, but you're going to think I am if you don't straighten up and act a little better about your business. This isn't the end of the world. It can work. Nobody told me that then. There were plenty of guys in your situation who went on to be great. And they didn't have to stand before some kid on a track ashamed because they didn't do what they should have."

TreShard looked over to the bleachers where his girlfriend sat studying and then back at Craig. "Man, whatever. By the time that baby comes, you won't even be here. You might have the rest of them fooled, but not me. You're all about the dollars. Always have been. And I ain't mad at you for it. Just don't block my way. I'm trying to get in there and take your spot."

A sudden rain ended practice for everyone but Craig. Though his knee was screaming in pain, the young boy's words were a fresher hurt, cutting all the way to the bone. He'd never thought about all those little boys watching him run down the field, boys who wanted to be like him in every way. Boys who thought that walking away meant being a man.

Boys God had sent Craig home for.

Chapter 8

Finding Brianna's father wasn't hard. He was cleaning the church bathrooms, faithful as always.

"Hey, Craig, good to see you," Mr. Davis said, without missing a stroke on the wall he was scrubbing. "I haven't heard much from Brianna if that's what you want to know. I told her that she should work things out with you, but you know how it goes. Girls now don't always listen to their fathers."

Craig paused to let his words sink in. And like the words of young TreShard, Mr. Davis's comments met their mark, a place deep in Craig's heart that he'd kept locked for years. A place of shame and regret.

"That's true. I remember you telling Brianna not to mess around with me. You said that I would hurt her . . . and you were right. Though I married Brianna, I never really got your blessing. I never truly apologized for everything that I put your family through. Can you forgive me, sir?"

The man stopped cleaning and wiped his forehead with the back of his hand.

"That's all I ever wanted, for you to be man enough to acknowledge that you got Brianna pregnant. These folks around here treated her bad over it. It was hard on me. In some ways, it's still hard. She was the oldest and, well, the rest of those girls after her didn't think too much of what I had to say, either. I forgive you, Craig. God does, too. Be free, son, whether you and Brianna get back together or not."

Craig grabbed a bucket and a rag and rolled up his sleeves. "Thank you, sir, but I don't think I'll truly be free until Brianna forgives me, too, and right now she's not talking to me. So just pray."

"I will," Mr. Davis said, moving over to make room for Craig on the wall. "I pray for the two of you every day. I have since the day she brought you home."

Craig closed his eyes for a second, then opened them again. "Thank you, sir. Don't ever stop. Those prayers have done more good than you'll ever know."

"Call us when you get there," Terrell said after putting Brianna's last bag into her car.

"Are you sure you don't want one of us to come along and help you drive," Clare said. "It's quite a ways to Tampa."

Brianna couldn't help but smile. "You're all like mother hens. Back up. I'm pregnant, not dying. If I'm tired, I'll get a hotel and I will call when I get there. I know it probably isn't the best timing, but I don't think this is something I should tell Craig over the phone. Not to mention that I need to pay Asia a little visit."

Terrell laughed. "All right, now. No Holy Ghost beatdowns, okay? You might want to stay away from that one. You know she's a little crazy."

"Aren't we all?"

The laughter quieted down.

"Pretty much," someone said. "Anyway, just be careful. We'll be praying."

They must have been true to their word because Brianna made it to Tampa in great time, even with all her bathroom stops. She tried Craig once, but he didn't answer his phone.

Good enough.

She had a stop to make anyway. . . .

Asia flung open the door with a squeal. "Bri-aaaana! Girl, I didn't know you were coming. I would have—"

"You would have what, sent a picture of my belly to the *National Enquirer*?"

Asia narrowed her eyes at Brianna. "I hadn't planned on that, but now that you mention it, we could make a little cash that way. Lift up your shirt—"

"Girl, stop playing. I'm on my way to see Craig, but I came here first because I need to talk to you."

"You're doing that already. Get to the point." Asia's tone was rising. A few more minutes like this and she'd be cussing like a sailor.

"The point is—did you send photos of me and Terrell to Craig and send a text from my phone to Terrell?"

Asia turned away. "Oh, man. I told him this wasn't going to work. Look, I didn't do all those things, but I did some of them and I did them for your own good."

Right.

"So you trying to get my husband—"

"Ex-husband!"

"Whatever. You trying to get with Craig was supposed to help me?"

Asia started laughing. Uncontrollably. "Is that what you think this was about? Me trying to get with Craig? Don't get me wrong, Craig is fine as all get out, but he can't stand me, and after all that has gone down, I'm not too fond of him—except to look at. It wasn't about that at all. It was about getting Craig to play. It was all Mr. Gunter's idea."

"Who?"

"The scout that wants Craig? He's a . . . friend from a few years back. He asked me to help him, and I didn't see any harm in it, especially since you two fight so much anyway. Craig Richards hasn't changed since he left you on that train track in eleventh grade. I don't care what you say."

Forgive as you have been forgiven.

"Asia, you don't have to hate Craig for me anymore. He has changed. We all have. In fact, I need to tell you that since we've seen each other last, I gave my life to Jesus."

"Again?" Asia stuck out her lip. "I hope it sticks this time."

Me too.

"Wait, did you tell Mr. Gunter about the baby?"

"No, I figured I'd leave that train wreck to you," Asia said, wiping lipstick from the corners of her mouth. "If you're done letting me have it, maybe you can catch Craig before he pulls up out of here."

"What do you mean?" Brianna loved Asia, but this whole thing was wearing her out. She just wanted to find Craig, tell him about the baby, and take a good, long nap.

"The tryout. Arman told me that the scouts moved things up. Craig is trying out today. Up at the school. . . ."

Brianna started running and didn't look back. She had to catch Craig before he did something they'd all regret. She knew exactly who "Mr. Gunter" was now. Arman the Bone Collector, the agent that brought men out of retirement and ran years off their lives. Craig was better than that. And worse yet, she knew that if he did it, it would be for her. It was time for both of them to stop making each other pay for the past.

Christ paid it all.

"Run it again."

Though his knee seemed like something had come unglued inside, Craig walked back to the start line for the forty-yard dash. He looked out over the stands, filled as though there was a game being played instead of a old pro trying to come out of retirement. As he did a quick stretch to prepare for his next run, he saw someone in the crowd, waving a pink handkerchief.

Brianna.

Years ago, that had been their signal. It meant, "I love you," and it was all Craig needed. He looked closer, and she was smiling. That was just icing on the cake. When the whistle blew, he ran like a madman.

Though Craig doubted that his ex-wife's hankie wave meant anything more than that she didn't hate him, it was enough fuel to help him run near his personal best.

"Nice!" Gunter screamed as he gathered the scouts around him.

The crowd seemed to hold a collective breath, but Craig had been in sports long enough to know that at least one of those scouts would have been impressed by his workout so far. That wasn't what concerned him at the moment.

TreShard stood near Brianna wearing his jersey with Craig's old number. The boy's girlfriend was sitting next to him, but she wasn't smiling. He couldn't be sure from here, but it looked like she'd been crying. . . .

One of the scouts gave Gunter a nod, and the agent approached Craig with a big smile.

"You did it, man. I knew you could. One mil for next season. I'll go and draw up the papers." He turned to the crowd and raised a fist in victory. Almost everybody went wild. TreShard climbed over the seat in front of him and started walking away. He stopped to look at Craig and shook his head.

Craig shook his head, too, at Gunter.

"No. I'm sorry to have wasted your time. I need the money, but there's something here that I need more."

Gunter scrambled to make peace with the agents while staring daggers at Craig. "I knew you would do this. Say goodbye to your wife, to the life that you had. Tell this crowd why you've turned your back on them!"

True enough, people booed Craig. Many of them just left the field, confused about what exactly had happened. TreShard came up and shook Craig's hand.

"Maybe I was wrong about you."

Craig gave the boy a nod and reached out to shake the

hand of the boy's pregnant girlfriend. They were standing together, holding hands.

"Maybe we were wrong about each other," Craig said as he told the boy good-bye. "See you Monday. After I get some rest, I'm going to run you all over this track."

The boy smiled. "After today, you won't be running anywhere for a good long minute, but when you're ready I'll be waiting."

As Craig laughed and said good-bye, he heard a beautiful and familiar sound behind him. Brianna's laughter.

"The boy didn't lie. That was one serious run. You're going to need some Ben-Gay for that, baby."

Craig hugged her close. "Bri . . . I've been trying to get in touch with you. I need to tell you something."

She smiled. "Me too. You go first."

He nodded, waving good-bye to his aunt, who blew him a kiss on the way to the car. She didn't look surprised or confused, but then she'd seemed to know how it would happen anyway.

"I'm sorry, Bri. About the baby. About leaving you. I didn't know what to do. I did love you, though, and I love you now. No matter what happens between us, though, I just need to know that you forgive me."

She looked up at Craig with a smile so big it made him shiver. "You are forgiven. We both are. That's part of what I want to tell you."

He hugged her again, and this time he didn't let go so easily. "You went back to church? To Jesus?"

She nodded. "I did. And God has been healing me so that I could come here today and ask you to forgive me, too. There's been so much hurt, so many things broken and I'm sorry. So, so sorry."

"Shhh . . ." Craig pressed a finger to her lips. When she had no more words, only tears, he put his hand on her stomach. It was too early to feel anything, but he knew that a baby was in there. He did know what he should have done all those years ago, when she came to him just like this and he'd turned away. Only this time, the baby wasn't his.

"Lord, bless this child. May he or she grow up to love You and walk in Your ways for all the days of his or her life. Bless Brianna with a healthy pregnancy and a quick recovery."

She wiped her eyes. "You knew? Who told you? Asia?"

Craig shook his head. "Nobody told me. I could see it. Congratulations. To you and Terrell, I mean. And don't worry, you're not showing yet. Not really. I can just tell. I I remember—"

Brianna kissed him quietly. "You should remember . . . Daddy. That was quite some shower if I recall."

Chapter 9

Shocked but thrilled, Craig closed his eyes as an ache traveled the length of his leg and settled into his knee. The wrestling was finally over. The struggle had hurt, but the blessing had finally been bestowed. A new beginning. He and Brianna were back at the beginning.

A baby.

"I guess I should have taken that money, huh?" Craig said as reality dawned on him: diapers, toys, books . . . college.

Brianna shook her head. "Nope. Somebody told me once that God does a pretty good job at taking care of his children."

Hearing Brianna talk about God like that was almost more than Craig could bear. It was just too good. "I still can't believe it. You, a Christian?"

Brianna nodded. "Believe it. Baptized and blood-bought."

Craig took Brianna's hand and walked off the empty field. Something dropped out of his pocket. The lottery ticket.

Brianna raised an eyebrow. "What's that about?"

Craig laughed as he picked up the ticket and put it back in his pocket. "It's a long story. I'll tell you on the way home. I bought it for Mrs. Wright—"

"Tenisha's mom?"

"Right."

"Don't even try to explain, then. That says it all."

There's something else Craig wanted to say, though. Something he had to say.

"Will you marry me?" he whispered into Brianna's ear.

Before Brianna could answer, her phone rang. She held it up so Craig could see.

"It's . . . Dante? I didn't even know he had my number."

"Tenisha," they both said together.

Craig rolled his eyes. That boy never did have any sense of timing. "I can't talk to him until you answer me, girl. For real, now."

Brianna laughed and gave Craig a kiss on the cheek. "I'd love to be your wife, now answer the phone."

"Hello?" Craig said, wanting nothing more than to toss the phone across the parking lot. "Man, what is it? I'm kinda busy—"

"Do you still have the ticket? The one you bought for Brenda?" Dante was screaming into the phone. He'd been at the field earlier but made no mention of what had happened or Craig's decision. "Where is it, man? This is urgent."

Craig fumbled in his pocket. "The lottery ticket? I've got it right here. Why?"

Someone was arguing in the background. "He probably threw it away."

"He didn't!" Dante screamed. "He's got it right there in his hand. Don't play my boy like that. He's not crazy."

"D, what's going on, man? Did we hit the lottery or something?"

"Exactly that, my brother. Exactly that. And since I told you to buy it, we only have to split it two ways."

Craig just started laughing. He didn't care how they split it. He just wanted to know one thing: "How much? And how do you know I won? Did you memorize the numbers?"

Dante smirked. "I didn't have to. Your wedding date, your birthday, your old football number, the combination to our rookie locker. You know I don't forget numbers. When I heard the number a few minutes ago and they said that no one had claimed it, I was like, that's my boy's ticket!"

The last date, the day that Brianna had lost their first child, Dante would have known, too, but he didn't mention it now. Craig leaned down and kissed Brianna's hair, surprised that she wasn't asking him a million questions. She looked as if she was almost asleep on her feet, so he perched the phone on his neck, picked her up, and carried her back to his car.

"All right, man. Tell me where I have to go. Brianna is almost sleep in my arms. I've got to get her something to eat, too. She's pregnant."

"Is it yours? I'm just saying . . ."

"Yes, fool. Now tell me where I need to go and tell me how much we won."

"Well, Miss Brenda is over here talking about what she won since she says the ticket is for her, but you know I'm not paying that any mind, right?"

"Dante!"

"Okay, right. The jackpot is thirty-two million. I believe that should hold a few things in place for a while. And you didn't even have to blow out your knee again for it."

Craig let his phone hit the ground. He stopped where he was and lowered himself and his woman to the ground. Brianna slept right through it.

"Lord, when you blessed me before, I didn't know how to handle it. But now I know that whatever You give me isn't just for me. It wasn't the way I thought it would come, but somehow You always come through. Thank you for a second chance."

Epilogue

One year later

"Welcome to the dedication of the Theresa Richards Family Life Center."

Craig held his infant daughter Melody up to his shoulder to be sure that she could hear. Brianna reached over and hugged both of them.

"I wish Aunt Tee could have been here today to see this," Craig whispered. His aunt had fallen ill not long after he and Brianna remarried, but she'd had a peaceful passing. Many times, like right now, Craig could almost feel his aunt's presence.

Pastor Green cut the ribbon on the building after a dedication prayer and called Craig and Brianna up to the front. "These folks won the lottery through an interesting set of circumstances. They thought that Soul Harvest wouldn't take the money since it came from gambling, but y'all know me better than that, don't you? We cleaned that money right on up, and with their gifts, we have completed the church building, this facility for families and young people, and helped twenty-six people get their GED, and double that for finding a job. So those of you who are still sitting around wondering what you should do, just do like Brother Richards and pray while you're running. God will show you the way to go."

While people made a line to shake Craig and Brianna's hands, Craig's mind was somewhere else. He had a bit of limp now and a few new gray hairs, but he wouldn't have traded his life for anything. For the first time in his life, Craig Richards was truly blessed beyond measure.

A Knight in Pink Armor

TIA MCCOLLORS

Chapter 1

"Go ahead and buy a lottery ticket."

"No. I'm not doing it." Dara Knight sat an orange soda, a bag of white cheese popcorn, and a tropical-flavored pack of Skittles on the counter. She had no intention of spending a single dime of her hard-earned money on a lottery ticket.

Besides, she wasn't one to play the lottery anyway. Dara considered it a waste of money even though the people who played on a regular basis could squeeze an ounce of justification out of every ticket they bought. Winning ten dollars from a scratch-off that they'd spent one dollar on was a respectable rate of return. But Dara didn't see why they always failed to calculate the money they'd blown over the last five years without cashing in a single penny.

"You act like God is gonna strike you down in this convenience store," India Lanier said. "We're practically in Booneville, Georgia. He probably forgot this place even exists."

Dara's cousin, India, turned the plastic display holding the brightly colored scratch-offs, all of them promising a one in a billion chance at wealth. "Let me get one of each of the ones on this side," India said, then slid a ten dollar bill under the opening of the bulletproof window. "And don't forget to add these." She held up a bottle of cranberry juice and pack of cashews.

Dara tried to block India from tearing tickets from the roll.

India reached over her. "We're in the middle of the boonies," she said, still trying to convince Dara. "This is the kind of town where winners hit it big. When's the last time you heard of a lottery winner that bought their ticket in a big city? As soon as we get to Atlanta, our chances are going to plummet."

"They're going to plummet anyway," Dara said, counting out correct change for her purchase. "Because I'm *not* going to buy a lottery ticket." Even if India does have a valid point. Stores like this transformed winners from being everyday people with respectable three-bedroom homes to millionaires with fourteen-bedroom mansions. But that didn't change Dara's mind. Her parents had taught her better.

India didn't seem to care what Dara said or thought. She was pulling out every excuse to debate her point.

Dara dropped her goodies in her purse. "While you try to convince everybody else in this store to follow your lead, I'm going to the restroom. I don't plan to make a stop on this highway again until we reach the city limits. I'll meet you in the car," she said.

"I know I'm not the only one who could use sixteen million dollars," Dara heard India tell someone.

Dara didn't waste any time getting in and out of the public restroom. Thankfully, India had already moved the car from the gas station pump to the first parking space in front of the store. Dara jumped in the passenger seat and immediately reached for her sweater because her cousin consistently blasted two things whenever she drove—the radio and the air conditioning.

"I've two gifts for you," India said, strapping on her seat belt. "One is that *I'm* taking the wheel and driving us home from here."

"Well it's about time," Dara said. "I *have* been driving the last six hours. Taking the last two or so is the least you can do."

"If I were you, I wouldn't have such a sassy mouth to somebody who might have made you a millionaire." She reached into the area of the console where they'd stacked a bunch of CDs and pulled out a lottery ticket, tossing it on Dara's lap.

"No, you didn't," Dara said. "And on a *Sunday*."

"Yes, I did," India said, shifting their rented SUV into reverse. "It's for the big one. The jackpot is sixteen million, so you can thank me by giving me half if you win. And just so you know, five of the numbers I picked had something to do with your life."

"What?" Dara said. She turned the ticket over and looked at the row of six numbers.

"The first two are your birth month and day, the next two come from the chapter and verse of your favorite scripture, and the last one is your age. Oh yeah, and I let the machine randomly pick your power ball number."

"You're one of the most hardheaded people I know," Dara said. "No wonder Aunt Latrice was always having to hem you up."

"My sweet little cuz," India said. "You can see with your own eyes that the housing market is slow as molasses, even for my clients who are sitting on plenty of bank. I'm just trying to open myself to other possibilities. Besides, you could buy as many Harleys as you want to if we win this money, and then you won't have to ride around on that pink scooter of yours."

"My motorcycle is *far* from a scooter, I'll have you know. It's a machine. You're just jealous because you don't have the guts to ride one."

"Call me what you want to," India said. "I just hope after Tuesday you'll be able to call me rich."

Dara stuffed the ticket in the bottom of her jean tote bag and threw it in the backseat along with her laptop bag. Surprisingly, she wasn't tempted to boot up her laptop. She didn't consider her vacation to be officially over until she walked inside her home.

When she first arrived in Destin, Florida, Dara would've been content soaking up as much air conditioning as possible and working from the hotel's balcony, but India wasn't having it. India had locked Dara's laptop in the room's safe and refused to give her the code until it was time for them to retire from the day's festivities. After their third day on vacation, Dara realized that she didn't miss having to stay on top of her client's schedules. But it would be back to business tomorrow.

"You know our next road trip will have to be to Augusta, right?" India said.

Dara groaned. "Don't remind me. I still don't see why Mama and Daddy act like they can't take a two-hour ride down the highway and come see me."

"You know what your daddy always says." India laughed. "People don't take a day off from dying so he can't take a day off from working."

"Believe me. The staff is trained well," Dara said. "It's not like his clients can give him any trouble."

"Oh. You have such a morbid sense of humor," India said, using her teeth to rip open her pack of cashews. "You've become so desensitized to death."

"Not true," Dara said. "But I know life is too short not to live."

"Well spoken from a chick who lives such a boring life. But I think I may have finally broken you out of your shell this week."

"My life isn't boring. I live a fulfilled life, if you ask me."

"Considering what it could've been," India said, laughing, "I guess you're right."

Dara agreed. Her predetermined destiny—according to her parents—was still a sore spot between her and them. While she was being groomed to carry on her family's mortuary business, Dara always had different dreams. She wanted to service the needs of the living and pursued a bachelor's degree in Restaurant, Hotel and Institution Management.

Dara's parents had never been pleased with her decision. "Let her get it out of her system," her mother, Thelma, had told her father, Hunter.

But she never did, and never would, get it out of her system. It was in her heart to help others, and to do it by playing by her own rules. When the entrepreneurial bug bit her, she used her training to start a personal concierge business, On Point Concierge. Dara had always earned a respectable living, but once India connected her to some of her wealthy real-estate clients her business catapulted to another level. Dara didn't want for much of anything, unless she counted a husband to share her life with one of these days.

That was, if Dara made it back home alive. India was driving as if she had biceps and brawn waiting for her at home. Which she didn't, either.

"India, I'd like to stay in the land of the living, if you don't mind," Dara said, and watched the odometer drop down five miles per hour.

India merged into the slower right lane. "Speaking of dead things, did that Bobby guy ever call you back?"

"Girl, that one date I suffered through was one too many. If you think *I'm* boring, you don't know the half of it. I can't perceive for the life of me why Isaac thought we'd have so much in common."

"No, what I can't believe is that he actually calls himself Brother Bobby. Who walks around saying that? If I hadn't had heard it with my own ears, Sister Dara, I would've thought you were exaggerating."

"I wish." Dara held her hands up as if they were an unbalanced scale. "I mean, if I date a man whose older than me, he tries to be my daddy, and if I go out with someone younger, it's like I have to be his mama. I don't have time to try to train a boy to be a man."

"Well, I refuse to give up hope on the perfect man for me," India said. "I'll wait for my knight in shining armor until I'm eighty years old if I have to because the word *settle* isn't in my vocabulary."

"If you're eighty, I guarantee you you'll have to settle for some old rusty, nasty armor." Dara gripped the side of the door as India jammed her foot on the gas pedal so she could pass an eighteen-wheeler. *Lord, help me get home.* India's erratic driving was one of the reasons Dara volunteered to drive during most of their road trips. If Dara had it her way, they would've flown to Destin, but India hated to fly.

Dara leaned her head back against the headrest and tried to relax. Maybe their driving time would pass quicker if she tried to catch some sleep.

She'd had her eyes closed for only for a moment when she felt a jolt to the side of the car. The car swerved to the shoulder of the road and Dara screamed out, "Jesus," the first word that came to her mind when she pictured the car plunging down the side of the grassy ravine.

Chapter 2

The driver of the semi either didn't notice or didn't care that he'd forced Dara and India onto the shoulder of the highway.

"My God," India screamed, gripping the wheel and easing the SUV to a stop. "Idiot," she said, resting her forehead on the steering wheel.

Dara rubbed her back. She could feel a tremor shaking India's body. "It's good, Indy. We're safe," she said, assuring her cousin. Dara made mental plans to reclaim the driver's seat. After a scare like that, India would gladly hand over the wheel.

"I can't believe that jerk ran us off the road and didn't even bother to stop," India stammered. She massaged her temples.

"Let it go," Dara said. "God protected us, and that's all that matters."

"What matters would've been me getting his tag and a phone number so I can turn his behind in."

Dara looked through the rear windshield and noticed a Mustang pulling up behind them. A man from the passenger's side of the sports car came to Dara's window. Even though it was broad daylight, Dara cautiously let the window down only enough to hear him.

"I saw that truck run you guys off the road," he said, poking a piece of paper through the slit Dara had opened. "Here's the tag number and the phone number that was on the truck. We wrote it down, then turned around at the next exit to make sure you were all right."

"See," Dara said, taking the paper and handing it to India.

The driver had joined his friend, who looked to be more concerned with scoping out Dara and India's beauty than ensuring their safety. He peered through Dara's window.

"You can roll the window down. We're here to help you, not hurt you. I'm Zebulon and this is Tyler."

"We're fine," Dara said, letting the window down an inch more. She kept her finger on the button in case Zebulon was up to some risky business. If he tried to stick his hand inside and pull off anything suspicious, she was prepared to trap his arm and pull him down the highway, all the way to Atlanta if she had to.

"Do you want to switch places?" Dara asked India. "I know you want me to drive."

"Yes," India said without a second thought about the intent of their highway heroes.

Zebulon opened Dara's door while Tyler eagerly jogged over to India's side. Of course, Tyler didn't know it, but Dara knew now wasn't the time to try to spread his charm over her cousin. Dara decided to let the man dig his own hole and try to climb out of it.

"Is the car okay?" Zebulon asked. He walked to the front of the car and around to the driver's side to survey for any damage.

Dara had a chance to get a good look at him, although up close she'd already seen his dimpled chin and the small mole beside his left eye.

"I didn't hear any odd noises when we pulled over, so prayerfully all is well," Dara said. "It's a rental anyway, so we're covered if something comes up later."

Dara was anxious to get back in the car and get home. She opened the back door to retrieve her shades from her bag.

"Where are you guys headed?" Zebulon asked.

"Atlanta."

"Us, too," Zebulon said.

"You can't tell me this isn't fate," Tyler said to India. He'd turned the brim of his baseball cap to the back, revealing a set of puppy dog eyes. He flashed a smile with a tiny gap between his two front teeth. He pulled his cell phone out of his pocket. "Why don't you go ahead and hit me with those digits?"

"You saw me almost get killed and you're trying to get my phone number?" India asked, with both disbelief and wit on her face. She specialized in giving men a hard time.

"Nothing like the present," Tyler said, shrugging. "What difference does it make? I just want to call you later and make sure you're all right."

"I'm fine. Nothing broken. Everything is in the right place."

"I can see that with my own eyes. If it ain't broke, don't fix it."

Dara laughed, and they all couldn't help but do the same. "You opened the door to that one," she said to India. "And he walked right in."

India crossed her arms and looked at Tyler as if she might be having second thoughts at his advances. "You're a cutie, but you're still leaving empty handed. Not to mention, we're out here in the way of danger."

"She's right about that," Dara said.

"Well, what about me?" Zebulon asked. "It would make my day if I had a way to get back in touch with you."

Dara reached into the front pocket of her laptop bag and pulled out her business card. "I'm a stickler for environmental issues," she said. "Don't let this be a waste of paper."

"You don't have to worry about that," Zebulon said.

Zebulon and Tyler waited for India and Dara to get back in their car and merge safely back into the flow of the traffic.

India adjusted the passenger seat as far back as it would go. "I can't believe you were trying to make a love connection on the side of I-85," she said, flipping through the stack of their CDs.

"You should take notes, Ms. I'ma-wait-until-I'm-eighty-years-old. Tyler could've been your knight."

India scrunched her nose. "Uh, the breath on that brother melted any armor that he had."

Dara shook her head. She wasn't going to get India started on her list of must-haves. Tolerable breath was understandable. But some of the things India insisted on, like a hairless chest and a second toe that was shorter than the big toe, were negotiable in Dara's book.

Too bad if India decided to miss out. Zebulon's breath was fine, and so was he. Dara hoped he took the time to call.

Chapter 3

It was back to business as usual on Monday morning. In hindsight, it would've been wise for Dara to tell her clients that she wouldn't be returning until midweek, giving her two extra days to get her bearings and click back into work mode.

India was right. She'd broken Dara out of her shell over the retreat week in Destin. It had been a welcome change to move spontaneously through the day instead of having her schedule, and everybody else's, dictating her moves when the tasks and reminders popped up in her BlackBerry messages like clockwork.

And like clockwork, Cassius Freeborn called her that morning at ten o'clock sharp. He acted as if he couldn't run his life effectively without Dara's help, but for some reason Cassius never forgot to call her for his weekly updates. Her duties for him doubled whenever it was football season, and despite his numerous pleas, she refused to come on as his full-time assistant.

What Cassius really needed was a stay-at-home wife. Right now, he was trying to pay Dara to be his spouse, minus the special marital benefits.

"Hello, Cassius," Dara said, using the speaker feature on her phone.

"I'm not feeling you taking these vacations, Dara, just so you know," he said, without even welcoming her back from her trip. "How am I supposed to function?"

"I already told you, I'm trying to get you married off so I can pick up some new clients. You take up way too much of my time."

"Shoot. Why do I need a wife if I have you? A wife is just another person to be pulling at my pockets. I've got enough jokers trying to do that already."

"When are you going to find a new excuse?" Dara asked, tapping the space bar on her laptop to awaken it from the sleep mode. She opened her online calendar program and scrolled through Cassius's schedule—including his appearances, charity work, and business-related appointments. Everything was already set to send him updates and e-mails directly to his phone. He lived, ate, and drank football. The rest was up to Dara.

Dara tolerated Cassius's extra cravings for attention because she knew he needed her to be more than his taskmaster. He always asked Dara to pray for him. He talked a lot about God giving him the wisdom to make tough decisions. And although Cassius externally joked in a lighthearted way about people asking him for money, he carried a heavy burden of being the financial provider for the majority of his family. For his mother, Cassius did it with a grateful heart. However, his siblings and the other family members who were along for the ride, had come to rely on *his* checks instead of them seeking employment to support themselves. After a season of repeated injuries two years prior, Cassius began to question not only his future football career but also his faith.

More money, more problems. Dara witnessed the old saying in the life of others, and unfortunately it was true.

"You've got an appearance at a youth football camp in South Carolina on Thursday afternoon and a fashion show benefit on Friday night. Other than that, you're clear," Dara said. "Oh, but you need to start thinking about your mama's birthday present."

"Mama can have anything she wants," Cassius said. "I'll call and ask her."

"Have you ever thought about being creative or watching her when you're together so you can see what she needs?"

"You've seen her house and her bank account. Ella Freeborn doesn't *need* anything," Cassius said. "I take that back. The only thing she *needs* is for her loud grandkids to get out of that house and stop bunking up in there like it's an extended stay motel. What my Mama *needs* is some peace and quiet."

Having just returned from a week full of it, Dara offered her suggestion. "Why don't you send her away on a trip? Or a cruise? Now, that would be nice."

"Perfect. I'll send her someplace tropical and let her take one of her friends. She'll love to brag about that."

Dara knew what was coming next. Thankfully, this was a task she could complete in one quick phone call. She already had connections with a preferred travel agent.

"You gonna handle that for me?" Cassius asked.

"I'll let you know where she's going and get the itinerary to you by the end of the week," Dara said.

"And you said I need a wife? Holla at me later this week," Cassius said, then hung up the phone.

Dara hated when he did that, but it wasn't up to her to change him. Like most men, she thought they had a few rough edges that only the grace and patience of a wife could smooth out. "Lord, bless her soul, whoever it'll be," she said, jotting down the travel agent's name on her task list.

Dara would call after her morning devotion and dream session, as she liked to call it. It wasn't like her to sleep past eight thirty or so in the morning, but her body was still on vacation. By the time she'd showered and slipped on a relaxing pair of wide leg linen pants and a vintage-looking spaghetti-strap top, Cassius had called.

Dara preferred that God be the first person she talked to in the morning. She found that when she did, the rest of the day was a lot less stressful. She walked out onto the balcony of her third-floor condo. The iron bistro patio set and potted plant enveloped most of the space, yet it was the perfect size for Dara to escape with her journal and her dreams.

Dara fell in love with the quaint and neighborly feel of downtown Decatur. It was the kind of city she'd read about in the novels of her childhood. Blossoming little girls could express their creativity by wearing a pair of angel wings strapped to their backs and red and black ladybug rain boots on a perfectly cloudless day if they so desired. Nobody would look at the girl twice, except to comment on how adorable she was. Then there were the things that made the town perfect for families—like the annual beach party on the square when the city dumped sixty tons of sand out for families to romp through.

It was a life that seemed worlds apart from the community where she regularly visited with the outreach team from church. Sometimes Dara's hearts ached for the people, and she wished her parents could see the passion she held not only for her concierge business but for the street evangelism that she enjoyed. Dara found pleasure in leading wayward souls to Christ. And even if they rejected Him at first, she knew love could melt even the most cold and stony heart. While her parents tended to the physically dead, Dara ministered to those who were spiritually dead.

Hunter and Thelma Knight thought that Dara could best serve her calling within the four walls of the church, or at least a ministry they considered to be safe. Her mother had admonished her to take part in serving at the homeless shelter instead. For years, Dara was expected to follow "the rules." And the rules didn't include riding a motorcycle.

As a teen, Dara was called the "P. K.," or preacher's kid. Now at thirty-five, the initials have taken on another meaning. Dara's love of riding motorcycles ran a close second to her first love for evangelism. To her pleasure, she'd been able to marry her two loves with a unique new ministry at her church—The Kingdom Knights. Thus her name, Pink Knight.

Dara had shirked her parents' conservative expectations. She'd once overheard her mother call her rebellious, but that didn't make Dara give up the speed of her custom-painted, pink Honda Crossover.

It wasn't easy being the daughter of a preacher who owned a funeral home. And as popular as she was, Dara was still the source of teasing and sometimes cruel taunting, like her mama used embalming fluid as perfume. On days when it felt like too much to bear, she'd pour out her thoughts on paper. Dara had been keeping diaries and journals for as long as she could remember. Flipping the pages of her treasured books could transport her back years. She could usually tell by her handwriting whether she was having a good or a bad day—either her i's were dotted with smiley faces or there was chicken scratch scribbled across the page. Like all children, she bumped heads with her parents, but they provided her and her brother with something the world couldn't take away—morals and memories.

The thought of her family made her want to call home. So when Dara finished her prayer and devotional time she called her mother at the funeral home.

Thelma Knight answered the phone in her signature grace-filled and peaceful voice. It was the kind of voice suited to calm storms, erase fears, and bring solace to families who were facing the daunting and draining task of preparing for the burial of a loved one.

"Hey, Ma," Dara said, wishing she was there to get one of her mother's squeezes.

"Dara? Is that you?"

"Yes, Ma. Who else do you think it is?"

"Nobody, honey. I was just playing with you. You know I know my own child's voice."

"I was about to say . . ."

"Say what? Say you're moving back home?"

Here we go again, Dara thought.

Chapter 4

Dara was barely ruffled by her mother's comments because she'd heard them so many times. She thought that after living in Atlanta for more than twelve years, her mother would get the point that she wasn't moving back to Augusta.

"What are you up to?" Dara said.

"Waiting for your father to come back from the church. We have a family viewing hour at two o'clock and your brother's handling the funeral for a young man that died in a car accident. Such a tragedy," she tsked.

Some would think Dara would be used to it by now, but death—more so the grieving families—always burdened her heart.

"But enough about that," Thelma said, probably sensing Dara's mood. "How was your vacation?"

"Sooooo nice, Ma. Me and India had a great time. You and Dad should take a few days and go down to Destin. He'd love staying at one of the golf resorts."

"I can barely get your father to leave Augusta," her mother said. "I told him I'm going to start traveling without him."

"You should," Dara said, remembering the time she'd convinced her mother to fly to New York for a few days so they could shop and go experience *The Color Purple* while it was on Broadway. It was her mother's first time in the Big Apple, and Dara could barely keep up with her.

Dara assumed her mother would tire of the constant walking and attempts to catch cabs, but she'd packed her walking shoes and gotten her full money's worth and then some out of them.

"Maybe he'll consider it if you tell him," Thelma said.

"You're his wife. You have more pull than I ever will," Dara said.

"I think if you tell him in person, he'll be more apt to think about it. Why don't you come up here this weekend?"

"I can't, Ma," Dara said, walking back inside from the balcony. "I have outreach on Saturday."

"Oh, Lord." Thelma sighed. "Are you still riding that bike out to that side of town?"

"Yes, Ma," Dara said. Yes, for the five hundred and eightieth time, she wanted to say.

"Aren't you scared somebody's going to try and hijack you for that thing? You know with the economy the way it is, people are acting real crazy. Crazier than they already were. Even doing stuff in the middle of the day.

"I saw on the news how these boys kicked in the door of this family's house in broad daylight. They didn't even care that the security cameras were around the house. I mean, they didn't try to cover their faces or anything."

Dara had seen the story on the news, too. But she couldn't live her life in fear. She prayed, tried to use caution and common sense, and went about doing what she needed to do.

"I'm always safe, Ma. And the other riders make sure we keep each other covered, especially in prayer."

"That's the other thing I don't like. You riding around the city with a bunch of grown men. That doesn't look right. And as much as I taught you about etiquette and carrying yourself like a lady, and you choose to ride with your legs sprawled out over a motorcycle seat. Those things were meant for men. Not women."

Dara chose to keep her comments to herself. She had her viewpoints, and no matter what she said it wasn't going to make Mrs. Hunter J. Knight take off her traditional blinders.

Dara heard her brother's voice in the background. James didn't know he'd swooped in yet again to save her.

"Give me a minute," her mother said to James. "'I'm talking to your sister."

Dara heard some more muffled words in the background, then the next voice she heard was her brother.

"What's up, Cookie?" James bellowed into the phone. Dara pulled her ear away from the phone.

"If you call me that again, I'm hanging up the phone," she threatened.

Dara's father had given her that nickname when she was a toddler. He said it was because she was the sweetest girl he knew. They used to tease that Dara was her mother's competition for her father's affection, doing things like bringing him his house shoes when he walked in the door. Dara carried the nickname Cookie in her family until she reached her thirtieth birthday. After that, she forbade everybody but her parents from calling her that.

"What do you want me to call you?" James asked.

"By my name, big head," Dara said.

"If my head is big, so is your mama's," he said.

"I know Mama didn't hear you say that."

"Of course not. I ran her out of here to go and make sure the limos were cleaned out."

"Where's my nephew and niece?" Dara asked.

"At camp until three. I had to get them out of here so they could burn up some of that energy. Especially since I found Kendrick using one of the caskets as a makeshift basketball hoop."

"Shut up," Dara laughed. She remembered those boring days at the funeral home. She and James had been just as inventive when their parents dragged them to work because they weren't old enough to stay home alone. She lived for the days when her Aunt Latrice would take days off from her job so she could bring Dara and James over to spend the day with India.

"I'm serious," James was saying. "Your niece and nephew are off the chain. And Amber? Talk about high maintenance."

"You started spoiling her from day one so it's most of your doing that she expects—and deserves—the best," Dara said, taking up for her diva-fied niece. "By the way, did she get the necklace I sent her for her birthday?"

"You're talking about that necklace that her and her mama had a falling out over this morning because she couldn't wear it to camp? Yeah, she got it. And a spanking to match it."

"Don't say that. I'll feel like it's all my fault. She really wanted a necklace like mine with her initial on it."

"She didn't want that necklace as much as she wants to see you for her birthday. We're having a party tomorrow."

"Who has a child's birthday party in the middle of the week? It's not normal."

"It is if you've got funerals to handle on Saturday. Plus, it's only her best friend from school and a couple of the girls from church."

Dara filled a glass with water and went over to soak her house plant that had sagged to the side in thirst. "Well, she won't miss me then," she said, moving the plant near the sunshine. "Her little buddies will be there."

"You can convince yourself to think that if you want to, but she keeps talking about her Auntie Dara coming for her birthday."

Dara reminded herself that she had to be more careful with her words. She'd told her five-going-on-twenty-five-year-old niece that she'd come and see her *around* her birthday.

"I just got back home from being away for a week. I can't come to Augusta tomorrow. I've got work to do."

"All right. I'll tell her," James said. "And when she falls out on the floor crying I'll let her call *you* so you can explain."

Dara knew James was exaggerating. Neither he nor her sister-in-law would let that go down in their household. True enough, Amber was high maintenance, but even that had its limits.

James knew which guilt buttons to push with Dara. As her older brother by four years, he knew *all* of her buttons to push. He knew how to irritate her until she'd finally give in. He knew how to anger her to the point that one time she'd thrown a drumstick at him. She missed him, but not their twenty-gallon fish tank. It hadn't been a pretty scene when her father returned home.

Dara closed the online file she'd opened for Cassius and clicked open her personal folder. Everything she needed to do for herself and for her clients could be handled by telephone. The beauty of being an entrepreneur with a business like hers was that as long as she could pack up her laptop and make the necessary phone calls, business could basically move forward without a hitch.

Maybe India will ride with me.

"If I come tomorrow, you better not tell Mama and Daddy. Let it be a surprise."

"Unlike you, I know how to keep secrets. Hold on a second," James said, and seemed to cover the phone receiver with his hand.

Whatever, Dara thought. *I can keep secrets better than you think.*

India was still the only person who knew about the tattoo of a cross that was inked on the lower section of Dara's shoulder blade. She'd made sure the tattoo artist positioned it where it wouldn't be visible even if she wore a spaghetti strap tank top. Her parents were bent out of shape by her riding a motorcycle—she could only imagine the ruckus if they knew she had a tattoo. She'd never seen her father walk on water, but by the way he acted sometimes a person would think he performed the miracle on a daily basis.

"Hello," James said, coming back to the phone.

"I'm still here," Dara said. "But I gotta go. Remember what I said. You better not spill the beans, Big Head."

"Cookie, if I've got a big head, then your mama's got a—"

Dara hung up the phone on James before he could finish his sentence. She knew she'd pushed *his* buttons with that one. But he deserved it. She'd warned him not to call her Cookie again.

Chapter 5

Dara realized that she should really go home more often. The ride actually wasn't that taxing, and she could make it to Augusta in less time than it took most people who lived in the outer suburbs to make it to their downtown Atlanta jobs.

India flipped her cell phone closed. "I could've been showing a million-dollar house right now, but I'm on my way to a six-year-old's birthday party. Something's wrong with this picture."

Dara put on her turn signal so she could merge into the right lane. "I thought you said they were free tomorrow morning. The house will be there tomorrow."

India scrolled through the messages on her BlackBerry. India worked hard so that she could play harder, she always said. "You don't keep people with money like that waiting. The money itches their palms, and you have to be on the top of their list when they're ready to spend it."

"Relax," Dara said. She turned her pearl white Mercedes-Benz into the H. J. Knight Funeral Home. After being around black limos and cars most of her life, Dara had vowed that she would never purchase a dark-colored vehicle. Thus the reason for her white Benz and hot pink motorcycle.

India slipped her feet in her sandals and finger-combed

her short cropped hair. "Take me through the side door so I won't have to pass by any rooms with bodies in them. I can't deal with that today."

"Come on, scaredy-cat," Dara said. She pushed the button above her head to close the moonroof. She waited to pop the trunk until she was ready to catch a possible runaway balloon from the seven pink ones she'd bought from the grocery store down the street. The seventh balloon would either be a "one to grow on" or the extra to replace mishap.

India started to lift the Easy-Bake oven out of the trunk. She hadn't bothered to wrap it, but at least she'd found a gift bag for the child-sized apron and chef's hat she'd also bought for Amber. With cooking clearly the theme for India's choice of gifts, Dara didn't see the connection with the cheetah-print child-sized purse she'd couldn't leave the store without.

"You can leave that stuff in there," Dara said, wrapping the ribbons from the balloons tightly around her hand. "The child's not having her party at the funeral home."

Dara entered the employee security code to unlock the side entrance door, then pushed the balloon bouquet through the door.

"Well what in the world?" Dara heard her mother's voice say.

Dara pushed the balloon bouquet aside so that her mother could see her face. "Hey, Ma," she said. "Surprise."

Thelma's mouth dropped open. She looked back and forth between Dara and India as if trying to determine if they were flesh and blood or a figment of her imagination. "I ought to whip y'all," she finally said. "Pull your pants leg up so I can get you real good."

Dara's mother clutched a stack of programs and funeral home fans to her chest until India brushed past Dara and peeled them out of her aunt's hands.

"I don't know about Dara, but I'm a little grown for all that," India said.

"You've always thought you were too grown for something." Thelma held her arms open for Dara. "I have to hug my daughter first or she'll pout all the way back to Atlanta."

Dara got the hug from her mother that she'd been thinking about the day before. Her meaty arms felt like the perfect body pillow that allowed Dara to sink into the contour of her mother's body.

Thelma was the kind of old-school woman that most people talked about as if they were an extinct species. Dara wasn't sure that anyone outside of their household had ever seen her mother's knees. Her skirt hems skimmed no less than two inches below her kneecaps, and the same was said of the capris she liked to wear on weekends. Her hair was impeccable, styled by her longtime beautician, Shirley, and between her biweekly visits she pinned it back into a tight chignon. Dara's mother still sent handwritten thank-you notes and didn't let the empty nest that she'd had for over a decade change the fact that she still cooked on Sundays like she had a crew to feed.

Thelma kissed Dara on the cheek, then wiped away the light pink lipstick smudge that Dara knew had stained her. "That's a cute blouse," her mother said, running her hand along the sheer fabric of the sleeve.

"An Atlanta shopping spree is calling your name," Dara said. "You could even pack your clothes this evening and come back with me until the weekend. I'll bring you back on Sunday evening after church."

"And what am I supposed to do all day on Saturday while you're in the projects?"

Dara took a deep breath. How could she want to lie on her mother's shoulder during one minute and walk out the door the next?

India pulled at her aunt. "I'm still waiting for my hug," she said, putting her arm around Thelma while they all walked into the administrative offices. Dara knew her cousin and best friend was taking her place in the verbal boxing ring so she'd be the subject of her mother's soft uppercuts.

"I still can't believe you cut all of your hair off," Thelma said, turning India around so she could inspect the shaved nape of India's neck.

"What, Aunt Thelma? You don't like it?"

"Too short for my taste," she said. "But I guess that's how they wear it in Atlanta."

"This is a popular style everywhere," she said.

Thelma adjusted one of her hairpins. "Everywhere but in my house. You know the Bible says a woman's hair is her crowning glory."

"I guess some people have big crowns and other people have smaller tiaras," India said. "And my hair is only a little shorter than Mama's."

Thelma sat down at her desk and begin to divide stacks of papers. "That's because my sister thinks she's your age. One of these days she'll realize that's not the case."

Thelma slid her divided papers into colored file folders and moved to another stack on the assembly line known as her desk. Her mother was extremely organized, a trait that Dara had inherited and learned to perfect by watching her mother.

Because the funeral business was integrated into the lives of the Knight family, Dara and James were expected to take care of their business—including homework and household chores—without constant prompting. Their mother made sure she handled that aspect of their lives, and the Reverend Hunter J. Knight ran a tight religious ship and made sure the family stayed financially secure. Whenever they questioned either of their parent's actions, they were met with immediate discipline. Most things didn't have an explanation other than, "Because I said so."

Dara untangled the ribbons of the balloons that had started to wrap themselves around each other despite her best efforts to keep them straight. "Where's the birthday girl?"

"She's in the Peace Chapel watching a movie with Kendrick."

Dara lifted her eyebrows. "In the Peace Chapel? Is it empty?"

"No," her mother said, "but something's wrong with the DVD player in the back office so I let them go in there."

Dara had to admit it. Their family *was* a bit strange. India didn't realize why it seemed so odd, and Dara hesitated to tell her. And she definitely wouldn't let India see it for herself.

Chapter 6

The funeral home's viewing rooms had been named according to some of the fruits of the spirit. During recent upgrades to the services the funeral home provided, James decided it would be a nice idea to compose for the families a photo DVD that would commemorate the lives of the deceased. After a tug of war between James and his father, Hunter had finally given in, and James proudly added flat screen televisions to each viewing room. And Kendrick and Amber were enjoying the feature. In the company of a deceased body.

"I'll go and get them," Dara volunteered.

India stood up. Dara knew India couldn't wait to see her youngest cousins in the family. It had been Christmas since she'd been to Augusta because her mother, Dara's Aunt Latrice, found an excuse to travel to Atlanta frequently. She'd come more often if India could tolerate her in larger doses.

"You might want to wait here," Dara informed India with a knowing chuckle.

India plopped back down in the seat and crossed her legs. "I don't know why, but I'll take your word for it."

"Smart decision," Dara said.

She walked out of the administrative offices and turned

down the first hall on the left. She could hear the animated music for the kids' movie immediately. It was loud enough to drown out that horribly depressing music that her father insisted be played at all times on the surround sound stereo system.

Sure enough, Kendrick and Amber had company in the room with them. From the name placard on the outside of the door, it was Mr. Lloyd Persimmons.

Dara stood back from the door and watched them. Kendrick looked up periodically between the movie and his handheld video game, pausing occasionally so he could recite the lines from the movie verbatim.

He's seen this movie way too many times, Dara thought, wondering what creative mastermind had come up with the personalities of the sarcastic and sometimes crude talking donkey and his best friend, the green ogre.

Dara looked at her niece. Amber looked like her parents had given her the liberty to style her own hair that morning. When given the choice, she liked it to fly free instead of being tamed in ponytails. And fly it did. Some sandy brown tresses in one direction and some in another. Her creative expression would last only until it was time for the party. Dara's sister-in-law, Demetris, would make sure of that.

"Is somebody in here having a birthday?"

Amber jumped to her bare feet and seemed to go airborne as she flew into Dara's arms and latched her arms around Dara's neck.

Dara stumbled backward a few steps, surprised at how much force a forty-something pounder could muster. "You know you're getting too old to do that, right?"

"Auntie Dara, you're too funny." Amber's feet dangled a few inches from the floor.

Dara eased her niece to the floor and kissed her on the forehead. She took her hand and smoothed down the bang that was standing at attention in the middle of her niece's head. Dara could tell she was spending a lot of time outside, because the sun had already kissed her usually pale skin to warm bronze.

"Uh. Excuse me?" Dara said to Kendrick.

"Hold on for a second, Auntie. I want to get to the end of this level. I've never gotten this far before," Kendrick said. He chewed on his bottom lip in concentration.

Dara looked down and noticed that Amber's toenails were painted bubble gum pink. Dara was relieved James wasn't as conservative as her father. Dara was thirteen before she'd been allowed to paint her nails, and even then it had to be clear or a very sheer color.

"Where are your shoes, little lady?"

"Over there," Amber said, then skipped over to get her sparkly pink jelly shoes from the corner near the casket. "Aunt Dara," she said, casually, "did you know that man's not even sleeping? He's dead."

"As a matter of fact he is," Dara said, figuring that Amber was finally maturing to the age that she could define death, even if she didn't completely understand it. Kendrick had been around the same age when he realized the bodies he sometimes saw in the embalming room weren't asleep, either.

"Aww, man," Kendrick howled. She sprawled out on his back on the floor, making an X with his husky limbs. He let his handheld game fall to his side, then slapped his hands over his eyes.

"That was the debacle of the decade."

Dara shook her head, wondering what other nine-year-old tossed around vocabulary words like that.

Once Kendrick's short-lived disappointment was over, he came to hug Dara, and she walked back to the office sandwiched between her niece and nephew. Her father and brother were there to welcome her.

"What's up with you sneaking up here, Cookie?" her dad said.

"She came for my birthday party," Amber proudly announced.

"I don't blame her," Hunter, Sr. said, picking up his granddaughter as if she were still in diapers. "It's the event of the century."

Amber scratched her temple.

"Duh," Kendrick said. "A century is the same as a hundred years."

James slipped his daughter's sandals on her feet. "It's a very long time," he said to Amber. "It's how long your mama is going to be mad at me if I don't get home and start getting you ready for your party."

Hunter, Sr. passed his granddaughter off to his son. In their minds, Amber was still a baby, and it wasn't anything to see them haul her around while she sat in the crook of their forearms like it was her personal cushioned throne.

"And please make sure she looks like she was born into the Knight family and not into a flock of roosters," Thelma said, using her hands to brush back the hair budding out like weeds around Amber's hairline.

"That's your aunt," Dara said to India.

"But it's your mama," India said.

James picked up his keys and waited for his kids to round up their stray belongings. "Do me a favor on the way to the house," he told Dara. "Stop by that convenience store that's across the street from the BP gas station and get a salted pickle. Don't ask me why, but Demetris loves those things from there."

Hunter, Sr. looked at his watch. "You better hurry up and get in there before the gamblers get off work. They'll have the line so backed up spending their money on lottery tickets that you can't half get in the door."

India cleared her throat and cut her eyes at Dara. She placed her hands where no one could see and ran one index finger on top of the other. Shame, shame, her fingers signaled.

By the mischievous look on India's face Dara knew her cousin was about to stir up some trouble.

Chapter 7

"That's a shame, isn't it, Uncle H?" India pushed. "Buying lottery tickets."

"A crying shame. And you can get it from the saints and the ain'ts."

Dara knew she was standing on the edge of the line that she knew better than to cross. Why not? India had already started something.

"Daddy, what would you do if one of your church members won the lottery and wanted to pay their tithes and offerings?"

"My church members wouldn't play the lottery," Hunter, Sr. said, protecting his flock.

There were other things Dara's father thought his church members wouldn't do, but Dara had seen some stuff with her own eyes. Deacon Troy shouldn't have been lighting up cigarettes, but Dara had seen one dangling from his lips on more than one occasion when he didn't know anyone was looking. Once he was supposed to be out behind the church washing the church van, but he'd also been taking a smoke break. He'd come back inside the fellowship hall sucking a peppermint and with breath that smelled as if he'd swallowed an entire bottle of mouthwash. Until then, Dara had thought he kept handfuls of candy in his pocket so he'd have some to divvy out to the children who behaved in Sunday School class.

Dara wanted to use that story as an example, but Deacon Troy's cigarette smoking habit was his business. That was between him and God.

Hunter, Sr. was still ranting when everyone else had left the room, leaving him an audience of two—Dara and India.

"Lottery money is the devil's money," he said. "I don't want anything to do with it, and I definitely don't want it in the collection plate. Not at my church."

Dara had forgotten how long it took to put out one of her father's fires once she'd stirred up the embers and thrown sticks on it. But with this conversation, it was like she'd saturated it with gasoline and lit a match.

"We'd better get going, Daddy. We'll see you at the house this evening. We won't be staying too late because we need to get back on the road."

"I'll be home around five thirty. We don't have any wakes tonight, believe it or not."

Dara and India couldn't get outside to the parking lot fast enough.

"More or less, your daddy just said you're going to hell."

"Me? You're the one who bought the ticket."

"You took it. Didn't your parents teach you not to succumb to peer pressure? It'll get you in trouble most of the time."

"You're living proof of that," Dara said, hitting the keyless entry for the doors.

"Well, don't forget to check your ticket tonight," India said.

"I haven't thought anything about that lottery ticket," Dara said. "I changed purses, so as far as I know I might have thrown that thing away."

"You could've thrown away a fortune," India said.

Right, Dara thought. *What are the chances of that?*

Chapter 8

Dara was in her element. She straddled the leather seat of her Honda Crossover and for a millisecond thought about what her mother had said about how ladies should sit.

Oh well, she thought, letting the bike cruise forward with the help of its engine and her tiptoes.

Isaac Reid, called by many as Sir Isaac, held his right fist in the air, signaling that he was ready to move forward. The others followed suit so he'd know everyone was ready to leave for the city.

Isaac rode a classic Harley to which he'd added a loud muffler so he could make sure everyone was aware of his arrival. Kids especially got a kick out of the rumbling, and he got the most requests from young boys who wanted to sit on the seat and pretend they were old enough to fly down the highway at ridiculous speeds.

If Isaac's bike wasn't the main attraction, it was Mario's sleek red and silver Suzuki sports model. He'd customized the side with lightning bolts, and when Mario put on his matching helmet, not only did he look like a super hero, but Dara thought he tried to act like one, too.

Dara received either the questioning look from the boys or an admiring look from at least one young girl who thought it was neat to see a woman riding a bike. An eight-year-old named Keysha always found her way to Dara whenever they visited the southside community.

The area had once been a sort of community utopia for African Americans, but over the years it had become a mainstay as one of the top stories in the evening news. About five years ago the gang activity had started slowly and quietly. Residents speculated about activity more than they actually saw it with their own eyes. It was a game of sorts to figure out whose child was involved. At least that's what Bettye Athena, the neighborhood watchdog, said. But those days were gone.

Now, overworked frustrated mothers threw their hands up in surrender when forced to make a choice on trying to keep their job or staying in the streets to look for their wayward children. Many had given up. On their children. On life.

Gang membership was a source of pride, and their not-so-silent threats had caused a dark cloud of despair to hover over the community. The police couldn't get the residents to talk. They were forced into silence by their circumstances, because few had the means to move out of the way of danger after being classified as a snitch. They settled for sealed lips in exchange for their family's protection.

Isaac had been spurred to action after a sermon from Dara's pastor, Reverend Sullivan. Everyone who had an interest in rolling with the Kingdom Knights was required to listen to that sermon. Dara always played it the night before there was an outreach. Her pastor's words were still fresh in her spirit from last night.

"How long are we going to sit back and let the enemy rule the streets? It's something wrong when the elderly can't rest on their front porches and watch our children play. It's something wrong when our kids are recruited into gangs and compromising lifestyles and all we do is come to church on Sundays and go back into our houses that have three alarm systems and fourteen deadbolt locks. Somebody's got to stand for something, because this generation is falling for everything."

With Reverend Sullivan's blessing, Isaac started the evangelism team that their pastor lovingly dubbed the motorcycle missionaries. As she was the only female in the crew, and because of her custom-painted bike, Dara carried her nickname with pride.

The Kingdom Knights pulled into the parking lot of a church building of four-sided brick that had been painted white. The burglar bars on the front door were latched for additional security with a padlock, a juxtaposition to the hand-painted sign tacked on the door that read ALL ARE WELCOME.

The entire church could've fit easily into the gymnasium at Dara's church, but what mattered most to Dara and the community was the size of the heart of their people.

When the church's pastor caught wind of the mission of the Kingdom Knights, he'd insisted that they use his parking lot to park their bikes when necessary. They also used his lot as a temporary distribution site when they had other outreach events.

Dara dismounted her bike and circled up for prayer with the other Knights. They interlocked arms, a sign of strength and unity for themselves and anyone else who may have been watching.

"I saw you hugging that road, P. K." Isaac joked.

"You all can't go one time without picking on me," Dara said.

"That's what big brothers do to their little sister," Isaac added. "But we wouldn't let anybody else mess with you," he said.

"For sure," Mario echoed.

"You roll with me today, P. K.," Isaac said. "I want to go by Ms. Bettye's house, and she seems more relaxed when you're around."

That didn't surprise Dara. Isaac had an intimidating presence that naturally came with somebody with his large stature. His dread locks looked like long, gray twisted ropes, and flared out like a lion's mane when he didn't have them tied down with a bandana. When he was twenty-five, he'd gotten his tooth knocked out accidently by a baseball and had never bothered to replace it.

"Okay," Dara said, hoping that Ms. Bettye had a fresh loaf of banana bread cooling on her countertop. She did all of her baking and Sunday dinner preparations on Saturdays.

Ms. Bettye fed her foster children and grandchildren better than a five-star restaurant, and the banana bread was the most requested item. That and what she called her "slap yo' mama" banana pudding. If the recipe called for bananas, Ms. Bettye could put her signature taste on it.

And today Ms. Bettye didn't disappoint. Dara stepped onto the screened-in porch and into a dancing mixture of baked goods that smelled like the oven door had just opened and they'd rushed out to do the tango with some Southern fried chicken.

"I know why you *really* wanted to come here," Dara said to Isaac. "You know Ms. Bettye won't let you leave without taking a plate."

"I'm here to serve some spiritual food, but you ain't never known me to turn down a meal," he said, then rapped on the inside door.

It didn't take long for a child to open the door. Ms. Bettye's home was a haven for foster children and the two grandchildren whose mother had been claimed by the street's drug problem. Once the foster children became accustomed to her care, they were upset when the system came to take them back to their families.

One of the children who came to the door announced who was on the porch and, after getting Ms. Bettye's approval, unlatched the lock.

Ms. Bettye peeked from around the kitchen wall. "Hold on a minute," she said, "Let me wash my hands."

Dara looked at the photo gallery of pictures propped along the top of an antique stereo console that looked as if it had been brought in and never moved since the first day Ms. Bettye moved into the house.

"Oooh, Lord," Ms. Bettye said, coming into the living room. Ms. Bettye didn't walk, she swayed, slow and even like a pendulum, and most of the time her hands were stuffed into the folds of her hips.

"It feels better outside than it does in this house," she said, fanning her face with a dry cloth from the kitchen. "Of all days, the air conditioning unit in the front window died." She turned up one of the three fans that were blowing in the room.

Dara didn't feel that it had helped any. "Are you going to be able to get another unit?"

"My brother's coming sometime today. He has a spare one that needs a knob or something put on it, but he said it works fine. The children will probably break the knobs off anyway. Long as it blows cool air." Ms. Bettye opened the door and went out into the small front yard.

Dara and Isaac followed her, and Isaac propped his size 15 foot up on the cement step. "How are things in the neighborhood?"

"I wish I could say things have changed, but it's all the same."

Dara noticed a group of five or six men that had congregated at the end of the street. It wasn't hard to miss the orange bandanas hanging out of their back pant pockets. Which pocket the bandana hung from signified their supposed rank in the gang, Isaac had found out.

Ms. Bettye swirled her skirt around her legs as if it helped to keep her cool. "At least the police cruise the community more often since some of us went down to the city council meeting."

"That's encouraging," Dara offered.

"Well, the hoodlums aren't stupid. They wait until the police are nowhere to be found before they do their dirt," she said, shaking her head. She lowered her voice to a whisper. "Speaking of dirt," she said. "These guys are scraped from the bottom of the barrel."

"They just need a little redirection, that's all," Isaac said in his always optimistic way.

Ms. Bettye huffed. "Well, somebody can redirect them all up out of this community. It didn't use to be like this, you know?" she said, cutting her eyes in the direction where the men were getting closer. "They're in and out of jail as it is. Somebody should've had their three strikes by now and not been able to step foot on free ground again. That's what needs to happen," she said, crossing her arms in indignation.

With the gang members about ten yards away, Dara could smell the stench of alcohol and smoke. Dara felt safe with Isaac, but she still knew that they were people who shouldn't be taken lightly. And they wanted everybody to know it.

Chapter 9

The foul language and disrespectful bander dripped like toxins from their lips with no regard for Ms. Bettye's presence. Dara noticed how the group slowed their stroll. They were used to people tensing up whenever they walked by. But Dara didn't flinch.

"How are you gentlemen doing?" Isaac asked. He stood upright, positioning his body as a barrier between the group and the women.

The man Dara knew to be one of the leaders used his tongue to move a chewed-up toothpick over his gold caps on his bottom row of teeth. She'd heard them call him Magnum.

"See y'all out again tryin' to change the world. Can't y'all find something else to do than passing out some Jesus tracts?"

Another stepped up beside Magnum and hoisted his sagging pants up by the crotch. "Look around. Don't you see God don't live here? This is hell on earth, not heaven."

"Couldn't be heaven." Magnum chortled. "'Cause I'd be lining my pockets fat as hell with the gold off the streets."

They laughed and gave each other high fives, but Dara took note of Magnum's words. She'd learned in evangelism how important it was to listen. People would—knowingly and unknowingly—give glimpses into their lives.

Sometime in Magnum's life he'd attended church, or at the very least been told something about God. How else would he know about heaven's streets being paved with gold? It was a small seed to work with, but at least it was something.

"Jesus paid it all on the cross just for you, brother," Isaac said.

Magnum sneered and spit the toothpick out of the side of his mouth. "Cross? A cross ain't nothing. I got my man, Cross, right here."

Cross stepped forward as if he'd been summoned to the front of the class by his teacher. It was amazing how much influence Magnum had on the others. They responded to his orders by the time he could finish his sentence.

"Lift up your shirt," Magnum told Cross. And he did.

Under his New York Knicks basketball jersey was what most would've considered astounding artwork if it had been painted on a wall and not inked on somebody's chest. An ornate cross was tattooed in immaculate detail starting at the top of Cross's chest bone and ending under his navel. He turned around to show a similar tattoo stretched across the span of his back.

"My man right here is the only cross I need," Magnum said, slapping Cross on the back.

Cross let his jersey fall down. While everyone else's attention had been on Cross's chest, Dara saw something she had in common with him.

Chapter 10

It was inked in the webbed skin between his thumb and forefinger. And it was identical to the one on Dara's shoulder blade. Even down to the John 3:16 scripture. It made Dara wonder if they'd been in the same tattoo parlor on the same day. Had their paths met in time once before? It was the tattoo artist who suggested that Dara add a scripture to her tattoo. Was it because he'd tagged Cross's body with the same thing?

If anybody could be reached, it would be Cross, Dara decided. When Dara looked back into Cross's face, he was staring at her. She could see it in his eyes. He was trying his best to make sure a scowl stayed on his expression, but Dara could see past that. He had a greater vision pulling at his life, and he was in the grip of being yanked between light and darkness. *All he needs is one encounter with God.*

Cross winked at her, but the smile Dara gave him said, "I know your story." He turned away and went to the edge of the curb to spit something out of his mouth.

Dara always returned home feeling empty after a day of evangelism. After leaving Ms. Bettye's house, she and Isaac had mounted their motorcycles and cruised through the neighborhood in silent prayer. Later they'd joined Mario and the rest of the Kingdom Knights in praying for a group of women who were caught in the stronghold of drug abuse. But God was stronger.

Nelda wasn't in that group. In fact, Dara hadn't seen Nelda in a few months, and no one was aware of her whereabouts. Dara had prayed with Nelda before, and had even taken her to get the dust and dirt shampooed from her hair, which had started to lock in knots. The stylist had cut off most of the damaged hair and braided the rest into neat cornrows the way Nelda had requested. By the time Dara took her to buy her three new outfits and get showered, no one would have known Nelda was entangled in a web of drug use. Unless they saw her smile. She rarely parted her lips in happiness, but that day she did, having no embarrassment at her rotted teeth and infected gums. Dara was surprised to find out that Nelda was thirty-four, just two years younger than she at the time. She'd thought her to be at least in her midforties.

Dara checked Nelda into a halfway house and left her with a bag full of things that all women enjoy having, like fra-granced lotion and body splash; a pocket-sized Bible; snacks; and Dara's phone number. The next morning when Dara called the halfway house to check on Nelda, they said she'd checked herself out. She'd seen Nelda once since then.

Dara was devastated but not surprised, because she knew the cycle. Yet it pained Dara's heart, and she continuously prayed and asked God what else she could do to make a greater dif-ference in the lives of the entire community. This evening in particular, she felt like she'd get an answer to her prayers soon.

After time to unwind and refill her spiritual tank, Dara prepared her clothes for church service. There was a cute yel-low sundress she wanted to wear, but her mother's discretion had worn on her choices of her Sunday's best clothing.

"A woman shouldn't bare her shoulders at church," she'd

been taught. Dara wasn't sure how her mother had ended up with the conservative ways and India's mother bucked most of the tradition that had ruled their household as children.

"I haven't worn this since last summer," Dara said to herself, taking a green dress off its hanger and throwing it across the ironing board in the hallway. When she looked on her shoe rack for the shoes that matched it perfectly—a pair of gold gladiator-style sandals—Dara realized India had borrowed and never returned them.

Dara called India to tell her to bring them over the next morning. They usually rode together to church, then went out for their customary Sunday brunch afterward.

"You have something at your house that belongs to me," Dara said when India picked up the phone. Actually, she'd had to yell it because the music was so loud in the background that it was a wonder that India's neighbors hadn't called the police to report her being a nuisance.

"What?" India screamed. "Hold on a minute," she said. India disappeared from the phone and returned after turning down the volume to the level for people who wanted to keep their hearing well into their elderly years. "Now what's so important that you had to interrupt my praise party?"

"My gold sandals, that's what. You know, the gladiator-looking ones."

"Do I have those shoes?"

"Stop playing." Dara dumped the contents of the three purses she'd carried that week out on the bed. Shoes, India could borrow. Clothes, she could borrow. But her cousin never had, and never would, be allowed to walk out of the door carrying one of Dara's purses. She was a purse connoisseur. She wasn't necessarily stuck on brand names, but she was a stickler for quality and uniqueness. "As a matter of fact," Dara said, "you've got quite a few things of mine over in your inventory."

"The way I figure, if you don't ask for it back in three months, then you don't want it."

"That's a good one. But the devil is a lie. So you and your stealing self need to bring my shoes when you come over in the morning."

"I will. They hurt my little toe anyway," India said.

While India complained about the fickle clients she'd been trying to please all week, Dara downsized the contents of her purse to the essentials she needed for church—her wallet, makeup compact, lipstick, lotion, and a tissue pack.

"Here's my ticket to hell," Dara said, picking up the lottery ticket India had purchased for her. It had only been forgotten in her purse for a week, but somehow a leaky red ink pen had stained the top of it. The numbers were still legible.

"Make sure it's a round-trip ticket," India joked. "But if it ain't, make sure you leave a will and testament about everything you want me to have."

"You know what?" Dara said, as her cell phone rang. "You need prayer."

Dara knew it wasn't anyone she knew. She'd assigned a specific ringtone to all the family and friends she talked to on a regular basis. Even all of her clients were grouped into a particular ring. "Let me see who this is," she told India, grabbing the phone off the dresser and unhooking it from the charger. "Be on time in the morning. If you're not here by nine thirty I'm leaving you."

"Yada, yada," India said, and hung up the phone.

Dara took her cell phone and walked into the hallway to iron her clothes. "Hello?"

"May I speak to Dara Knight, please?"

Dara hesitated before she answered. Who would ask for her by her first and last name on a Saturday evening? "This is she," she said. "May I ask who's calling?"

"This is Zebulon. Remember the guy who was trying to pick you up on the side of the highway?"

Remember? How could I forget? "Hi, Zebulon. Nice to hear from you," she said.

"I told you I was going to call. I'm a man that keeps my word," he said.

That's what they all say, Dara thought before chastising herself. She wasn't going to lump him in the category with the men she'd been encountering lately. "And I appreciate you keeping your word," Dara said.

"I wanted to call and check on you. See if you'd made it in okay."

"After a week?" Dara teased.

"Charge it to my head, not my heart," Zebulon said. "It's been a crazy week."

"I know how it is," Dara said, leaving her dress to finish ironing later. "I'm just teasing you."

"So what made your week so busy?" Zebulon asked. "Tell me about yourself. By what's on this card, you must be a woman who knows how to handle business."

Dara stretched out across her bed. "I can't say you're wrong about that," she said. She picked up the lottery ticket that was lying on her pillow and folded it into a paper airplane. "Hello?" Dara said, when there was nothing but silence on the other end of the phone.

"I'm here," Zebulon said. "Waiting for you to tell me about your week. Or about you."

"Oh, you really want to know? Because if you get me started I'll talk all night."

"And I'll listen all night," Zebulon said. "Well, not really. I need to get at least a few hours sleep so I won't fall asleep in church."

"I feel you," Dara said.

Dara didn't expect her conversation with Zebulon to flow so easily—and for such a long time. They'd covered a whole gamut of topics from their preferences in food to their careers, future aspirations, and their mutual affinity for crime and forensics television shows.

From how Zebulon talked, he sounded like he'd been

raised in a home much like Ms. Bettye's house, but instead of foster children, his home was a revolving door for family members who needed help while they got back on their feet.

"Can you believe it's after midnight?" Dara said, looking at the clock on her end table for the first time since she'd gotten on the phone with Zebulon. "It's past my bedtime," she said.

"I don't want to hold you," Zebulon said. "But I would like to see you sometime soon if that's okay."

"That would be nice," Dara said. "I'll wait for your call."

"You won't be waiting long," Zebulon said. "Good night."

"Good night, Zebulon," she said, and then hung up the phone. Zeb. Zebbie. Lon. She went through his possible nicknames.

Dara flipped on the switch for the ceiling fan. Even though she faithfully ran the air conditioning during the summer months, she enjoyed the feeling of the soft breeze over her head while she slept. After turning back the sheets, Dara picked up the miniature paper airplane and unfolded the lottery ticket.

She picked up her phone and called the automated line listed in tiny print on the back of the ticket, following the prompts that the computerized voice gave her. Dara figured she might as well put India's mind at rest, because if not, she'd get hounded until she found out she *hadn't* won.

Dara listened to the numbers from the Mega Millions. She didn't think much of the match with the first two numbers, but when the third number was the same—she took a deep breath and tried to stop her heart from turning over in her chest.

Chapter 11

One in a billion, Dara thought. The fourth number matched. And the fifth.

Until that moment, she'd never known what it was like to feel as if she was about to faint. Dara sat down on the edge of the bed and steadied herself.

There's no way I heard what I thought I heard. No way. I'm just tired.

Ministering in the streets had taken a lot out of her, and evidently it had affected her hearing, too. Dara disconnected the line and dialed the lottery's automated number again. Followed the same prompts. Heard the same numbers. *Her* numbers.

One more time, she said to herself, hands trembling. She pushed the keys on the phone slowly and said each number aloud. And again, everything was the same.

Dara wanted to call India, but anxiety paralyzed her from doing anything but sitting on the couch.

What if the automated line had the ability to track her phone number to her address? She always thought technology far surpassed the capabilities that the average citizen thought about. She wouldn't be surprised if she was on the radar of some authority somewhere. Her phone could very well already be tapped.

Not knowing what else to do, Dara folded the ticket into fours and slid it into the side of the box of her granola crunch cereal on the top shelf in the pantry. She sat down on the couch in the middle of a stunned silence. She jumped at the slightest sound.

"This is crazy," Dara said, turning on the television. She was in her own home, and yet she'd never felt this fearful. She evangelized on the streets in one of the roughest parts of Atlanta and had never been this nervous.

For hours she watched television and the clock, yearning for daybreak when she could call India. Dara watched a man trying to sell a microfiber towel that could supposedly soak up a bucketful of water without dripping. After fifteen minutes' worth of hands-on demonstrations, he had her convinced. Right about now Dara believed anything was possible. She picked up the phone and ordered two of the towels.

He even made Dara believe the putty he pitched in the next segment could aid in helping a pickup truck pull a tractor trailer truck fifty yards. Dara picked up the phone again, then her rationale kicked in. She was turning into her father's sister, Aunt Charlene, who watched only home shopping programs. The UPS driver on Aunt Charlene's route came to her house so much that she had invited him and his family to Thanksgiving dinner. They'd squeezed into the dining room with Dara's cousins and the ceiling-high stacks of unopened boxes.

Dara could see how a person could be seduced by the promises of the products. Before she was cast under the spell again, Dara turned to the twenty-four-hour Christian channel. At four o'clock in the morning, the only thing playing was a track of instrumentals behind rotating video of nature scenes.

Finally, at five o'clock, she turned to the early morning

news. It was her sign that daybreak was just a few hours away. India would arrive soon enough and they'd figure out what do to.

But Dara didn't witness the sunrise of that Sunday morning.

Chapter 12

"Dara!"

Dara felt the catch in her neck as soon as it happened. She jerked forward so abruptly that her entire right side had twisted in a way that normally would've seemed humanly impossible.

"Girl, don't scare me." India was clutching her chest. "I thought you were dead."

Dara winced when she tried to tilt her head to the right. "Why did you scream my name like that? No, I'm not dead, but you almost killed me with a heart attack."

India dropped her purse on the coffee table. "I've been knocking on the door for the past five minutes and couldn't get you to answer the phone. I had to run downstairs to my glove compartment and get your spare key."

"You were knocking?" Dara asked, stretching her mouth wide with a yawn.

"And calling on every phone you have," India fussed. "What's going on? Have you been in here getting your sip on or something?" she asked, walking into the kitchen and doing an inspection in the sink and trash can.

"I've been up all night," Dara said, rotating her right arm to see if that would help relieve the pain in the side of her neck. "You're not going to believe this." She walked into the kitchen and pulled the cereal box out of the pantry.

"What I *don't* believe is that you're about to eat cereal when you were getting on me about being on time." Despite her fussing, India opened the cabinet and pulled out two bowls. "And then you have the nerve not to have any clothes on," she said, holding out Dara's shoes, each one of them hooked on the tip of one finger.

Dara shoved her hand into the side of the cereal box and produced the small paper square. She put it into India's empty hand. Either India would call the lottery phone number and tell Dara she'd been hearing things or she'd tell her that both of their lives had officially changed. Dara was prepared for the former. Becoming a millionaire in one day was too good to be true.

"Call the number on the back of the ticket," she told India.

"Ticket? What kind of ticket?" India asked, unfolding the paper.

When her cousin realized it was the lottery ticket, she nearly went into an immediate stupor.

"Don't do it," Dara said. "Don't go there. At least not now. Just call the number." She hovered over India's back as her cousin tried to call the lottery number.

"Please stop. You're making me nervous," India said, looking around.

Dara could imagine that her cousin was going through the same thought process that she had when she'd first called. And Dara was right.

"Is the door locked?" India asked. "Check the door."

Dara did as she was told because Dara knew India wouldn't push a single, solitary number until then. Dara unlatched, then relatched both locks on the front door and shook the handle to assure India that they were safely bolted inside.

"I swear, if you're playing with me, I'm gonna—"

"Call the number, India," Dara screamed. She bit into her fist.

India dialed the number, and when her mouth dropped open in disbelief, Dara had her first confirmation that it was true. She'd hit the lottery. *They'd* hit the lottery.

"You won," India whispered frantically.

"No. We won," Dara said. She gripped India's shoulders and shook her back and forth. "We won."

"We won," India repeated. She covered her mouth and held in a squeal. She set down the lottery ticket in the middle of the coffee table and backed away from it. "That's the ticket that I bought last—"

"That's the ticket," Dara said. She picked up the ticket again and folded it back into fours. "Why are we whispering?" she asked.

"Because," India said. She looked around the room and began to throw back the sheers and open the blinds. "I don't know why. We can buy this entire building if we want to," she said, kicking each of her legs so that her shoes flew off and hit the wall. One of them left a black scuff mark on its fall to the floor.

"Put it on my half of the tab," India screamed, her voice finally escalated to normal. Then with each word it raised an octave.

Dara stuffed the ticket back in the box. "Okay, shut up already," she said, even though she wanted to do the same thing. "You keep it up and the whole city is going to know."

"Once people get ahold of this news, you know we're going to have all sorts of new friends and family."

"Nobody is getting word of anything because we're not telling a soul yet."

"My thoughts exactly. And especially not Uncle Hunter."

"Not unless you want me to get written out of the will," Dara said, not wanting to think about her parents' reaction to her windfall fortune. Dara twisted off the childproof top of her multivitamins. Her inadequate sleep was already taking a toll on her, and now wasn't the time to make her body susceptible to illness. "We might be going to the grave with two secrets between us."

India was helping herself to a breakfast bar from the pantry. "That microscopic cross tattoo on your back is nothing compared to this," she said.

Dara perched her feet up on the coffee table and leaned her head back against the couch pillows. The muscle strain on her right side prevented her from getting as comfortable as she wanted to.

"I know you're not trying to kick back and relax. We've got to get to church. We'll be a little late, but not that much."

"You're going to church?"

"This is not the day that I want God to decide to strike me down with lightning because I didn't go to church because of a lottery ticket. Throw that cereal box in the pantry and get moving," India directed. "If you think I was having a praise party yesterday, you wait until I get to church."

Chapter 13

Dara was still waiting for India's praise break. It seemed more like someone had pushed the pause button on her usually bubbly cousin, because she'd barely moved.

"What's wrong with you?" Dara whispered when Sister Renee got up to read the weekly announcements.

"I feel like somebody's watching me." India pulled out a pen and filled out her offering envelope.

"Relax. There's no way anybody knows anything. God is about the only person paying attention to you right now."

India shifted in her seat. "If that was supposed to make me feel better, it didn't work. I can hear Uncle Hunter in my head."

Dara didn't want to think about it. She had been fighting the urge to day dream. When the praise leader, Warren, entered the pulpit, he'd admonished everyone to lift their hands. Dara had closed her eyes and tried to focus her thoughts on magnifying God, who was bigger than everything she faced and any decision she had to make.

When Dara had opened her eyes, tears streaming down her face, the view from the back pew had stirred her spirit. The arms of the congregation reaching heavenward had looked like extended eagle wings.

Dara wasn't one to quickly attribute her thoughts and say

that God has spoken to her, but at that moment the words "Eagles Pointe" came to mind. She'd envisioned building a new subdivision, and Ms. Bettye would be the first to receive a new home.

Reverend Sullivan picked up his microphone, walked down the side steps of the altar, and stood in front of the first pew.

"I feel a leading in my spirit that there are many of you in the congregation who are facing situations where you need God's wisdom, above anything you can hear from man. Now I'm not saying that you shouldn't seek wise counsel," he said, holding onto the gold medallion cross that he always wore draped on top of his robe. "But God's word never changes. And you're going to need to know you had a word from Him if the going gets tough."

Reverend Sullivan stretched out his hands, and Dara felt drawn to the altar. Both she and India stood up and walked to the front together.

If they ever needed wisdom, now was the time. They locked arms, and Dara was glad they did. She was going to need someone to help cushion her fall if she collapsed to the ground under the weight of this enormous responsibility that had come her way. She prayed her legs wouldn't give way, and by the end of the altar call Dara felt strengthened instead. She was still floating on a spiritual high at the service benediction.

"How are you feeling?" Dara asked India as they walked back to India's car. They'd headed straightway for the exit instead of milling around after church like they usually did. The Kingdom Knights typically had a brief debriefing on the Sundays after an outreach, but Dara decided to catch up with them later or read the newsletter that Isaac dutifully e-mailed every week.

"A hundred percent better," India said, unlocking the car doors. "But you know, I was thinking about something."

"What's that?" Dara slid her shoes off and dropped them on the floor in the back. No wonder she'd been so quick to let India borrow them. They hadn't shown any mercy to her little toe, either.

"We might be going through all of this drama for nothing. You never know how many people will have to split that money. You could walk out with a few thousand dollars."

"I hadn't thought of that," Dara said.

It's not like she walked around hitting the lottery on a daily basis. As a matter of fact, before last Sunday Dara had never had a ticket in her possession. Her family was so adamantly against gambling of any sort that when she'd attended college she was clueless about how to play spades, bid whist, tonk, and the other card games that kept her dormmates engaged in tournaments well into the night. After trying—and failing—to learn all of them, Dara had given up. But she was the champion at UNO and Go Fish. And to think her first experience at a game of chance could very well yield her millions. Dara knew God had awesome plans for her, but she never fathomed it could come this way.

"We'll just take it one day at a time," Dara said. "Right now, let's go eat. What do you have the taste for?"

"A couple of million," India said, laughing. "And a box of some granola crunch cereal on the side."

Dara was glad India was getting back to herself. She didn't even bring up the thought that she was sure they could find out if there were other winners simply by checking the Internet or calling back the automated line. In their haste, neither of them had listened to the prompt past the announcement of the Powerball number.

"Why didn't we have prizes like that in our cereal when we were growing up?" India asked, pumping up the music.

Chapter 14

Dara picked up Cassius's call on the first ring.

"You sound like a woman who's ready to talk to me," he said.

"Because I am. I need your help. How's your accountant and financial advisor working for you?"

"Charles McGlothen has been with me since day one and I haven't been locked up or had the IRS come after me, so evidently he's doing a pretty good job."

"Well, that's not a rule of standard," Dara said. She ignored the comments that India was making in the background. They'd decided yesterday it would be a good idea if India picked up some clothes and stayed with Dara indefinitely. But they didn't anticipate indefinitely lasting more than a few days.

Once they were aware of how much money they had coming, they'd both go back and figure out how they were going to adjust to their new life. Last night they'd let their imaginations run wild. Dara had her construction plans laid out and told India that she needed to call her best real estate contacts so Dara could contract with Atlanta's best to get the Eagles Pointe housing subdivision moving forward.

Of course India believed that the money could be better served elsewhere, but Dara didn't burst her cousin's bubble when she outlined the traveling excursions she wanted to take, especially her newfound interest in going on an African safari. The only thing Dara had said was, *"You know you can't drive to Africa, right?"*

Dara heard a clanking in the background and guessed that Cassius must have been lifting weights in his downstairs gym.

"In all seriousness, the man knows what he's doing. I wouldn't steer you wrong, especially not when it comes to money," Cassius said.

"I trust you," Dara said. She took down the accountant's information, gave Cassius his weekly updates, then closed down the screen of her laptop. There was one appointment this morning that she couldn't handle by phone. If she walked out of the lottery district office as a millionaire, then Cassius may have to find someone else to be his walking calendar.

Dara stood up and slung her purse over her shoulder. "You ready to go?"

India walked to the door ahead of her. Dara usually had to peel India from under the covers, but this morning she'd been the first up and the first dressed, welcoming Dara into the kitchen with a Mexican omelet.

"As ready as I'll ever be," India said.

It was a short ride from Dara's downtown Decatur abode to the lottery's district office. Dara thought how millions—or at the least thousands—of dollars probably traded hands there during a week while the folks in the Southside were trying to make ends meet.

"Did you bring your social security card?" India asked as they rushed into the building.

Dara clutched her purse to her chest. "Girl, I even got my birth certificate. I wasn't sure what they'd need, so I brought it all."

★ ★ ★

They contained their emotions until they were alone, and when they'd closed both the driver and passenger doors, they let the emotions erupt. It was the first time Dara had screamed, and once she started, she realized she couldn't control herself. When she felt a soreness tickle her throat, she stopped. But India didn't.

"We're millionaires," India said, beating the steering wheel. "You might have to drive back home. I'm not sure I can take it."

Dara held out her hand. "Look at *me.* I'm shaking. Did you see how my hand was trembling when I was trying to fill out that claim paper? That man probably thought I was crazy."

"When's the last time you laid claim to nine million dollars?" India pounded the steering wheel again. "Nine million dollars."

If she keeps it up, nobody is going to be driving the car home, because this girl is about to beat the thing out of the console, Dara thought. They were carrying on for so long neither noticed that someone had approached the car.

The man's face and hair were just as dusty as his blue city-issued uniform. He wrapped his knuckles on the driver's-side window and pressed his nose against the window like a hound dog trying to get a whiff of the action.

"You hit the big one?" he asked. He pulled at the car door handle like Dara and India were crazy enough to let him slide onto India's lap and share in their joy and their winnings.

Without a second thought about her nervousness or any of the man's body parts, India threw the gear shift in reverse and slammed on the gas pedal. The force threw Dara against her right side. She clenched the seat and reached for the seat belt while India ripped from the parking lot. She didn't slow down until she slipped in front of incoming traffic, sped through a yellow traffic light, and stopped at the corner.

"What in the—?" Dara looked at India as if she'd lost her mind.

"What did you expect me to do? We're millionaires. We can't be entertaining every little vagrant that sticks his face on the window. Shoot, if he got something knocked off, let the city pay for him to get it put back on."

Laughter shook Dara's body so hard that she forgot about her right side that was still slightly sore from India busting in on her. India laughed until she couldn't catch her breath, but an impatient driver behind them didn't find anything funny. He blared his horn to remind India that there was such a thing as turning right on red, which only heightened their laughter. Infuriated, he sped around their car and shot them the bird.

"Let's go chase him down," India said, turning down the street and pulling up behind the man who, despite his rushing and harried disposition, had gotten stopped at the next traffic light.

Dara caught hold of India's arm. "You better not," she warned India. "If you get yourself killed right now you're going to miss out on your four and a half million, and I know you don't want to go out like that."

"Child, please. I'm not thinking about that man. He's probably late for work. Something that I'll never have to do again unless I *want* to. I'm going to make that money work for me, even while I'm on my trip to Africa," she said, and let out a shriek as if she were carrying a spear and wearing animal fur.

Dara reclined her seat. She was going to let her money work for her, too. It was going to help her accomplish all the dreams that she'd penned during her devotion and dream sessions in the mornings. If this was the way God wanted to see the work He'd given her accomplished, who was she to argue with the means of how it had come about? Like Reverend Sullivan had said, Dara was going to need a word from God to stand on, and for her it was coming from Isaiah 40:31, her favorite scripture: *"But those who hope in the Lord will renew their strength. They will soar on wings like eagles; they will run and not grow weary, they will walk and not be faint."*

Dara raised her arms above her head.

"What are you doing?" India asked.

"Mounting up on wings like an eagle," Dara said.

"Speaking of birds," India said, "I want to stop and get a chicken sandwich."

"Well, hurry up because I have work to get home to."

"Work?"

"You can take a leave of absence from your broker's office if you want to, but I'm putting you on *my* payroll. I'll pay you twice as much as I'm paying you now."

"You don't pay me anything."

"Exactly. So double that. You've been telling me to put things on your tab since we were in elementary school, so I'm about to make you cash it in. I was serious about what I talked about last night." Dara looked in the side mirror, then turned around to assess the traffic. The street was clear of cars, and she didn't see a police car.

"Get over in the left lane and make a U-turn," she instructed. "I need to show you something."

India merged over, then circled the car around the median. "Are we going to the hood? Because I don't have bulletproof windows."

Dara slapped her shoulder. "Shut up and drive."

Chapter 15

India slowed her car as she bumped over an orange extension cord that snaked from the rear window of one of the dilapidated houses, ran across the street, and went into the front window of another boarded-up house. Neither place was inhabitable, but evidently one of the homes still had the power connected. Dara had seen it before, especially in the vacant houses that the area's homeless and drug addicted used as places to lay their heads. As soon as the payee received the bill, he'd come looking for the source of his outrageous bill, and that would be the end of the free power.

Dara had been watching the look on India's face since they'd turned into the community. It was going to take more than Dara's commentary to make India see the vision of Eagles Pointe and any other hope for revitalization, for that matter.

"These people have the same dreams for themselves and their families as the people who live five minutes down the road in half-a-million-dollar condos but have never driven to this side of the tracks, so to speak." Dara motioned for India to pull over in front of a house with stained beige siding and blue shutters.

"You don't have to preach to me, Dara. I know all of that. But you can't make me have the same passion as you do."

"I'm not trying to. I just want you to respect the decisions I make."

"And I will. But I know that sometimes you have more faith in people than they have in themselves. Then you come down hard on yourself when things don't turn out the way you expected."

Dara knew she had the tendency to take on other people's burdens, but she'd always been that way. She was the one her younger cousins came running to when the older bunch used their seniority or strength to muscle them around. She guessed compassion ran in her family, and Eagles Pointe was going to be her way of pouring it out to fill someone else's life.

"Don't worry about me," Dara assured her. "You have to look at the bigger picture."

India watched a woman cross the street who seemed to be having a lively conversation with an invisible friend. Without warning the woman started to slap and scratch at the side of her face. She stopped for a moment in front of the car where they were sitting, turned around in a circle, and kept walking in the direction she was headed.

"I'm not trying to be funny, but can we leave now?" India said. "I'll help you however you need me to. I promise."

"Let's go." Dara reached in the side pocket of her purse for her ringing cell phone. "And thank you."

Dara hadn't programmed Zebulon's number into her phone, but she recognized it. "This is Zebulon. The guy who stopped for us on the highway," she told India. Dara answered the phone before he was transferred to voice mail.

"Hello?"

"What's up, Dara? I didn't think you'd answer the phone."

"Hi, Zebulon." She used hand gestures to direct India out of the neighborhood maze. "My cell phone is like my child. Always with me," she said. "What's going on with you?"

"Me and Tyler are headed out to lunch for a bite to eat."

"Is that so?" Dara jabbed India in the arm. "How's Tyler doing?"

"He's straight," Zebulon said.

India shook her head and waved a hand in front of her mouth. "Don't do it," she whispered. "You do and you're going to pay big time."

Dara covered the phone's receiver with her hand. "What? Zebulon and Tyler are on their way out to lunch."

India ignored Dara.

"Zebulon, can you hold on for a second?" Dara put the call on mute. "Listen. The last man I went out to eat with was Brother Bobby, and let's not talk about Mr. El Cheapo that took you out last month."

"But Mr. El Cheapo didn't have breath that smelled like a sewer."

"I'm not asking you to kiss the man. We'll just grab something to eat if they happen to be near our side of town. What are the chances?"

"Just go ahead," India said, giving in. "Whatever will make you happy."

Dara unmuted the call and silently hoped their taste buds were bringing the two men to a location that wasn't too far out of the way. She wanted to see if the picture of Zebulon she'd stored in her memory was as attractive as he really was. Their conversation had definitely made her want to see him again.

"Okay, sorry about that," Dara said to Zebulon. "I was wondering . . . what side of town are you on?"

"Right now we're in the area near Stonecrest Mall. We're going to see if we can find something to eat somewhere between here and Conyers."

"Would you like some company? I'm with India and we were just on our way to eat, too."

"I'd rather have your face to stare at than Tyler's mug any day."

Dara laughed. "We're headed in that direction. Call us when you decide where you're going to eat and we'll meet you there."

"That'll work. I'm glad I called when I did."

"He's such a charmer," Dara said when she hung up the phone. "It's too early to even think about something jumping off between us, but even if it doesn't, it seems like he'd be a nice person to know."

"He's not that nice if he hasn't told his friend about his problem," India said, following the signs to Interstate 20. "You need to be praying that Tyler's breath doesn't melt the skin off my face or you'll be using some of your half of the money for my reconstructive surgery."

Chapter 16

The pieces were coming together quicker than Dara expected. It had been only two weeks and India had already found a suitable architect and builder for the project.

"I told you cash is king," India said, handing a roll of blueprints to Dara. "Things move forward faster when you don't have to deal with the red tape and egos of some of those lenders. I'm telling you. I've seen the difference between the 'haves' and the 'have-nots.' That's why I work with the 'haves.'"

They'd move their production to India's home because she claimed she was able to work more efficiently when she was at home. And keeping to her promise, India decided not to renew the office space she was renting from her broker's office so she could help Dara.

Dara knew India was one of the top-selling agents in the company, but she didn't see how she got anything done with stacks of contracts offers, MLS printouts, and directions to properties strewn all over the floor. Dara wanted to dive in and color code and file her papers, but India had already warned her that if Dara moved anything from its designated spot, she was prone to lose a limb.

Dara took the roll of blueprints downstairs to the dining room table. With the exception of her office that looked like it had been turned upside down, India's house looked like a decorated model home.

Dara pushed the place settings and center arrangement to one end of the table so she could spread out the three designs she'd chosen for the twelve ranch-style houses she planned to build. If phase one was completed as planned, she'd launch another community somewhere close to it.

India came downstairs with a legal-sized folder of contracts. "I need you to sign these so I can fax this back over."

"Gladly," Dara said, scribbling the business name across the highlighted lines as if she were a celebrity with thousands waiting in line for her autograph. Dara cloaked her identity behind her business name, H. J. Holdings, LLC, before bidding for the plots. The city had been anxious to sell them at a ridiculously reduced price. The market downturn had worked in Dara's favor, and it looked like she'd also be closing on two adjoining plots at the end of next month.

"Remember, you're a silent investor," India said. "You don't need to go down there every day trying to check on stuff. Let the contractors do their work and let Zebulon handle any issues that come up. That's what you're—well, the business—is paying him for. Even though you could probably pay him with kisses and he'd be just as satisfied." India laughed. "I mean, he's coming on strong."

"Can you blame him?" Dara said. "But regardless of how he pursues me, that's not going to happen right now. I don't mix my business and personal lives."

"Good. Because if he uses those eyes of his on you, he might be able to hypnotize you out of our secret. And a man you've known for less than a month doesn't need to know you're sitting on four and a half million stacks."

"You don't have to worry about that," Dara said.

Of everything that could've come out of their roadside swiping, Dara would've never guessed it would be a project manager for Eagles Pointe. After lunch two weeks ago and her subtle way of digging into his background and more of his character, Dara had been confident in Zebulon's abilities. He had prior experience in property management and construction, and although he hadn't used it yet, he had obtained his general builder's license in Georgia.

After a few days of prayer, Dara brought her decision up to India, who'd always been her second set of ears and eyes. India acted as a human resource manager and called Zebulon to request his resume with references, and had him sign a release for her to perform a criminal background check. His record was spotless and his references raved about his work ethic and performance. That was enough for both of them to pull him onboard. Which meant Tyler would come aboard, too. Zebulon and Tyler, like Dara and India, were tight in blood and friendship.

And since it seemed that Tyler's breath issues had only been a fluke on the first day they'd met him, India had agreed to work with him. Still, she wouldn't let him get his expectations up that there was a future for them. She'd seen him with the top button of his shirt undone, she'd said, and he had mounds of chest hair. A no-no in her book.

"Can you ride with me out to the supply warehouse? I want to look at some granite countertops."

"Granite countertops?" India picked up the signed contracts and stuffed them back in the legal folder. " No. I'm not letting you do it. Find some nice laminate and call it a day. You don't even have granite countertops in *your* condo so why put them somewhere where they're going to be messed up anyway."

"India!"

"I'm sorry, I'm sorry. I know my mind-set about some things is jacked up, but I'm working on it. I'm serious. I prayed about it and everything. With God's help, I'll do better. I want you to put your money into things where you're sure to get a return on your investment, that's all."

"Returns on investment don't always come back to you in money," Dara said, leaning over the first three-bedroom, one-and-a-half-bath design. "And what kind of investment do you expect to get on this African safari you're going on?" She still couldn't believe India was actually going to do it.

"Connecting with my people," India said.

"Your people live in Augusta, Georgia," Dara said, reaching for her cell phone. It had been ringing nonstop all morning. Dara had also opened a business phone line and had the calls forwarded to her cell. To prevent her name from being tied to the project, she'd removed her personal greeting from her voice mail box and had India record one of her professional sounding messages.

"Oh, it's Zebulon," Dara said.

"You better watch him," India said. "He's tipping over to the stalker side," she teased.

"We're supposed to be meeting today."

"Meeting? That's what you call a date these days? Shoot, I need a meeting, too."

"This is *business*," Dara said, answering the line. She knew it would raise India's suspicions when she disappeared into the spare bedroom that had been her home for the past week, but she'd seen India headed toward her iPod. That thing was small, but when India hooked it up to her speakers, you couldn't tell it.

"Hey, Zeb," she said, adopting the nickname that Tyler always said.

"I hate to call and cancel at the last minute, but something came up with my mama. I need to go and help her handle some family business. Can we reschedule for tomorrow? I'll make it up to you with lunch."

"Actually, tomorrow is good, but let's have dinner. I have outreach that lasts all day."

"If you don't mind, I'd like to come with you. Unless your church shuns outsiders."

"Don't even try it," Dara said, impressed that he'd even offered. "That's perfect, because it won't just be the evangelism team this week. Some of the other ministries are joining us for a back-to-school bash. Anybody's welcome, and we'll need all the help we can get." She snapped her fingers. "That's right. You know where it is. It's the same community where the investor is going to build Eagles Pointe." Investor, also known as me, she thought.

"Maybe I can convince Tyler to ride out with me. Sometimes he acts like he grew up in a penthouse."

"I know what you mean," Dara said, since she'd been trying to make India change her plans to go shopping at the outlets and come with Dara to shop for souls for God's Kingdom instead.

"So I guess I'll call you tomorrow morning," Zebulon said. "Is eight o'clock all right? I can meet you out at your church. That'll be closer for me."

"That's fine," Dara said, wondering how Zebulon was going to react when he found out she was a motorcycle lover, and most of all rider. Dara hadn't yet told him, but she wouldn't be able to conceal it when she mounted up with the Kingdom Knights. Some men thought it was attractive, but she knew some who thought it was borderline masculine.

Dara stuffed her duffle bag with her dirty clothes and only the necessary items she needed to take home for the weekend. It was nearly two o'clock and she wanted to get on the road headed toward home before the three o'clock traffic thickened as all of Atlanta scrambled through the downtown area.

Dara heard the shower running in India's master bathroom. She walked into her bedroom and knocked on the cracked door. There was enough steam heating the room to run a dry cleaning business.

"I'm about to leave. I need to go home and get ready for

tomorrow. Instead of meeting today, Zeb and I are going to hook up tomorrow down at the outreach."

"Okay. Call me later and lock the door behind you."

Dara noticed the clothes spread across India's bed. It wasn't the kind of thing she wore lounging around the house. "You've got plans?"

"I thought I told you Mama was coming down. She called last night and said she wanted to hang out. I didn't invite you because I know you typically stay in and prepare the night before when you have your evangelism days."

"I'm too tired for all of that, anyway. You and Aunt Latrice have a good time. Don't get too wild."

"I'm not the one you need to be telling," India said.

"I'll call Aunt Latrice and tell her myself," Dara said. She also planned to tell her that she wanted to see her so she needed to come down to the outreach tomorrow. Dara was sure her aunt Latrice would do it because Dara was her favorite niece, and the one she depended on to keep India out of trouble.

Tomorrow would prove to be an interesting day if everyone she invited actually showed up.

Chapter 17

Dara had let her neighbor's teenage son, Nathan, wash her motorcycle. Oftentimes he came through to ask the neighbors on their floor if they needed any odds-and-ends jobs done. Nathan's mother complained that instead of saving the money, he used it to buy tennis shoes and used video games, but Dara didn't care what he did with the money as long as he was earning it legally.

When Dara walked to the parking lot to inspect his work, Dara found that he'd washed and shined it as if it were his own. She paid him fifty dollars for his extra attention to details, and he volunteered to wash her ride every week if she wanted him to. She told him every three weeks would be sufficient, and she counted it as a blessing for a boy who excelled academically and steered clear of trouble. She couldn't promise him fifty dollars every time, but she'd pay him fairly.

All of the Kingdom Knights were posted on rides with sparkling chrome and buffed leather. Dara waited in the lineup of motorcycles in her usual position while Isaac instructed the remaining volunteers who were still at the church on what needed to be done. She assumed Zebulon had stood her up, until she noticed his car coming around the bend from the front steel gated entrance. He slowed down for the speed bumps, but pulled hastily into the first parking space he saw.

Zebulon stepped out the car wearing jean shorts, a sleeveless basketball jersey, and matching tennis shoes that looked like they'd never been worn.

He pushed his dark shades up to the top of his head, and Dara knew he was looking around for her car. He walked up to Isaac, who happened to be standing nearby barking orders. Isaac turned toward the motorcycles and pointed in Dara's direction.

Dara dismounted her bike and walked toward him. He had a half smile on his face, and Dara could tell by his expression that he was the kind of man who appreciated a woman who could handle a machine.

"You've been holding out on me," he said, giving her a hug.

"You didn't ask me."

"Well, it's not a question you typically ask a woman."

"There's a lot about me you don't know," Dara said, pushing a stray strand of hair out of her eyes. She made sure she was wearing her full matching regalia that morning when she got dressed, from her hot pink riding jacket to her coordinated pink and silver Nikes.

"I plan on being around long enough to find out," Zebulon said, confidently. He gently nudged her shoulder so she'd turn around so he could see the back of her vest. Other than the unique color that set her apart, the Kingdom Knights wore identical vests for special events with their names and the crest embroidered on the back.

"Pink Knight," Zebulon read. "I like that."

I bet you do, Dara wanted to say. "Thanks," she said, then noticed Isaac mounting his Harley. "I need to go. But you can follow us down there if you don't remember the way."

"I think I'll ride behind you so I can see how you handle that thing," Zebulon said, still looking at her with astonishment.

When Dara looked in the direction of Zebulon's car, she noticed Tyler hanging out the window. With Zebulon's slightly mirrored tint on his windows, she hadn't seen him before and figured Zebulon hadn't been able to talk his cousin into doing a good deed that morning.

"Hey, Dara," he yelled. "India rides a motorcycle, too?"

"No way that'll ever happen," India said.

"I was about to say. She's got me for life if she did. I wasn't ever going to give up on her," he said.

You might as well give up, Dara thought to herself. Before India had pointed it out when they were at lunch together, Dara hadn't noticed the chia pet growing out the top of Tyler's shirts. Even from where she was standing, she could attest that he *was* indeed very hairy. It looked like fresh breath hadn't helped his chances after all.

Chapter 18

The Kingdom Knights cruised to a stop at the traffic light on the overpass. Dara noticed two young girls staring at her from the backseat of a minivan. She lifted her helmet's visor, winked at them, then gave them a thumbs-up signal. Tickled at the attention, they waved ecstatically and got their mother's attention for her to look out the window.

When the traffic light turned green, Dara followed the lead of the men in front of her. As always, she was fourth in line. Because she was the only woman, the men insisted that she ride in the middle of the pack—three in front of her, and three in back.

After twenty minutes, the motorcade exited into the neighborhood that had become accustomed to—and even expected—their presence. They'd blanketed the areas with flyers over the past few weeks, so Dara knew both those who liked and didn't like their presence would be out today with no thought of the searing temperatures.

The first Saturday Dara had participated in the inner city outreach two years ago it happened to be the Knights' annual "Soul Survivors" event. A truck bearing all the necessary items for a block party had arrived before them. Church volunteers unloaded crates of food, fired up the grill, and constructed a small stage for entertainment. It wasn't their spring affair, but today was no different. And as always, the children were the most excited.

Dara couldn't wait to see their faces when Cassius arrived. She pulled into the area roped off for their motorcycles and immediately saw the line that had begun to wrap around the block. Ms. Bettye stood in front with five children. A toddler whom Dara had never seen was propped on Ms. Bettye's left ample hip, holding on to a dripping grape Popsicle. Her lips were rimmed in purple, and Ms. Bettye didn't seem to mind the sticky juice that was trailing down the toddler's arm and to Ms. Bettye's wrist.

While Zebulon found a place to park, Dara went to talk to her favorite resident.

"How are you doing, Ms. Bettye?"

Ms. Bettye wiped her forehead with the scarf that was hanging around her neck. "I feel like my skin is frying," she said. "It's hot as Hades out here, so you know I don't plan on the devil seeing my face." Her double chin jiggled as she laughed.

"Maybe the kids will have some mercy on you and not want to stay outside all day."

"It doesn't matter either way. My brother never did get that air conditioner to work. We've got plenty of fans, but during the day, they blow more hot air around than anything else. It's a little better at night, though."

That makes no sense, Dara thought. Here Ms. Bettye was with a household full of children and no air on a day that was forecasted to peak in the midnineties, and Dara had slept through the night with central air *and* a ceiling fan. By the morning, she'd do something about it.

"Lord Jesus, this chile is going to have a trail of ants following us home," Ms. Bettye said, wiping her wrist and the little girl's arm with the same scarf that was keeping the sweat at bay from her nose.

"I'll have somebody bring you some wet paper towels," Dara said, when she noticed Zebulon and Tyler coming her way.

Ms. Bettye grabbed Dara's arm before she had a chance to walk away. "You're an angel around here," she said, "and don't let anybody tell you different. As pretty as you are, you don't have to come down here and fool with these folks, but if I don't know nothing else, I know God sent you."

"Yes, ma'am," Dara said, her heart touched more than it had ever been before. People thanked the Kingdom Knights collectively all of the time, but it was the first time someone had singled Dara out.

If Ms. Bettye only knew what was in her future, Dara thought. She deserved a first-rate place to cool her banana bread. If Dara didn't buy those granite countertops for anyone else, she'd get them for Ms. Bettye.

Only my aunt would come to an outreach wearing high heels.

Dara didn't know how her aunt Latrice had already lasted two hours with her feet strapped into a pair of four-inch heels, but she walked around as comfortably in them as she would a pair of house slippers.

"It hasn't been that bad, has it?" Dara said to India. "I can tell you're enjoying yourself."

Unlike her mother, India was reasonably—yet fashionably—dressed in a pair of shorts and a daffodil yellow short-sleeved shirt. And Tyler still swarmed around her as if he were a bumblebee looking for a flower to pollinate.

"I have to say it's been very rewarding. I take back everything negative that I said," India offered, humbly. In the next breath she mumbled, "But if Tyler finds his way over here one more time, he's fired. He won't step foot in Eagles Pointe. I know Mr. Zebulon is a church boy, but Tyler's got more than Jesus on his mind."

Dara fanned a fly away from the table. "With the way

you're treating him, his fascination should wear off soon. Unless of course he's attracted to women who emotionally abuse him."

"I'm not even going to dignify your comment with a response," India said, ripping open three more packs of hot dog buns. She'd chosen to serve at the food table, and it was her responsibility to keep the assembly line of grilled hot dogs moving. Dara stood beside her and used one gloved hand to put potato chips on plates and the other hand to squeeze a ketchup bottle.

A woman with a recognizable scowl on her face approached the table with her three small boys behind her. Dara wondered what her face looked like without her forehead and mouth twisted in anger, because every time she saw the woman, she was always wearing the same look. Dara figured the stress of life had etched the expression on her face to the point that the woman didn't realize it had taken permanent residence there. Dara hated that she couldn't put a name to the face, but the woman had refused to tell any of the Knights.

Thinking that she'd be more comfortable with talking to a woman, Dara had approached her once during a Saturday evangelism, but the woman had adamantly resisted all of Dara's conversation.

"I don't want to hear nothin' 'bout no Jesus, no Allah, no Buddah, nobody. 'Cause whoever really is running this earth never done nothing for me," she'd said. She'd turned and stomped down the sidewalk with her kids waddling behind her like ducklings.

Her sons always trailed behind. Never beside her. Like they were an afterthought.

Dara dropped potato chips on their plates and squeezed ketchup on the hot dog of the one boy who requested it.

"Eat good now 'cause that's all for the rest of the day," she told the one who looked to be the youngest. And then to the one who seemed to be oldest of the bunch, "Get another hot dog, Little D. I'm telling you don't come crying to me when you get hungry. And if you don't finish, you better not throw it away," she fussed. The woman wrapped up her own plate and stuffed it in the bottom carrier of a stroller she was pushing, even though there wasn't a child in the seat.

Dara made a mental note to ride by the woman's house so she could write down the address. She knew the zip code for the neighborhood, so the only thing she needed for her act of kindness was the house number. In fact, while she was at it, she might as well write down the house numbers for every house on the woman's street, even if she didn't know their names. Addressing the envelopes to "Resident" would still let Dara accomplish her goals.

No matter their names, everyone had to eat. There was a major grocery store within walking distance and riding distance on the bus line. Tonight, Dara would stop by and buy enough gift cards to ensure that the residents of that street could eat for the month.

Dara's aunt Latrice walked up to the table and clapped her hands at the girls. She always caught everyone's attention, not because she was loud and demanded it, but most were attracted to her natural magnetism.

"Come on, ladies. Keep that line moving. We've got kids here that need to pick up their backpack full of school stuff. There are some future doctors, lawyers, and business owners that are counting on you to do your job," she shouted, getting laughs from some of the people in line.

"Please get your mother under control," Dara said, knowing that her aunt meant no harm.

India pulled up the plastic glove that was slipping off her hand. "Have I *ever* been able to do that?" she asked.

"She might be bossy today, but at least she's looking cute while she's doing it," Dara said. Her aunt was wearing a sleeveless tunic that she'd gathered at the center with a belt that snuggled her waist. It was paired with some trendy jeans that all of the teenagers were wearing now. All of the teenagers, and her aunt.

"She went on a shopping spree last night," India said.

"She came to Atlanta just to spend her money?" Dara asked.

"No, she came to Atlanta and ended up spending *my* money," India said, then shooed her mother back to her post where she was supposed to be.

Dara lowered her voice. "You didn't? Tell me you didn't tell."

Dara knew they couldn't keep their secret forever, but she didn't want India to spill the beans before it was time. India and Aunt Latrice had a close relationship, and Dara knew they probably had some secrets that were shared only between mother and daughter.

But it wasn't time . . .

Chapter 19

India ripped off the cheap pair of plastic gloves that had been slipping off her hands. She dropped them in the trash bag under the food table, then put on another pair.

"Of course, I didn't tell," India told Dara.

The man in front of Dara held his plate out for a handful of chips, but he could barely balance his paper plate because he was too busy watching every move of Dara's lips.

"Here you go, sir," she said, and waited until he was at the end of the table and digging through the cooler for a soda. "We'll talk later," Dara told India.

Dara's cell phone buzzed on her hip. She pulled off her gloves and asked the volunteer beside her to help India take up the slack for a while.

It was Cassius. She'd told him to call her when he was five minutes away so she'd have time to round up the Kingdom Knights who were going to act as his unofficial body guards and help control the crowd that she was sure to rush him.

"Hi, Cassius," Dara said.

"Doing like you told me," he said. "I'll be there in five minutes. I'm getting ready to exit off the highway now."

"You can actually do right when you want to," she said. "And I didn't even have to text you a reminder this morning."

"I'm on my best behavior. After you tried to break up with me, I figured I'd better get it together."

"Break up with you? You're funny," she said, knowing exactly what he meant.

Dara had successfully transferred four of her five clients to a mentee who was building her own personal concierge business, but Cassius refused to let Dara go. She knew why. They were tied together by more than the inked signatures penned on their contract. He leaned on her for spiritual guidance, and after praying about it, she realized it wasn't time for her to stop working for him.

Dara alerted Isaac of Cassius's pending arrival and Isaac called the men he had chosen into order. And just in time.

Though Cassius usually drove his Hummer on a daily basis, Dara had asked him to drive his midnight black Ferrari. He cruised down the street, his customized-inch rims spinning separately from the tires. And just as Dara thought, the children were mesmerized. They ran beside the car, trying to peer inside. The tint on Cassius's windows were just as dark as the car, and it wasn't until he'd parked in the spot designated for him that the children's guessing games ended.

"Man, that's Cassius Freeborn," one of the kids yelled. They bounded toward his direction, and try as they might, the volunteers could barely contain them. They pounced on Cassius, but remarkably kept their distance from his car. They only walked around it in awe as if it were a priceless museum exhibit.

"Man, that's the kinda car I'm gon' have."

"You crazy. You gon' be riding with me."

"I'ma be following behind y'all on a motorcycle like Ms. Dara's. Except mine gon' be purple," Dara's admirer, Keysha yelled out.

Dara pushed her way through Cassius's pint-sized fans. "Thank you so much for doing this," she said. "You don't know how much this means to me."

Even though she had access to Cassius's ear and his schedule, Dara didn't take advantage of his time by asking him to make celebrity appearances at events that she was involved in. In their three years knowing each other, this was only the second time she'd asked for a favor.

Dara opened Cassius's passenger door and lifted out the plastic bin on the seat. She kept a stash of glossy photos and felt tip markers packed for him and lined against one of the walls of a closet in his office. Whenever he had an appearance, he simply picked up a bin and put it in his car.

"All right, y'all get in a single-file line or Mr. Cassius is leaving," Isaac said, throwing out an empty threat.

The volunteers helped corral both children and adults into the best semblance of a line that they were going to get. They set up a card table and chair so he could sit down and sign autographs for the seemingly endless line.

"This isn't your boyfriend, is it?" Zebulon said, walking up to Dara. "You said there were things I didn't know about you."

"Cassius is my client. And a friend," she said.

Dara hadn't seen Zebulon for more than an hour. Soon after arriving, he'd disappeared inside the church to help unemployed men find suits for interviews. Dara could tell he was used to serving others, because he didn't wait for someone to hold his hand and give him instructions on every little thing. He stayed committed to his area, unlike Tyler who roamed from station to station—especially to the food table to hound India.

Zebulon said, "He almost lost his career about two years ago. One injury for an athlete can take away his career and endorsements. I don't envy him."

Dara didn't completely believe that. Jealousy for her was as big a turnoff as hairy chests were for India.

Since the food line had cleared after Cassius's arrival, Zebulon and Dara made themselves a plate and found two spare folding chairs to rest on.

"I think this is going to have to count as our dinner," Dara said. The heat was taking everything out of her, and the only thing she could see herself doing after the outreach was taking a cool shower and a nap.

"I feel you," Zebulon said. "I'm tired myself." He turned up a bottle of water to his lips, gulping it down until it was half-full, then looked around the area.

"I wonder why the guy who wants to build in this area doesn't want anyone to know who he is."

Guy? I might ride a motorcycle, but I'm far from a guy. "Some people aren't worried about public recognition," Dara said. "They just want to touch people's lives."

"Well, whoever it is is doing it in a big way," Zebulon said, downing the rest of the bottled water, then getting up for another one. "They must really trust you to keep a huge secret like this."

"I'm a trustworthy woman," Dara said.

"That must mean men can trust you with their hearts."

Dara wagged her finger at Zebulon. "From the day I asked you to come onboard with Eagles Pointe we had this talk. I can't think about being in a relationship with somebody I have to work with on a business level."

"You just said Cassius was your friend."

"Exactly, *friend*. And that's been after knowing each other for three years. We've known each other for how long? A little over one month?"

Zebulon stood and balled up his empty paper plate. Dara didn't even remember him eating his food, so he must've scoffed it down with barely chewing.

"Good thing for me it doesn't take forever to build houses," Zebulon said.

Isaac called to Dara from where he was standing beside Cassius. "Dara, can you bring Cassius some water? The brother's almost dehydrated. We need him next season. We need to make sure he stays healthy."

Everyone within hearing distance of Isaac cheered.

"Come with me to meet Cassius," Dara told Zebulon.

"For a minute. Then I need to get out of here," he said.

Dara wasn't the kind to be starstruck to the point of being dumbfounded around celebrities, and working with Cassius she'd been around her share. Still, most people showed a hint of excitement being around someone who most people in the world considered a celebrity, especially if he was a popular athlete.

But not Zebulon. If he was the least bit impressed with Cassius, he didn't show it.

"What's up, man?" Cassius said when they were introduced.

" 'Sup," Zebulon said.

They pounded fists, but their conversation didn't extend beyond the brotherly exchange of respect. Yet when Cassius turned to speak to Dara, his entire demeanor changed.

"Whaddya say we grab something to eat when we finish here?" he said, scribbling his autograph on a picture and flashing a million-dollar endorsement smile for a photo.

"I can't do it today," she said. "We'll talk after you finish here. I have something I want to show you that you might be interested in."

"All you have to do is say the word," Cassius said. "And I'm all yours. You don't ever have to worry about that."

Dara felt her face flush when the Kingdom Knights and volunteers who were helping to man Cassius's table looked her way. Dara walked around and decided to see if anyone needed prayer or another type of assistance. She bent down to tie the shoes of a little girl since the girl's mother's hands were full from carrying a plate of food and her daughter's new backpack.

Standing back up she saw Magnum, leaning against a stop sign, its white letters blacked out by spray paint. As always, he had something hanging out of his mouth, and even though he didn't say anything to Dara, he looked like the wheels in his head were spinning, coming up with something evil to plot.

Nothing but trouble, Dara said. But his time was short lived. Light and darkness couldn't inhabit the same place, and it was her plan to bring as much light to the community as possible.

Chapter 20

India had said she couldn't resist buying the gold leaf charger plates that she'd put on the table to replace her former table place settings. Evidently she hadn't been able to deny the voice of the hand-painted wall plates calling her name, either.

"You need to do something for *yourself*," India said.

"This *is* for me. It makes me feel good. You saw how it was out there today."

"No, I mean buy something for yourself that you're not going to give away."

"It's more fun to leave surprise gifts for people," Dara said.

After the outreach, Dara went home and bathed, changed clothes, and waited until dusk to purchase and secretly deliver Ms. Bettye's two window air conditioning units to the front porch. She'd also bought enough gift cards to bless the residents on the street she'd chosen, but she was going to mail them when she had time to write a word of encouragement and a scripture in the note cards she'd also bought to mail them in.

Despite Dara's plans to collapse in her bed after her clandestine errands, Aunt Latrice had insisted that she come over to India's for dinner. After eating, Aunt Latrice had challenged them to a game of Scrabble that was going on forever. Tired of arguing about India's questionable words, her aunt had gone into India's office to find the unabridged dictionary.

India rearranged her letter tiles. "It's like you're their knight in shining armor," she told Dara. "No . . . their knight in pink armor."

"Oh, I like that," Dara said.

Aunt Latrice walked back into the room. "Did I tell you how prosperous you're looking today?"

"Thank you," Dara said. She kicked India's leg under the table.

"Mama, you're always talking about somebody looking prosperous," India said, letting Dara know that was her mother's usual comment and hadn't come from India letting their secret slip.

"God's children should always look prosperous. If you were an heir to the throne, wouldn't you walk around acting like it?" She shook the bag of unused letter tiles. "My baby has me looking like a queen these days, doesn't she, Dara? I know that much. Did you see the stuff she bought me? I told her that she needs to earn commissions like that all the time because if it means I'll be treated like this, then I'll be back every week. And I'll convince your mama to come with me," she told Dara. "You let me get on her when I get back. She'll be here before you can blink."

Chapter 21

It had taken longer than a blink. Getting her sister to leave Augusta had taken Latrice a month. And as thrilled as Dara was to have her mother's company, it couldn't have come at a more inconvenient time.

They'd finally finalized the contracts, gotten the required permits, had environmental tests completed, and received the long list of approvals from the city. With Zebulon and India's assistance, they'd ripped through all of the red tape with fierceness. Ground breaking was this week, and Thelma had decided to visit.

But that wasn't Dara's biggest concern and the only reason why she wanted her mother to leave. No, *needed* her to leave.

It was eating Dara up inside. What kind of person could continue to act as if she was still bound by the limits of her normal paycheck when she knew she was a millionaire?

When Dara's confession bubbled to the surface, she called India. As soon as it was time for the ribbon-cutting ceremony at Eagles Pointe, she'd let her parents know. She'd let them see the "good" being done with her riches.

But it still wasn't time. . . .

Thelma held the stems of the bundled spring flowers under

the running waters in Dara's kitchen sink. She diagonally cut each tip and placed them in a crystal vase on the countertop, arranging each flower with the skill of an expert florist. Thelma was a believer in fresh flowers in the kitchen. Dara believed it was because she was used to the smell from the floral wreaths at the funeral home.

"It feels good to be away from home," her mother said. "Usually I'm the one taking care of everybody else, but this has been my kind of weekend."

"You deserve it, Mama." Dara took two of the flowers out of her mother's hand and stuck them in the vase. "Consider it my gift to you for finally leaving the city limits of Augusta."

"When your daddy sees that fondue set and those fancy baking dishes you bought me, I bet he'll drop me off more often. I can't wait to get home and try some recipes. You know I watch Paula Deen all the time. She's got this baked French toast casserole that James printed off her Web site for me. I'll probably try that this week."

"Now that sounds good," Dara said.

She'd tried to buy her mother more than cooking tools for her kitchen, but Thelma had refused, saying Dara needed to save her money so she'd have enough to pay the bills and then put some away for a rainy day. She didn't know Dara had enough put away for a whole line of storms. The accountant, Charles, had advised both Dara and India on how to shelter and invest their money.

"Do you think you'll be able to make it for me and your daddy's anniversary? James had talked about getting a dinner catered for us."

"I actually talked to James about that," Dara said. "We're going to work out the entire family coming to Atlanta because I have a gift here that I want to present to you."

"What kind of gift? You can just bring it to Augusta."

"If I told you it wouldn't be a surprise," Dara said. "And no matter how hard I try, I can't bring it to Augusta."

If everything went according to schedule, Dara hoped to be celebrating her parents' anniversary and the ribbon-cutting ceremony for Eagles Pointe in two months. She'd already had a corner stone engraved in her parents' honor that would sit at the subdivision entrance as a testament to her family's legacy. That was her gift to her parents. She hadn't taken on the family business, yet she'd still been able to serve others. She didn't know whether they'd ever come to terms with her lottery win, but in this case maybe it wasn't where the money came from, maybe it was more about what Dara was doing with it.

"Who's going to run the funeral home if we're all here?" Thelma asked, starting to worry already.

"We'll worry about that later. Mark it on your calendar, and we'll both work on getting Daddy to come. I promise you won't be disappointed," Dara said. Or at least she prayed not.

Thelma pulled back the glass door in the living room and walked out onto the balcony. For the past week, Dara noticed that her mother had been enjoying the area just as much as she did. Almost every morning, Dara found her sitting outside with her Bible and a cup of coffee

"I can't believe India and Latrice are taking off to Africa," her mother said. "I've never known India to go anywhere she couldn't drive to. How long is the flight going to be?"

"I'm not sure, Ma. But India still has a few months to realize what she's done," Dara said. She'd ridden with India before on a three-hour flight to Los Angeles. It wasn't pretty. "It might not hit her until it's time to board the plane."

"I'll tell you one thing. She's making some good money selling houses. One minute she was complaining about the slow housing market, and the next she's booked a trip to fly to the other side of the world. God is good. There's a special favor you walk in when you serve the Lord," she said.

"I'll be back, Ma," Dara said. She went into her bedroom and closed the door. Dara flung herself across her bed, buried her head in her pillow, and screamed at the top of her lungs.

"How am I going to last another two months?" she said to herself. She stood up and walked over to the full-length mirror hanging on her closet door. "I'm a liar. A big, fat liar."

Dara picked up the phone on her nightstand and called India. She could hear trucks rumbling in the background and a voice that sounded like Zebulon's yelling over them.

"I can't do it anymore," Dara said.

"What? What are you talking about?"

"This is too stressful. I've got millions in the bank, I'm trying to rebuild a community, and I don't have the courage to be an adult with my own parents."

"Hold on," India said. "Let me go to my car so I can hear you."

"Dara?"

She heard her mother's voice ring out. Dara opened her bedroom door and stuck her head out. "Let me finish taking this phone call. I'll be out in a minute."

India was evidently in her car, because the construction bustle outside had been closed out. "All right. Now what's going on?"

"I can't do it anymore," Dara whispered. "I'm about to bust."

"Tell her." India said it so easily. "What can they do? Make you give the money back?"

Dara sighed deeply. It was more complicated than that. She wanted to make sure they saw what she could accomplish first. She couldn't risk their being disappointed in her again.

"Never mind. I'll be okay," Dara said. "I think I just had to get it off my chest." Dara blew out a stream of air. "How are things going today?"

"The construction is moving along as planned. Zebulon runs a tight ship. But you've got some of your gangsta friends out here who've decided to bring their party to the sidewalk across from the construction. I'm the only one they try to verbally hassle, but you know I'm the queen at ignoring ignorance."

"How long have they been there?"

"All week."

"All week? And you're just now telling me."

"I didn't want you to get all hysterical. Aunt Thelma never comes in town, and I wanted you to focus on her while she was here."

"Maybe we should call the police."

"Legally, they're not doing anything. They're not *on* the property, they're *across* from the property. If you make a ruckus you'll give them what they want. Attention."

Dara had to do something about it. She knew it had to be Magnum who was the ring leader. If there was one thing she'd learned as a country girl, it was that the only way to kill a snake was to go destroy the head first. If not, it could regenerate another body. Magnum was the head, and without him, the others wouldn't survive.

"How's everybody else in the community?"

"Quite a few people came out to watch the workers. But again, that group of guys ran them back into the house after too long."

"It's ridiculous. Can you get the police over there?"

India huffed. "Dara, I've been here so much this week only to make sure things move forward. I'm not the security for the neighborhood watch program."

"All right, all right."

Thelma called out again from the living room. "Dara, how do you get this thing to come on? I want to watch Judge Joe Brown."

Technology was not her mother's friend.

"I need to go," Dara told India. "But do me a favor. If I get a box of books to you, can you take them out to the site tomorrow? Have one of the workers drop them by the community center. I heard they didn't even have anything for the kids to read in the after-school program."

"Whatever you want, Dara. You're the knight in pink armor and I'm your trusty sidekick," she said. "But let me warn you, you can't save all the dames and damsels in distress."

"No. But I can do my part." Dara hung up the phone. All she could do was what God asked of her. She only had to run and not get weary. She only had to mount up on eagles' wings.

Chapter 22

God answers prayers. It was the only reason Dara could think of why it had been four weeks and Magnum and his groupies seemed to have crawled back into their hole in the ground. Ms. Bettye let her grandchildren and foster children play in the front yard, and today Dara had gotten her first smile out of the woman with the three small boys. She'd even found out her name was Chantrelle.

Dara walked around with Zebulon to chart the progress.

"I hope the investor is pleased with everything," Zebulon said, kicking clay off the tip of his steel-toe boots. "I know I have to send you the photo updates, but there's nothing like seeing it with your own eyes."

"Trust me. The investor knows everything that's going on."

Dara had taken Zebulon's digital camera from him and was taking shots of the first four homes that had been completed. Other than the front yard landscaping, the homes were move-in ready. She'd pushed the builders to complete the first four houses on the new block, and she'd called in painters, electricians, and other contractors in the community to put on the finishing touches. Everyone in the neighborhood was pitching in, especially after they heard that Ms. Bettye had received a letter stating that the first house was being built for her.

Nobody knew what it was going to take to be a recipient of one of the new abodes, but that didn't stop them from being elated about the peace and feeling of renewal that had swept through the streets.

This Monday was one of the best in Dara's life. First came Cassius's ten o'clock call that he was donating twenty thousand dollars to build a playground and recreation field in the area. Dara zoomed the camera in on Ms. Bettye's house. Now this.

Zebulon walked Dara to the back of one of the worker's pickup trucks where there was a cooler of water. He flipped the spout and the water flowed into the cone-shaped paper cup.

"You always talk about how you're a trustworthy woman. So it's only fair that I be a trustworthy man," Zebulon said, handing her a cup.

Dara was puzzled. As thirsty as she was, she couldn't put the cup to her lips until she knew what Zebulon had to say.

"I know that you put the money up for Eagles Pointe," he said. "My curiosity got the best of me, and I did a little digging around, and used my knowledge and city contacts."

Dara shrugged. What else could she do now that the secret was out?

"It's safe with me," Zebulon hurried to say. "Even Tyler won't know. But I thought I should tell you."

"Thank you for being honest, and thank you even more for keeping your mouth shut," she stressed, praying that he'd actually do what he said. She turned the cup up and let the water wash her dry throat.

So Zebulon knew. Her parents still didn't. If that was the worse that had happened in a day, she still considered this Monday one of the best ones in her life.

Chapter 23

Dara wasn't watching the ten o'clock evening news. Although her television was turned on, she had the volume on mute. She was still trying to gather her senses around the call from Zebulon that two of her finished properties had been vandalized. Right after nightfall, he'd gotten word from Ms. Bettye that there was some suspicious activity going on in the area. She wouldn't say who'd told her, but whoever it was must've known that Ms. Bettye—of all people—would be able to contact someone who was in charge. That person was Zebulon.

Dara was both disappointed and furious. She let Zebulon and Tyler go back to the properties to secure the door and board up the windows. Now she wished she hadn't called India, because she wasn't helping the situation.

"Just because you change a person's environment doesn't mean you've changed their mindset," India said. "Money has power, but it doesn't have that much power."

Zebulon beeped in on the other line. Dara had talked to him an hour ago so she knew the properties had already been secured. He probably wanted to call her again to make sure she felt better. Whey they'd last talked, she was still shaken up.

"It's Zeb," she told India. "I'll call you in the morning. Try not to go to bed angry." It was what Dara had been telling herself for the last two hours. "We have to pray our way through this one. Zebulon said it's nothing that can't be repaired or replaced."

"I'll do my best," India said. "As long as you're okay, I'm okay."

"Don't worry about me," Dara said, "God's got my back on this one."

She flashed over to Zeb's call on the other line. "Dara, I'm on my way over." He sounded as if he was running through his house. "Turn on the news."

Chapter 24

Dara should've known better than to play with God. From a child, her father had told her that she should listen to her parents, because they were right more than they were wrong. Toying with the devil's money was causing Dara's pain. She didn't know how much she could take. She tried to take slow, even breaths as she watched her dreams go up in smoke. Dara didn't know if she could replace the three homes. She didn't know if she *wanted* to.

The news anchor turned toward the burned and smoldering frames. "Investigators returned tonight to new construction in a southwest Atlanta neighborhood where three houses were gutted by fire. Police investigated the same area less than three hours ago when a manager for the project reported that houses were being vandalized.

"It's too early to know how the fire started, but neighborhood residents suspect that it was an act of not-so-random violence. One woman refused to appear on camera for fear of retaliation from a gang. However, she said off camera that this area was starting to look a little brighter when they built these homes, and she hoped the cloud of despair didn't return. Unfortunately the cloud did return, and it brought a billowing fire with it."

"If this wasn't what you wanted me to do, God, why did you let me get this far?" Dara cried out. "Maybe I wasn't listening. Maybe I was too busy trying to make a change instead of being changed."

Dara threw her hands in the air. "You want my attention? You got it."

Dara's phone rang incessantly. She knew it was either Zebulon or India. However, she didn't want to talk to anyone unless it was someone who could tell her how to dump this money, and her problems, out of her life.

Chapter 25

Dara stared at the charred rubble and gray ashes of what used to be Ms. Bettye's place. Specks of ash floated around her face like an unexpected summer snow. The distinct scent of fire hung in her throat, and Dara was sure it had already attached itself to her hair, too.

She'd cried a million tears—both joyous and painful—but none of them had been enough to prevent the flames that had destroyed this house . . . while she sat watching it on television.

"How dare they?" Dara said, knocking a tear off her cheek as if it were the one that had betrayed her. "How dare they destroy my dream."

Dara walked around to the only property that hadn't been touched by the fire, although it had visible smoke damage.

Dara followed the thin stone path she'd had laid from the backyard to the front porch. The door was closed but not locked. Dara wasn't surprised. Why would she expect a vandal to extend an act of courtesy and lock the door?

Mahari, one of Ms. Bettye's foster children, rode up to the house on a BMX dirt bike that was about three years too small for him. Most of Ms. Bettye's foster children had ridden that same bike.

"Hey, Ms. Dara. Were you here the other night when those houses were burning down?"

"No, I wasn't," Dara said. "Were you?"

Children always seemed to be the eyes of the neighborhood. And although they weren't prone to being voluntary snitches, she'd found that a little coaxing could provide valuable information.

"Yep. Me and Mama Bettye watched it. We were standing right over there until the fireman and police made us move down the street. My grandma said she bet it looked like hell on earth."

Dara had heard that before, long before the fire had taken the houses.

"She's probably right," Dara said, looking over to the sound of the screeching school bus pulling against the curb. The children filed off the bus with reckless abandon. Most of the boys dropped their backpacks—and all thoughts of homework—on a concrete slab near the bus stop.

"See you, Ms. Dara," Mahari said. He kick-started his bike with one foot, then went racing down the sidewalk so fast that it looked like his stick-thin legs would slip off the pedals and get tangled in the wheel spokes.

Dara kept the door open while she was inside the house. It had been two days since the fire, but the stench was still detectable, and it mingled with the slight smell of fresh paint. She thought it was from the eggshell colors she'd chosen for the rooms, but then she noticed the new graffiti markings on the hallway wall.

Dara unclipped her cell phone from her pocket and dialed her painter. She refused to let them win. She'd called the contractors so many times that she knew most of the numbers by heart.

"Hey, Ed. This is Dara."

As always, he answered, "What you know good, baby girl?"

"I've got a job for you," Dara said. "Hopefully that's good for you."

"You know you always an answer to my prayer," Ed said. He unloosed a round of phlegmatic coughs. Ed looked to be in peak physical condition for his age, except for his complaints about his throat. Ed attributed it to allergies and popped over-the-counter allergy meds like candy, but Dara thought it was from years of inhaling paint dust.

"You heard about the fires, didn't you?"

"Yep. That's too bad. Them gangs don't want nothing coming to their neighborhood."

"Well, there's one house that's still standing," Dara said. "And if there's not too much smoke damage I believe it can be saved."

"I can get out there tomorrow first thing in the morning," Ed said.

"Thanks, Ed. I'll have Zebulon meet you, all right?"

Dara never heard Ed answer. She didn't have time to fight back against the arm that wrapped itself around her neck. She tried to break the grasp, but whoever it was that had snuck up behind her acted like he had no plans of letting her take another breath.

She gripped her nails into his dark, sweaty arm and gasped for air. He loosened his grip enough for her to swallow but not enough for her to wiggle out of his grasp. She did a donkey kick with her left leg, hoping it would paralyze him with a blow to the groin, but evidently she missed. And his grip on her neck tightened.

"You do that again and I'll snap your neck in two." He growled through his whisper.

Dara tried to slide her hand between his arm and her neck . . . let off the pressure. But when she tried to do that, another hand came from the back and covered her eyes. Dara feared the worse. She'd gotten too comfortable in the neighborhood. This wasn't her world.

The children's screams from outside sounded like they were coming closer to the door. She prayed they'd stay away and not let their childhood curiosity bring them to inspect what she was doing inside. This wasn't their fate, either.

"Leave her alone and let's go," a voice pleaded. Dara hadn't known there were two.

"So you want to punk out now?"

"She ain't done nothing."

"Maybe not now, but she's been too busy around here." He breathed a musty breath on her ear. "Yeah, I know you," one of them said to Dara. "I seen you riding through here with you and the other holy rollers trying to save the world. Then you cruise over here in your Benz and try to show us we ain't nothing. Like we can't do nothing for ourselves."

"No," Dara managed to say. The tears stung her eyes, and they fell down her cheeks and salted her lips. Her nose was beginning to run, too. But there was no moisture in her mouth. The grip he had on her neck was causing her to pant.

"Stop all that damn crying. You probably ain't never seen nothing in your life to make you cry."

Dara did her best to stop her tears. Every move she made was for her own survival.

"Man, leave her alone. Let's get out of here."

"Why don't you shut up before I leave you and Holy Roller in here together so the police can come draw a chalk line around your bodies."

Oh God, Dara said, pleading silently. The last words of the Lord's prayer was the only thing running through her mind, so she kept repeating it to herself.

> Deliver us from evil. For thine is the kingdom, and the power, and the glory. For ever and ever. Amen . . . Deliver us from evil . . . Deliver us from evil . . .

Dara felt her body slump to the floor before her world started to go black. But she'd seen it. She saw a hand holding hers. And it had a cross tattooed on it.

Chapter 26

It was a strain for Dara to open her eyes at first. The light pierced the slit in her eyelids, but she could still see the faint, blurry outline of people in the hospital room.

A hand touched her shoulder, then rubbed the side of her face. It was soft and smelled like bananas.

"As soon as you get out of here I'ma fix you the biggest pan of banana bread that you want. It'll take you all year to eat it."

Now Dara was sure it was Ms. Bettye. Sweet, smelling-like-bananas Ms. Bettye.

Dara turned her head slowly to the left to see Cassius and Zebulon standing by her bedside. Both of them looked as if they wanted to sweep her up in their arms and carry her away. They were the last people she wanted to think about. Truth be told, she had a thing for both of them, which was why she'd pushed both of them away. And if they were still attracted to her after seeing her in the worst condition she'd ever experienced, then there was something to be said of both their characters.

Dara reached to feel the knot on the back of her head. It was covered by bandages, but she faintly remembered India telling her something earlier about getting stitches. That was before she'd pressed the button to administer herself another shot of pain medication. She didn't remember much after that . . . like how all of these people had wound up in her room . . . but she did remember how she'd gotten here. The slight concussion the doctor said she had didn't take away the vision ingrained in her mind of the houses that were burned to the ground. It didn't erase the glimpse she'd caught of the hand . . . and the cross tattoo.

"Pink Knight."

Isaac, Mario, and three of the other knights walked up to her bed. Isaac didn't look as intimidating as he usually did, Dara thought, but that could've been because the medicine was giving her a warped sense of reality.

"I must say, you're a real ride-or-die chick," Isaac said. "But I'm telling you now, as your big brother, not to let this happen again. And that's an order."

Dara held up a thumbs-up sign, then she heard India's voice.

"And just in case you're wondering, Isaac's the reason we're all in the room. You're only supposed to have three visitors at a time, but have you ever heard anyone tell him no?"

Everyone in the room chuckled softly. Dara gripped the side of the bedrail and tried to pull her body up.

"Not so fast," India said, using the controls on the side of the bed. Once she was sitting more upright, she noticed Ed in the room. He stood up and walked to the side of the bed. He was wringing his cap between his hands, which were stained with paint. "I heard it all through your cell phone. I didn't know what was going to happen, but I told one of my partners to call 911 and tell them to get out to the properties."

"Thank you, Ed," Dara said. Dara didn't know why she expected her throat to be sore, but it wasn't. Maybe she'd assumed it would be painful like every other part of her head.

Everyone looked toward the door as it swung open. Dara's parents rushed inside, and the nurse asked for everyone to clear the room.

"India," Dara said. "Stay in here with me. It's time."

Thelma ran by her daughter's bedside and gripped Dara's forearm. "It's time? What do you mean it's time? Lord, Jesus."

"Mama." Dara stopped her mother before she started calling down fire from heaven and petitioning healing angels to Dara's bedside. All of Atlanta and Augusta would be holding a prayer vigil outside on the hospital sidewalk if her mother got started.

"Calm down, Ma. It's not what you think."

India sat down in the chair by the bed. "*Really* not what you think," she said.

Dara leaned her head back and closed her eyes while she told her parents the story. She couldn't bear to look at their faces.

"Actually, I bought the ticket," India said. "So, technically if you're mad at anybody, it should be at me."

Hunter, Sr. clenched his lips in a tight line. Dara wished he'd say something. Anything. Thelma was still holding onto her daughter's forearm as if she was waiting to hear her husband's comments before deciding how to react.

After a few long moments, he spoke. "I ain't never told my children to be scared of the devil's tactics. There are a lot of people who are scared to stand up for anything. Most people wouldn't have this many people come out to see them at a hospital unless they were already dead. But you must've touched their lives or they wouldn't be here."

Dara paused before pushing the button for more medication. She wanted to make sure it was really the Reverend Hunter J. Knight talking and not the medicine.

He shook his head. "I'm still not for folks playing the lottery. What I'm saying doesn't change that. But if you're investing your money in the people who are ignored, I can't see how God wouldn't honor your heart."

"So you're not mad?" Dara asked.

"Oh, I'm mad. But I'll get over it. As long as you move back to Augusta."

Dara moaned, and her father bent down and gently kissed her head. "I'm just teasing you, Cookie. You know you're still sweet as you can be."

India sniffled in the corner, and Hunter, Sr. turned his attention to her. "What are you over there crying for? I oughta whip you right now for buying the ticket," he said, pulling his niece into his chest and giving her a bear hug.

Zebulon pushed the hospital room door open and asked if he could come in. "Excuse me. I didn't want to interrupt your family time, but I thought you'd like to know this."

What else does he know? Dara thought. She didn't have any more secrets for Zebulon to dig up.

"Two guys were arrested for the vandalism and fires. Ms. Bettye said you'd know them by Magnum and Cross, but their real names are . . ." Zebulon unfolded a paper he was holding. "Quinton Barrow and Christian Taft. Christian 'Cross' Taft actually turned himself in to the police and led the authorities to the guy, Magnum. It was Magnum's third strike so he'll be locked up for a while. Believe it or not, it was Cross's first offense so they might not be as harsh on him. It looks like Cross was more along for the ride."

"God killed the snake by crushing the head," Dara said. "That's incredible. Absolutely incredible."

That was Dara's sign. After taking some time off she'd start back where they'd left off. There was still one house standing. And *she* was still standing.

"Thanks, Zebulon," Dara said as he left the room. "Ma, can you help me get to the restroom?" she asked. Her mother held the bottom of Dara's hospital gown together while she and India eased her out of the bed.

Dara felt her mother's fingernail scratch an area on her shoulder blade. Christian Taft wasn't the only "cross" that had been revealed.

"Dara, what's that on your back?"

The newest member of Pastor George Landris's church stirs up more troubles than blessings when he decides to rededicate his life to God in . . .

THE TRUTH IS THE LIGHT

by Vanessa Davis Griggs

Coming in June 2010 from Dafina Books

Here's an excerpt from *The Truth Is the Light*. . . .

Chapter 1

The stone which the builders refused
is become the head stone of the corner.
—Psalms 118:22

"Crown me!" said the ninety-nine-year-old dark-chocolate-skinned man who didn't look a day over seventy. He sat back against the flowery-cushioned chair and folded his arms, all while displaying a playful grin.

"Crown you?" a match in tone, thirty-five-year-old who resembled a slimmed-down teddy bear said. Shaking his head, he mirrored the old man's grin. "*Crown* you?"

"That's what I said. So quit stalling and get to crowning me."

The younger man first started to chuckle before it turned into a refrained laugh. "Gramps, I've told you twice already: we're playing chess, not checkers. The rules are different. There's no crowning a piece when it reaches the other side, not in chess."

"You say that there is my queen, right?" Gramps touched the game piece that represented his queen.

"Yes."

"Well, if there's a queen, then there's *got* to be a king with some real power a lot closer and, frankly, better than this joker here." He touched his king. "So quit bumping your gums and crown me so I can get some real help in protecting my queen." Gramps nodded as he grinned at his favorite grandson, proudly displaying his new set of dentures.

Clarence Walker couldn't do anything but smile and shake his head in both amusement and adoration. "I've told you. Because there's already a king on the board"—he pointed to the king—"we don't crown in chess. Just admit it. You don't really want to learn how to play chess, do you? That's why you're acting this way."

"I tried to tell you from the git-go that I'm a checkers man and strictly a checkers man. When you get my age, it's hard for an old dog to learn new tricks. I know how to fetch. I know how to roll over and even play dead. But all this fancy stuff like walking on your hind legs and twirling around . . . Well, you can take that to some young pup eager to learn. Teach the young pups this stuff. With checkers: I move, I jump, and I get crowned when I reach the other side. Just like Heaven." He pointed his index finger and circled it around the board. "I get enough kings, I set you up, trap you, wipe the board with you, and like normal—game over." Gramps stroked his white, trimmed beard.

Gramps was now on a roll. "All this having to remember pawns, knights, rooks, and bishops, which direction each moves in, how many spaces they can move when they move . . . I ain't got time for all of that. Then to have a king that's less powerful than his queen? Check and checkmate? Nope, I can't get with that. You know what your problem is, don't you? You don't like me whuppin' up on you like I normally do. You're trying to find somethin' that'll confuse old Gramps. Now is that check or checkmate?"

"No, Gramps. I'm merely trying to help keep you sharp. That's all. Studies show that when you do something new and different, it exercises your brain. You *do* know that your brain is a muscle, so it needs working out just like the rest of your body does."

"Humph!" Gramps said. "If I was any sharper, merely passing by me too closely would cut you." Gramps sensed his grandson had something more on his mind he wanted to talk about other than chess. Gramps leaned forward and placed his elbows on the table as he put his clasped hands underneath his chin. "Okay, so what's going on with you?"

Clarence sat back and became more serious. "Gramps, I'm getting baptized this coming Sunday night. I gave my life to Christ . . . for real this time. It wasn't just going forward to shake a preacher's hand like when I was twelve and my daddy made me do it to get it over with. Do you think you'd care to come and see me be baptized on Sunday?"

A smile crept over the old man's face as he leaned back against his seat. "So you done finally seen the light, huh?"

"Yeah, Gramps. I've finally seen the light. And I'm not running from the Lord anymore. Something happened to me on Sunday. I can't explain everything about it. But I know that the same man that walked into that building is not the same man that walked out. Something changed on the inside of me; it was an inside job. *I* see a difference."

The old man nodded. "Oh, you preaching to the choir now. I understand exactly how you feel. I ran from the Lord for a long time myself, both physically and figuratively." Gramps readjusted his slender body more comfortably. "I know your mama is happy about all of this. My baby girl has been doing some kind of praying for you, yes she has. And knowing your daddy like I do, I'm sure he acted like the father of the biblical Prodigal Son who finally returned home after wallowing for a time in a pigsty."

"Mom is *too* excited. She kept grabbing my face and pressing it in like she used to when I was a little boy. Like she wanted to be certain that I was really real—that it was actually me she was talking to and not some dream or figment of her imagination. Now Dad, on the other hand, probably would have been happy had I done this at *his* church."

Gramps leaned in. "Hold up there, whippersnapper. You mean to tell me you were somewhere else when this miraculous conversion occurred? You telling me this didn't take place at your daddy's church?"

"No, Gramps. It didn't happen at my daddy's church."

"Well, look out below! I'm sure *that* went over like a boulder falling off a tall building in New York City during lunchtime."

"You know my daddy."

"Yeah. Me, of all people, knows your daddy. Not one of my favorite folks in the world, that's for sure. No need in me trying to pretend he and I are bosom buddies, especially not after the way he treated my daughter. But Clarence, your father did give us you and your older brother, Knowledge. So I don't count him being in her life *all* bad."

Clarence tried to force a smile. "I told him about me being saved and about my scheduled baptism for Sunday. I asked him to come."

Gramps scratched his head. "You don't even have to tell how *that* conversation went. To him, you getting saved—and in another preacher's house at that—had to be the ultimate openhanded slap to his face. In his superreligious eyes, you are officially and publicly humiliating him. And everybody who's anybody knows your father loves the spotlight and equally detests being disgraced—intentional, accidental, or otherwise."

"That's the part of this that I don't understand. The greater point should be that I've repented of my sins and that I'm changing my ways. What difference does it make where it happened and with whom, as long as it happened? Daddy took it like I was deliberately trying to make him look bad . . .

like I was purposely trying to embarrass him by getting saved under another pastor's leadership instead of his. But I heard God speak to my heart just as clearly. And in that moment, I knew I had to move right then and there. I realized where I end up spending my eternity depended on my receiving Jesus."

Gramps picked up his bishop's piece off the chessboard and held it up. He began to make air circles with it. "Are you following what God is telling you to do?" he asked.

"Yes, sir."

"Then Clarence Eugene Walker, in the end, that's all that really matters." Gramps set the bishop back in the same spot he'd picked it up from with a deliberate thud. "Marshall Walker ain't got no Heaven nor a Hell to put nobody in. 'Cause the Lord knows, if he had, I'da been in need of an eternal air conditioner ages ago. In fact, on more than a few occasions Marshall has flat-out told me which of the two places I could go, and believe me, it wasn't Heaven. But"—Gramps smiled—"as you can clearly see, I ignored both him and his hearty request. That's what *you* gonna have to do if your father is bothering you about this. Don't let him get you off track, you hear." Gramps struggled somewhat as he made his way to his feet with slight assistance from his grandson.

"I'm all right," Gramps said, asserting his independence to get up without help. "I've told you I can stand up fine. It just takes me a little longer to get my motor started, that's all. Eventually, I get it going, then watch out." He looked at Clarence, now shaking his head and grinning. Gramps nodded. "You can come pick me up Sunday evening," Gramps said as they left the activity room of the nursing home that he, for a year now, had called home. "If the Lord be willing and the creek don't rise, I'll be here waiting on you. There's nothing I'd love more than to see you be baptized." Gramps beamed.

They walked to Gramps's room. Inside, Gramps started

grinning like a Cheshire cat as he looked down at Clarence's attaché case. "So, did you bring my stuff? I don't want you conveniently leaving here without giving it to me. I might be old, but as I just told you, my mind is still sharp. I ain't forgot, in case you're counting on me forgetting."

"Gramps, you and I both know I shouldn't be doing this."

"Boy, what did I tell you? I'm grown . . . past grown in case you've failed to notice. Now, did you bring my stuff in that fancy case of yours or not?" Gramps gingerly sat in the tan, leather recliner with a built-in massager his daughter, Zenobia, had given him Father's Day. He reached over and turned on the blue retro-styled radio, a modern-day replica of a 1950s automobile engine, that sat on his dresser. "Stand by Me" by Ben E. King was playing. Gramps closed his washed-out, brown eyes and began to sway as he softly sang—his voice as strong as when he was twenty and just as smooth and calming as milk chocolate. There was no question where Clarence had inherited his singing voice.

"Now that's some real singing right there," Gramps said as the song trailed off. "Ben E. King, Nat King Cole, Otis Redding, Sam Cooke, Mahalia Jackson, Bessie Smith, Josephine Baker, Billie Holiday, Sarah Vaughan, Marvin Gaye, Aretha Franklin, Frankie, Ella, and Lena. And those are just a fraction of some of the greats of my time." Gramps held out a hand to let Clarence know he was still waiting on his "stuff."

Clarence opened his black case. "Gramps, we have some great singers in our time, too. Stevie Wonder, Michael Jackson, Patti LaBelle, Janet Jackson, Beyoncé, Mariah Carey, Alicia Keys, Vickie Winans, Tramaine Hawkins, goodness! Smokie, Donnie, Kirk, Yolanda, Babyface, Raheem, Whitney, Celine . . . don't get me started." Clarence pulled out a blue, insulated lunch box. "Then there are groups like Earth, Wind and

Fire and En Vogue, who I hear are back." Clarence handed the lunch box to Gramps. "Here. But I want to go on record that I don't feel right about this. I just want you to know."

Gramps unzipped the lunch box, looked inside, and began to grin as he pulled out its content as though the wrong move might cause it to explode. "Ah," he said, placing the still warm, wax-papered-wrapped item up to his nose. He inhaled slowly and deeply, then exhaled with a sound of delight. The smoky aroma escaped into the room. "Just the way I like it, wax paper and all."

Clarence nodded. "Yeah, three rib bones with extra barbecue sauce, the sweet not vinegar kind, between two slices of white bread, wrapped in your favorite BBQ Joint's signature paper." Clarence shook his head. "You *know* you're not supposed to have that."

"Yeah, well, you just make sure you keep your mouth closed about this. Don't tell your mother and we'll be fine. She's the only one trying to keep me from my barbecue rib sandwiches. Like I got these teeth, which incidentally cost a pretty penny, merely for show. Waste not, want not—I'm putting these bad boys to work." He clacked his teeth together. "You're a good grandson, Clarence. You really are. Now sing that song I love."

"You mean the one by Douglas Miller? 'My Soul Has Been Anchored'?"

"Yeah, that's the one." Gramps placed the sandwich on the dresser and handed the now-empty lunch box back to Clarence.

Clarence put the lunch box back in his attaché case, then began to sing—holding back his full voice so as not to disturb any neighboring or passing residents of the home.

Gramps closed his eyes briefly as he seemed to take in every note and every word with a methadone-like ticktock of his head. When Clarence sang the final note, Gramps opened his teary eyes and nodded. "Yes," he said, pumping an open hand upward, "*my* soul's been anchored"—he swung a fisted hand while smiling and said—"in the Lord!"

Clarence nodded, hugged his grandfather, told him that he loved him, then left.

Chapter 2

If thieves came to thee, if robbers by night, (how art thou cut off!) would they not have stolen till they had enough? If the grape gatherers came to thee, would they not leave some grapes?
—Obadiah 1:5

Twenty-seven-year old Gabrielle Mercedes and thirty-year old Zachary Wayne Morgan were at Gabrielle's house in the kitchen cooking fajitas. They'd gone to a highly acclaimed play Sunday night and had a wonderful time. Few Broadway plays made their way to Birmingham, Alabama, whenever those plays happened to travel outside of New York. Afterward, Zachary surprised Gabrielle with tickets to *The Color Purple* scheduled for the BJCC Concert Hall in October. Gabrielle couldn't believe after all of these years of wanting to, she was finally going to get to see this live Broadway hit.

The doorbell rang. Gabrielle glanced at the digital clock on the stove. "I wonder who that could be." She cut down the heat on the gas stove to simmer and rinsed her hands at the sink, drying her hands on the large dish towel she kept draped across the handle of the oven door for just that purpose.

"I'll watch the food," Zachary said, turning the heat back to medium as he took over stirring the rectangular strips of marinated steak in the large cast-iron skillet with plans to add fresh sliced red, yellow, and orange sweet peppers and red onions at the end, to maintain the vegetables' firmness. The doorbell rang again, this time repeatedly.

When Gabrielle saw who was standing there pressing the doorbell, she practically yanked her front door open.

"Well, it took you long enough," Aunt Cee-Cee said as she fanned her face with her right hand and stepped inside. "You must have been in the bathroom or something."

Cecelia Murphy was Gabrielle's aunt on her father's side. She'd taken Gabrielle in—raised her since she was three (close to four) years old after her mother was killed and her father convicted of her murder and sentenced to twenty-five years in prison.

"No. But I *was* busy. I have company in case you didn't notice the car parked outside when you pulled up," Gabrielle said, trying hard not to show her own frustration.

"You mean that black, two thousand and something Lincoln Town Car? I just thought you'd bought yourself another vehicle." Aunt Cee-Cee tilted her head back, nose up. "What's that I smell? Smells like it's coming from the kitchen?" She started walking in the direction of the scent. "It smells like someone's sautéing onions and peppers."

"We're making fajitas," Gabrielle said, still holding the opened door since she hadn't asked her aunt to come in. She was now hurriedly trying to figure out what she needed to do to lure her aunt back toward her and out of the door.

"Well, it smells to me like I have fantastic timing," Aunt Cee-Cee said as she continued, undeterred, toward the kitchen. Gabrielle closed the front door and hurried to catch up with her now uninvited, unwelcomed, and undeniably unpredictable guest.

"Seriously, Aunt Cee-Cee, this really isn't a good time right now—"

Aunt Cee-Cee stepped into the kitchen and saw Zachary

just as he was turning off the stove and lifting up the cast-iron skillet. He raked a little of the steak, onions, and colored peppers mixture onto a flat flour tortilla.

"Well, hello there," Aunt Cee-Cee said as she walked toward Zachary. "Well, well, aren't you something? You must be the Handsome Chef." She let out a slight chuckle. "There's the Iron Chef. So I can only conclude you *have to be* the Handsome Chef who makes house calls." She scanned him from his head to his chest as she smiled.

Zachary looked at Gabrielle, who now stood next to the frumpy-looking visitor.

Zachary set the skillet back down on the stove. "No, but I thank you for the compliment. I'm Gabrielle's friend, Zachary Morgan."

"I'm Cecelia Murphy"—she extended a hand—"Gabrielle's aunt. But everybody calls me Cee-Cee."

Zachary quickly wiped his hand on the towel and shook Aunt Cee-Cee's outstretched hand. "All right then, Cee-Cee. It's a pleasure to meet you."

"Ah, that's what you say now. Give it some time." Aunt Cee-Cee laughed, then hopped up on a bar stool at the kitchen counter. "That sure does look good. I'm *starving*. Gabrielle, why don't you fix me one of those things Zachary's making. Oh, and can you get me something cold to drink? I need to wet my throat." She fanned her face again with her hand. "You wouldn't happen to have a beer or wine cooler around here, would you?"

"No, I wouldn't." Gabrielle's response was stern and cold.

"I would be glad to go and get you something," Zachary said, obviously wanting to make a good first, impression. "There's a Quik Mart about five miles from here—"

"You don't have to do that," Gabrielle said before Zachary could finish his sentence. "I have something to drink in the refrigerator. She can drink one of those." Gabrielle turned and looked squarely at Aunt Cee-Cee. "Besides, she'll not be staying long enough for you to go get anything and make it back."

Aunt Cee-Cee glared at Gabrielle only briefly before she broke her stare with a warm (though obviously phony) smile. "Gabrielle's right. I won't be here that long. So"—Aunt Cee-Cee turned her attention back to Zachary—"are the two of you dating?"

Neither Gabrielle nor Zachary answered.

"I said are you two dating?"

"Yes," Zachary said when he realized Gabrielle wasn't planning on answering the question. "But we're actually calling it courting." He couldn't hold back his own blush.

"Courting? Oh, how cute! You don't hear that word much these days. I suppose it's better than wham, bam, thank you, ma'am." Aunt Cee-Cee slid down off the bar stool and sat in a chair at the glass-top kitchen table. She looked at Gabrielle, her way of letting her niece know that she was still waiting on both her food and something to drink.

"Gabrielle is a special woman. We want to do things right," Zachary said. Once more he looked at Gabrielle, who still hadn't moved to get her aunt a plate or anything to drink.

"So, Mister Handsome Chef, what do you do for a living?"

"I'm a d—"

"Aunt Cee-Cee, why don't I fix your fajita to go?" Gabrielle promptly went and picked up the plate with the fajita Zachary had already begun making.

Aunt Cee-Cee fastened her gaze on Gabrielle like a laser. "Because I'm not *going* yet. And honestly, the quicker I get something to eat, the quicker I'll get *out* of here. I'm hungry, and I don't care to eat while I drive. Like texting, it's dangerous to drive and eat. In fact, there should be a law against both." Aunt Cee-Cee softened her face with a smile.

After rinsing her hands, Gabrielle hurried to finish rolling the fajita for her aunt.

"Now," Aunt Cee-Cee said, turning her full attention once more toward Zachary. "You were saying. What is it you do for a living? Because I hope you know I wouldn't want my niece, who's like a daughter to me . . . raised her myself, hanging out with no scrub. That's what they call a guy without a job who lives off others, right? A scrub."

Zachary laughed a little. "Well, you know, you could call me a scrub."

Aunt Cee-Cee pulled her body back and placed her right hand over her heart.

"Hold up," Zachary said with a chuckle. "Before you conclude I'm not good enough for your niece, allow me to clarify. I'm a doctor. So technically speaking, in my line of work, I wash my hands a lot, a whole lot, i.e., making me somewhat of a scrub."

"A doctor." Aunt Cee-Cee's words were flirty and sweet. "Oh, my goodness. Mercy me. My Gabrielle is courting a *doctor*, a real doctor. Well, isn't that something." She smiled at Gabrielle before turning back to Zachary. "What type of doctor are you?"

"A burn specialist. I specialize mainly in burn victims, although lately I've been spending my share of time equally in the emergency room when I've been needed."

"A multitasker," Aunt Cee-Cee said. "Gabrielle, why haven't you called and told any of us that you're *courting a doctor*?"

Gabrielle set the plate with the fajita and a can of Pepsi down in front of her aunt. "The last few times I've called, you haven't taken or returned my calls," Gabrielle said.

Aunt Cee-Cee eyed the can. "You got Coca-Cola instead of Pepsi? I prefer Coke."

"All I have is Pepsi. But I can give you water if you'd prefer that. Water is wet." Gabrielle smiled, knowing full well her aunt never drank water, not even with medicine.

"Oh, no. Pepsi is fine. I was just asking. I think somewhere in the Bible it says we don't have because we don't ask." Aunt

Cee-Cee picked up her fajita and took a cautious bite. "This is really good," she said. "Handsome Chef, you're a great cook. The meat is so tender and moist and has such a marvelous flavor." She took a bigger bite.

"Actually, Gabrielle did all the work. The tender and taste is from the marinade. Lime juice breaks down the meat to make it tender and give it that flavor. She marinated it overnight. I merely stirred and added the vegetables when she went to open the door."

"I'm sure you're giving Gabrielle way too much credit. I'm willing to bet you did a lot more than you're letting on. The peppers and onions are perfect." She took another bite, then opened her can of soda. A hissing sound escaped when the cap popped. "Aren't you two going to eat before it gets cold? It's really delicious." She smacked as she spoke.

Gabrielle was about to say something when Zachary moved over to her, put his arm around her shoulders, and pulled her in close. "We *like* ours cold," he said.

"Suit yourself," Aunt Cee-Cee said. When she finished that one, she asked for another. She chatted on about how terrible things were at their house financially and her not knowing what they were going to do as she woofed down a third fajita. She then asked for yet another one. "Oh, but could you wrap that one up for me as a to-go?" she said. "Those are *so* good." She licked her fingers, then wiped her mouth with a napkin.

Both Gabrielle and Zachary looked at what remained in the skillet. Originally, there had been enough for them to have *at least* two full fajitas each. Aunt Cee-Cee had now eaten three and was asking for one more to take home with her. If they made her the one she was asking for now, there would only be enough left for one of them. Gabrielle made the last two fajitas and gave them both to her aunt.

"Oh, aren't you the sweetest thing!" Aunt Cee-Cee said when Gabrielle handed her the wrapped fajitas. "Would you mind putting them in a bag for me? And if it's not too much to ask, would you put two cans of sodas in the bag as well? Your uncle Bubba will need something to wash his fajita down with." Aunt Cee-Cee stood up as she waited on Gabrielle to finish.

Gabrielle put the fajitas and drinks in a grocery bag and walked her to the door.

"I'll call you later tonight," Aunt Cee-Cee said. Then she whispered, "Is the doctor spending the night tonight?"

"No, Aunt Cee-Cee. We won't be doing things like that. There'll be none of that."

"You mean he's not spending the night *right* now. But you don't mean you're not planning on doing *anything* with that man until or unless you get married, now, do you?"

"You mean sex before marriage . . . fornicating?"

"Well, you don't have to be so graphic with it. But yes, that's exactly what I mean. Listen, honey, you don't need to let a man like him get away. That's a real catch you have in there." She pointed her head in the direction of the kitchen.

"Aunt Cee-Cee, I'm a Christian now. I told you that. I gave my life to the Lord. God frowns on fornication. Zachary and I agreed we want to do things God's way, and only His way. And that means keeping ourselves pure until we're married to *whom*ever."

Aunt Cee-Cee started laughing. It sounded more like an animal in severe pain than human. "Yeah, well, trust me: I know plenty of Christians, and being a Christian doesn't seem to be stopping most of them from fornicating *or* committing adultery. I'll tell you this: You'd better take care of that man and his needs or he'll find someone who will. Take it from Aunt Cee-Cee. I know how men can be. Sure, in the beginning they'll tell you they're in total agreement about something like being chaste. But men are wired totally different from women. Men don't need as much emotional bonding as we do to move to the next level. That man is tall, light-skinned enough, handsome, can cook, or at least will pick up a spoon and help out, he has a job, *and* he's a doctor to boot. Oh, you'd *better* at least let him sample the cake batter and not have to wait for the baked cake."

"Good night, Aunt Cee-Cee." Gabrielle opened the front door.

"I'm going to call you either later tonight or tomorrow. Better yet, why don't you just call me when you're free so I won't interrupt anything. You'd best heed what I just said. Call me, now. I have something I *desperately* need to talk to you about. It's important, so don't take long in getting back with me. It can't wait any longer than a day."

Gabrielle mustered up one more smile. "Good night," she said.

After Aunt Cee-Cee left, Gabrielle closed the door. She stood there for a few minutes, her forehead resting softly on the door as she quietly listened for her aunt's car to crank. Hearing the car drive away, she exhaled slowly.

"Wow, what a character," Zachary said.

Jarred slightly by Zachary's presence, Gabrielle turned around and forced herself to smile yet again. "Oh, you don't *even* know the *half* of it."

"Just from those thirty-five minutes, I believe I received a pretty good introduction," Zachary said. "So . . . where would you like to go eat?"

Gabrielle put her hands up to her face to compose herself, then took them down. "I'm so sorry. I can't believe she did that. Wait a minute; yes, I can. That's classic Aunt Cee-Cee. And the funny part is, she has no idea that what she just did was totally wrong or completely selfish. No idea at all."

"Oh, she knows," Zachary said. "I get the distinct feeling Aunt Cee-Cee knows *exactly* what she's doing. *Exactly*."